BRET HARTE'S GOLD RUSH

BRET HARTE'S GOLD RUSH

"Outcasts of Poker Flat," "The Luck of
Roaring Camp," "Tennessee's Partner,"
and Other Favorites

Introduction by Reuben H. Margolin

HEYDAY BOOKS
BERKELEY, CALIFORNIA

Introduction © 1997 by Heyday Books

Editing: Kim Bancroft
Interior Design and Production: Wendy Low
Cover Design: Jack Miles, DesignSite, Berkeley
Printing and Binding: Publishers Press, Salt Lake City
Thanks to Amy Arnett for her help in selecting stories.

Please address orders, inquiries, and correspondence to
 Heyday Books
 Box 9145
 Berkeley, CA 94709
 (510) 549-3564

ISBN 0-930588-88-6

Printed in the United States of America

10 9 8 7 6 5 4 3 2

Front cover painting, "Sunday Morning in the Mines" by Charles Christian Nahl, 1872, courtesy of Crocker Art Museum, Sacramento, California; E.B. Crocker Collection. Back cover photo of Bret Harte courtesy of the National Archives Still Picture Branch (#111-BA-1084); date and photographer unknown.

CONTENTS

INTRODUCTION

T he California Gold Rush! Even now, 150 years later, that era still captures our imagination, and nowhere does it come to life with such vibrancy and humor as in the short stories of Bret Harte. Each of the fourteen stories in this anthology throws us into that turbulent world Harte witnessed in the 1850s. Including such long-time favorites as "The Luck of Roaring Camp" and "The Outcasts of Poker Flat," this collection contains the best of Harte's sentimentality, his keenest observation of human nature, and his unabashed love of local dialect and color. The host of roughly clad heroes that here leap into the present shows why Harte remains to this day a master of the short story.

Bret Harte was born Francis Brett Harte in Albany, New York, August 25, 1836. His father, a perpetually destitute tutor of Greek, died in 1845, leaving a widow and four children. Harte's childhood was bookish, and he suffered more than his share of illness. Having left school at age thirteen, Harte went to work in a law office and then in a counting house. During that time, his mother journeyed to San Francisco where she remarried in 1854. Harte and his youngest sister arrived shortly thereafter, enduring terrifying storms at sea and a difficult overland crossing in Nicaragua. Over the next few years, between the ages of eighteen and twenty-one, the young man wandered around Northern California, pursuing a number of odd jobs, including stints as a schoolteacher, druggist, Wells Fargo stagecoach messenger, and even a miner. It was during those years that he became saturated with the jagged landscape and the equally jagged social climate that would dominate the best of his work.

Even at the beginning of his wanderings, Bret Harte had already begun to assume the fastidiousness for which he would be remembered. He sported a mustache that he kept curled at the tips. With his vaguely effete mannerisms, and standing only medium height, he was something of a dandy compared to the long-haired, unshaven, buckskin-fringed and swaggering bullies he would meet and eventually mythologize.

Thirty years later, Harte recalled in an interview that California seemed to him "a land of perfect freedom, limited only by the instinct and the habit of law which prevailed in the mass."[1] Passions unhinged from the "civilized" East Coast exploded in the wilderness. A slightly offensive angle to the hat might land a man, derringer in hand, in a duel at sunrise. Vigilantes took the place of courts to dispatch wrongdoers. Being a stranger, as Harte noted in one story, might be considered a peculiar "moral deficiency." The actors in this new social order were mostly young men, many of whom had escaped a cultured upbringing in the East, all of whom could boast their toughness, having survived the treacherous trip to California. Yankees, Indians, Mexicans, Chinese, Australians, and more jostled for land, gold, and status, with all the expected frictions and unexpected sympathies between them. Indeed, as Harte reveals, frontier fraternity sometimes ran to profound depths. Women were so rare in those early days that a female's arrival in a mining camp would invariably cause enough commotion to fuel a thousand stories.

And what stories abounded! By 1854 more stories could be dug out of the hills than gold. Already half a dozen years had passed since the cry of "Eureka!" first attracted hordes of gold-fevered pioneers. Families were beginning to settle. Stores, theaters, hotels, and newspapers took root. Camps turned to villages, and villages to towns. As early as 1854, the frontiersmen viewed with nostalgia the passing of California's most rugged early years. They bragged about "the good old days" to newcomers. The makeshift communities began to reflect on their experiences, which inevitably inspired "lies" and stories. The communal cries of self-definition from the many mining camps in the throes of transformation fueled Bret Harte's popular tales.

Returning to Oakland in 1857 where his mother and stepfather had settled, Harte announced that he intended to be a writer. He promptly consumed a complete set of Dickens, his all-time favorite author. Soon he relocated to Arcata where he acquired a job at the Humboldt County weekly, the *Northern Californian*, quickly moving from a position as typesetter to that of editor. This job lasted until 1860 when he was run out of town after publishing an article he wrote condemning a white attack on unarmed Indians. Harte then moved to San Francisco to work for another newspaper, *The Golden Era*, contributing a plethora of poetry and literary criticism, as well as articles of purely local concern. In 1862 he married a young woman from New York named Annie Griswold, and shortly thereafter took a job at the U.S. Mint, which provided both the income and free time to write on his own. His first collection of stories, *Condensed Novels and Other Papers*, published in 1867, consisted mainly of parodies of his favorite contemporary writers. A year later, considered one of San Francisco's leading writers, Harte was made editor of the brand-new *Overland Monthly*.

Part of the agenda of the *Overland Monthly* was to convince more Easterners to settle in California, so it was with some trepidation that the owner allowed Harte to publish his story "The Luck of Roaring Camp" in the second issue. The owner's worst fears were realized when most of the local population denounced the tale as immoral and vulgar. However, the story drew so much praise from the East Coast, as well as generous offers from the *Atlantic Monthly* for future publication, that San Francisco changed its mind and stood behind its newly discovered hero. The next few years proved that Harte had struck a rich vein. His subsequent stories are among his very best, and he established himself at the forefront of California writing.

In 1871, however, Harte and his family left California for good, heading to New York with the promise of greater success ahead. The literary elite, including Longfellow, Emerson, and Lowell, hailed his arrival, and Harte signed a ten-thousand-dollar, year-long contract with the *Atlantic Monthly*. Nonetheless, the next years proved disastrous. The famous Westerner lost his popularity as he adopted a breezy, arrogant attitude. He borrowed considerable sums of money without paying them back, meanwhile living in more comfort than he could afford. Late in fulfilling his contract, he was not offered a new one. And, most importantly, Harte failed to achieve the quality of writing that had made his previous stories jump off the page. Driven by both financial and marital difficulties, Harte commenced a tumultuous year on a lecture tour. Later he claimed he would have been more successful in these talks if he had appeared as colorful as his hard-living heroes.

In 1875 the struggling writer completed and sold *Gabril Conroy*, a full-length novel. After writing a flop of a play called *Two Men of Sandy Bar*, Harte collaborated on another play, *Ah Sin*, with a friend he met in California—Mark Twain. This work also received little acclaim, and Harte's inconsistency and rudeness dissolved their friendship. The kindest words Twain had for him later were: "Bret Harte was one of the pleasantest men I have ever known. He was also one of the unpleasantest men I have ever known."[2]

In his later writing, Harte continued to explore the exact same vein he had already exploited. He seemed unwilling or unable to reach deeper than the inspiration of his original successes. In 1877, feeling unloved by all, the frustrated author left his family and the United States to accept a job as U.S. Consul in Germany, never to return to the United States. By 1885 Harte had settled in England where he was well loved, if not idolized. Until his death in 1902, Harte continued to write romantic short stories, many of them excellent, about California in the 1850s.

Altogether Bret Harte filled 20 volumes with prose, poetry and literary criticism, virtually all about California. This selection of short stories is collected from the whole span of his career and is presented in chronological order. The first six were written in San Francisco, the next four in the East, and the final five in England. To some degree this span reveals a sense of the author's growth. The later stories tend to have subtler and happier endings, and present a more lenient Nature, although the sheer energy of his earlier stories remained unsurpassed. More importantly, such a span shows Harte's steadfast love for the quintessential early California experience. Even his last tales seem to come to us directly from the campfire where the spinning of yarns and swapping of lies enjoyed the status of being the highest form of entertainment.

Over time, Harte has had immeasurable impact in shaping our perception of the "Old West," so much so that we greet his archetypal characters with a kind of warm familiarity. In these stories we become acquainted with the self-possessed gambler, like Mr. John Oakhurst, always calm and chivalrous in the face of danger. We wade through "slumgullion" and dodge "permiskus shootin'" to meet cattle- and sluice-robbers, drunkards and iron-willed women. Preachers tote six shooters as they face off with highwaymen, horse thieves, and self-sacrificing prostitutes. Harte rounds out this wonderfully rich and complex social jungle with a motley arrangement of mules, dogs, bears, and goats that occasionally claim a leading role.

Whether Harte is describing the beauty of California—her pine-perfumed forests and the majesty of the Sierra—or the catastrophic power of her floods, snowstorms, and earthquakes, he records the images with a precision that opens our eyes anew to the natural wonder of this state. But looking even deeper, Harte delves into human nature in confrontation with the strange turnings of fortune to which the California Argonauts were supremely susceptible. With cruel irony always softened by humor, Harte places at the center of his stories the question of fate, and that sensitivity to fate we call superstition. In a land where freak gold strikes and equally freak tragedies were the norm rather than the exception, gamblers were respected as wiser prophets than priests. The Argonauts applied a unique logic to luck which they articulated with the language of poker and gold panning. As in "The Luck of Roaring Camp," where "the strongest man had but three fingers on his right hand; the best shot had but one eye," paradox and irony seem to be attributes of the territory rather than a literary device.

While Harte's narrowness of topic and style may not have earned him a place among the very greatest of writers, no one can pack as much feeling and amusement into a single shot as he can. And because he never gets lost in an abstract intellectual mode, his stories are refreshingly visceral in language, bold in plot, lively in character, and just plain funny. Ultimately, the characters in these stories draw us in because of the non-judgmental and utterly moving tenderness with which Harte embraces the best and worst of them. No matter whether they cause half sobs, full chuckles, or glimpses into the romance and moral ambiguity of early California, these stories are always high spirited and fun to read.

From Harte's stories sprouted countless legends and tall tales, eventually the stuff of Westerns and TV serials. Yet it must be admitted that some of the characters created in the context of the 1850s "wild West" make the modern reader wince. The disparaging racial and ethnic slurs and the stereotyped portraits of women must be seen as a product of a past time and a raw place. As offensive as they are, such attitudes were very much a part of the Gold Rush era, and if we are to achieve any understanding of this period, we need to look them squarely in the face.

We also need to come to terms with some aspects of the Gold Rush experience that Harte left out of his stories entirely. As we now know, the wealth extracted from the Gold Country came at a horrendous expense. Rivers which once bore abundant runs of salmon and trout were polluted beyond repair, game was shot indiscriminately, forests were ravaged for building materials and firewood.

Furthermore, the modern reader cannot help but be aware that while the miners in this collection of stories might gather to shed tears and make maudlin speeches over the death of one of their own, in the hills and valleys around them thousands of native people were dying of starvation and sometimes outright violence. The literature of the time did not allow for the inclusion of such facts, and perhaps the mentality of the time did not even allow for deep consideration of them.

Modern historians sometimes conclude that the widespread violence against Indian people was committed by brutal, hate-filled men devoid of human feeling. The stories of Bret Harte, however, imply something else. Could it be, one wonders, that the atrocities and neglect that so devastated the native population were perpetrated, or at least condoned, by people capable of great tenderness, sentimentality, humor, and even love? Could it be, indeed, that these unspeakable atrocities may well have been committed by people who, as we see from these stories, were in essence not that much different in their range of emotions from those of us who live in California today?

The stories of Bret Harte were, of course, not written to answer big questions, but to provide entertainment, and in this they succeed admirably. Here one will find a cast of astonishing characters, clever turns of plot, and ample opportunity to laugh aloud or even choke down a sob. For many readers this will be enough. For those, however, who want to look deeper these stories offer an opportunity, both in what they depict and perhaps in what they fail to include, to learn something important about those turbulent times which have shaped our history and even today hold such sway over our imaginations.

Reuben H. Margolin
Berkeley, California

[1] J.W. Dam, in *McClure's Magazine*, December 1894.
[2] See *Bret Harte: A Biography* by Richard O'Connor (Boston: Little, Brown and Company, 1966).

THE LUCK
OF ROARING CAMP

T here was commotion in Roaring Camp. It could not have been a fight, for in 1850 that was not novel enough to have called together the entire settlement. The ditches and claims were not only deserted, but "Tuttle's grocery" had contributed its gamblers, who, it will be remembered, calmly continued their game the day that French Pete and Kanaka Joe shot each other to death over the bar in the front room.

The whole camp was collected before a rude cabin on the outer edge of the clearing. Conversation was carried on in a low tone, but the name of a woman was frequently repeated. It was a name familiar enough in the camp—"Cherokee Sal."

Perhaps the less said of her the better. She was a coarse and, it is to be feared, a very sinful woman. But at that time she was the only woman in Roaring Camp, and was just then lying in sore extremity, when she most needed the ministration of her own sex. Dissolute, abandoned, and irreclaimable, she was yet suffering a martyrdom hard enough to bear even when veiled by sympathizing womanhood, but now terrible in her loneliness. The primal curse had come to her in that original isolation which must have made the punishment of the first transgression so dreadful.

It was, perhaps, part of the expiation of her sin that, at a moment when she most lacked her sex's intuitive tenderness and care, she met only the half-contemptuous faces of her masculine associates. Yet a few of the spectators were, I think, touched by her sufferings. Sandy Tipton thought it was rough on Sal, and, in the contemplation of her condition, for a moment rose superior to the fact that he had an ace and two bowers in his sleeve.

It will be seen also that the situation was novel. Deaths were by no means uncommon in Roaring Camp, but a birth was a new thing. People had been dismissed from the camp effectively, finally, and with no possibility of return; but this was the first time that anybody had been introduced *ab initio*. Hence the excitement.

"You go in there, Stumpy," said a prominent citizen known as "Kentuck," addressing one of the loungers. "Go in there, and see what you kin do. You've had experience in them things."

Perhaps there was a fitness in the selection. Stumpy, in other climes, had been the putative head of two families; in fact, it was owing to some legal informality in these proceedings that Roaring Camp—a city of refuge—was indebted to his company. The crowd approved the choice, and Stumpy was wise enough to bow to the majority. The door closed on the extempore surgeon and midwife, and Roaring Camp sat down outside, smoked its pipe, and awaited the issue.

The assemblage numbered about a hundred men. One or two of these were actual fugitives from justice, some were criminal, and all were reckless. Physically they exhibited no indication of their past lives and character. The greatest scamp had a Raphael face, with a profusion of blonde hair; Oakhurst, a gambler, had the melancholy air and intellectual abstraction of a Hamlet; the coolest and most courageous man was scarcely over five feet in height, with a soft voice and an embarrassed, timid manner.

The term "roughs" applied to them was a distinction rather than a definition. Perhaps in the minor details of fingers, toes, ears, etc., the camp may have been deficient, but these slight omissions did not detract from their aggregate force. The strongest man had but three fingers on his right hand; the best shot had but one eye.

Such was the physical aspect of the men that were dispersed around the cabin. The camp lay in a triangular valley between two hills and a river. The only outlet was a steep trail over the summit of a hill that faced the cabin, now illuminated by the rising moon. The suffering woman might have seen it from the rude bunk whereon she lay—seen it winding like a silver thread until it was lost in the stars above.

A fire of withered pine boughs added sociability to the gathering. By degrees the natural levity of Roaring Camp returned. Bets were freely offered and taken regarding the result. Three to five that "Sal would get through with it"; even that the child would survive; side bets as to the sex and complexion of the coming stranger.

In the midst of an excited discussion an exclamation came from those nearest the door, and the camp stopped to listen. Above the swaying and moaning of the pines, the swift rush of the river, and the crackling of the fire rose a sharp, querulous cry—a cry unlike anything heard before in the camp. The pines stopped moaning, the river ceased to rush, and the fire to crackle. It seemed as if Nature had stopped to listen too.

The camp rose to its feet as one man! It was proposed to explode a barrel of gunpowder; but in consideration of the situation of the mother, better counsels prevailed, and only a few revolvers were discharged; for whether owing to the rude surgery of the camp, or some other reason, Cherokee Sal was sinking fast. Within an hour she had climbed, as it were, that rugged road that led to the stars, and so passed out of Roaring Camp, its sin and shame, forever.

I do not think that the announcement disturbed them much, except in speculation as to the fate of the child. "Can he live now?" was asked of Stumpy. The answer was doubtful. The only other being of Cherokee Sal's sex and maternal condition in the settlement was an ass. There was some conjecture as to fitness, but the experiment was tried. It was less problematical than the ancient treatment of Romulus and Remus, and apparently as successful.

When these details were completed, which exhausted another hour, the door was opened, and the anxious crowd of men, who had already formed themselves into a queue, entered in single file. Beside the low bunk or shelf, on which the figure of the mother was starkly outlined below the blankets, stood a pine table. On this a candle-box was placed, and within it, swathed in staring red flannel, lay the last arrival at Roaring Camp.

Beside the candle-box was placed a hat. Its use was soon indicated. "Gentlemen," said Stumpy, with a singular mixture of authority and *ex officio* complacency—"gentlemen will please pass in at the front door, round the table, and out at the back door. Them as wishes to contribute anything toward the orphan will find a hat handy." The first man entered with his hat on; he uncovered, however, as he looked about him, and so unconsciously set an example to the next.

In such communities good and bad actions are catching. As the procession filed in comments were audible—criticisms addressed perhaps rather to Stumpy in the character of showman: "Is that him?" "Mighty small specimen"; "Hasn't more'n got the color"; "Ain't bigger nor a derringer."

The contributions were as characteristic: A silver tobacco box; a doubloon; a navy revolver, silver mounted; a gold specimen; a very beautifully embroidered lady's handkerchief, from Oakhurst the gambler; a diamond breastpin; a diamond ring, suggested by the pin, with the remark from the giver that he "saw that pin and went two diamonds better"; a slung-shot; a Bible, contributor not detected; a golden spur; a silver teaspoon, the initials, I regret to say, were not the giver's; a pair of surgeon's shears; a lancet; a Bank of England note for £5; and about $200 in loose gold and silver coin.

During these proceedings Stumpy maintained a silence as impassive as the dead on his left, a gravity as inscrutable as that of the newly born on his right. Only one incident occurred to break the monotony of the curious procession. As Kentuck bent over the candle-box half curiously, the child turned, and, in a spasm of pain, caught at his groping finger, and held it fast for a moment. Kentuck looked foolish and embarrassed. Something like a blush tried to assert itself in his weather-beaten cheek. "The d——d little cuss!" he said, as he extricated his finger, with perhaps more tenderness and care than he might have been deemed capable of showing.

He held that finger a little apart from its fellows as he went out, and examined it curiously. The examination provoked the same original remark in regard to the child. In fact, he seemed to enjoy repeating it. "He rastled with my finger," he remarked to Tipton, holding up the member, "the d——d little cuss!"

It was four o'clock before the camp sought repose. A light burnt in the cabin where the watchers sat, for Stumpy did not go to bed that night. Nor did Kentuck. He drank quite freely, and related with great gusto his experience, invariably ending with his characteristic condemnation of the newcomer. It seemed to relieve him of any unjust implication of sentiment, and Kentuck had the weaknesses of the nobler sex.

When everybody else had gone to bed, he walked down to the river and whistled reflectingly. Then he walked up the gulch past the cabin, still whistling with demonstrative unconcern. At a large redwood tree he paused and retraced his steps, and again passed the cabin. Halfway down to the river's bank he again paused, and then returned and knocked at the door. It was opened by Stumpy.

"How goes it?" said Kentuck, looking past Stumpy toward the candle-box.

"All serene!" replied Stumpy.

"Anything up?"

"Nothing."

There was a pause—an embarrassing one—Stumpy still holding the door. Then Kentuck had recourse to his finger, which he held up to Stumpy. "Rastled with it—the d——d little cuss," he said, and retired.

The next day Cherokee Sal had such rude sepulture as Roaring Camp afforded. After her body had been committed to the hillside, there was a formal meeting of the camp to discuss what should be done with her infant. A resolution to adopt it was unanimous and enthusiastic. But an animated discussion in regard to the manner and feasibility of providing for its wants at once sprang up. It was remarkable that the argument partook of none of those fierce personalities with which discussions were usually conducted at Roaring Camp.

Tipton proposed that they should send the child to Red Dog—a distance of forty miles—where female attention could be procured. But the unlucky suggestion met with fierce and unanimous opposition. It was evident that no plan which entailed parting from their new acquisition would for a moment be entertained. "Besides," said Tom Ryder, "them fellows at Red Dog would swap it, and ring in somebody else on us." A disbelief in the honesty of other camps prevailed at Roaring Camp, as in other places.

The introduction of a female nurse in the camp also met with objection. It was argued that no decent woman could be prevailed to accept Roaring Camp as her home, and the speaker urged that "they didn't want any more of the other kind." This unkind allusion to the defunct mother, harsh as it may seem, was the first spasm of propriety—the first symptom of the camp's regeneration. Stumpy advanced nothing. Perhaps he felt a certain delicacy in interfering with the selection of a possible successor in office. But when questioned, he averred stoutly that he and "Jinny"—the mammal before alluded to—could manage to rear the child.

There was something original, independent, and heroic about the plan that pleased the camp. Stumpy was retained. Certain articles were sent for to Sacramento. "Mind," said the treasurer, as he pressed a bag of gold dust into the expressman's hand, "the best that can be got—lace, you know, and filigree-work and frills—d——n the cost!"

Strange to say, the child thrived. Perhaps the invigorating climate of the mountain camp was compensation for material deficiencies. Nature took the foundling to her broader breast. In that rare atmosphere of the Sierra foothills—that air pungent with balsamic odor, that ethereal cordial at once bracing and exhilarating—he may have found food and nourishment, or a subtle chemistry that transmuted ass's milk to lime and phosphorus. Stumpy inclined to the belief that it was the latter and good nursing. "Me and that ass," he would say, "has been father and mother to him! Don't you," he would add, apostrophizing the helpless bundle before him, "never go back on us."

By the time he was a month old the necessity of giving him a name became apparent. He had generally been known as "The Kid," "Stumpy's Boy," "The Coyote" (an allusion to his vocal powers), and even by Kentuck's endearing diminutive of "The d——d little cuss." But these were felt to be vague and unsatisfactory, and were at last dismissed under another influence. Gamblers and adventurers are generally superstitious, and Oakhurst one day declared that the baby had brought "the luck" to Roaring Camp. It was certain that of late they had been successful.

"Luck" was the name agreed upon, with the prefix of Tommy for greater convenience. No allusion was made to the mother, and the father was unknown. "It's better," said the philosophical Oakhurst, "to take a fresh deal all round. Call him Luck, and start him fair."

A day was accordingly set apart for the christening. What was meant by this ceremony the reader may imagine who has already gathered some idea of the reckless irreverence of Roaring Camp. The master of ceremonies was one "Boston," a noted wag, and the occasion seemed to promise the greatest facetiousness. This ingenious satirist had spent two days in preparing a burlesque of the Church service, with pointed local allusions. The choir was properly trained, and Sandy Tipton was to stand godfather.

But after the procession had marched to the grove with music and banners, and the child had been deposited before a mock altar, Stumpy stepped before the expectant crowd. "It ain't my style to spoil fun, boys," said the little man, stoutly eying the faces around him, "but it strikes me that this thing ain't exactly on the squar. It's playing it pretty low down on this yer baby to ring in fun on him that he ain't goin' to understand. And ef there's goin' to be any godfathers round, I'd like to see who's got any better rights than me."

A silence followed Stumpy's speech. To the credit of all humorists be it said that the first man to acknowledge its justice was the satirist thus stopped of his fun. "But," said Stumpy, quickly following up his advantage, "we're here for a christening, and we'll have it. I proclaim you Thomas Luck, according to the laws of the United States and the State of California, so help me God."

It was the first time that the name of the Deity had been otherwise uttered than profanely in the camp. The form of christening was perhaps even more ludicrous than the satirist had conceived; but strangely enough, nobody saw it and nobody laughed. "Tommy" was christened as seriously as he would have been under a Christian roof, and cried and was comforted in as orthodox fashion.

And so the work of regeneration began in Roaring Camp. Almost imperceptibly a change came over the settlement. The cabin assigned to "Tommy Luck"—or "The Luck," as he was more frequently called—first showed signs of improvement. It was kept scrupulously clean and whitewashed. Then it was boarded, clothed, and papered. The rosewood cradle, packed eighty miles by mule, had, in Stumpy's way of putting it, "sorter killed the rest of the furniture." So the rehabilitation of the cabin became a necessity.

The men who were in the habit of lounging in at Stumpy's to see "how 'The Luck' got on" seemed to appreciate the change, and in self-defense the rival establishment of "Tuttle's grocery" bestirred itself and imported a carpet and mirrors. The reflections of the latter on the appearance of Roaring Camp tended to produce stricter habits of personal cleanliness.

Again Stumpy imposed a kind of quarantine upon those who aspired to the honor and privilege of holding The Luck. It was a cruel mortification to Kentuck—who, in the carelessness of a large nature and the habits of frontier life, had begun to regard all garments as a second cuticle, which, like a snake's, only sloughed off through decay—to be debarred this privilege from certain prudential reasons. Yet such was the subtle influence of innovation that he thereafter appeared regularly every afternoon in a clean shirt and face still shining from his ablutions.

Nor were moral and social sanitary laws neglected. "Tommy," who was supposed to spend his whole existence in a persistent attempt to repose, must not be disturbed by noise. The shouting and yelling, which had gained the camp its infelicitous title, were not permitted within hearing distance of Stumpy's. The men conversed in whispers or smoked with Indian gravity. Profanity was tacitly given up in these sacred precincts, and throughout the camp a popular form of expletive, known as "D——n the luck!" and "Curse the luck!" was abandoned, as having a new personal bearing.

Vocal music was not interdicted, being supposed to have a soothing, tranquilizing quality; and one song, sung by "Man o' War Jack," an English sailor from her Majesty's Australian colonies, was quite popular as a lullaby. It was a lugubrious recital of the exploits of "the Arethusa, Seventy-four," in a muffled minor, ending with a prolonged dying fall at the burden of each verse, "On b-oo-o-ard of the Arethusa." It was a fine sight to see Jack holding The Luck, rocking from side to side as if with the motion of a ship, and crooning forth this naval ditty. Either through the peculiar rocking of Jack or the length of his song—it contained ninety stanzas, and was continued with conscientious deliberation to the bitter end—the lullaby generally had the desired effect.

At such times the men would lie at full length under the trees in the soft summer twilight, smoking their pipes and drinking in the melodious utterances. An indistinct idea that this was pastoral happiness pervaded the camp. "This 'ere kind o' think," said the Cockney Simmons, meditatively reclining on his elbow, "is 'evingly." It reminded him of Greenwich.

On the long summer days The Luck was usually carried to the gulch from whence the golden store of Roaring Camp was taken. There, on a blanket spread over pine boughs, he would lie while the men were working in the ditches below. Latterly there was a rude attempt to decorate this bower with flowers and sweet-smelling shrubs, and generally someone would bring him a cluster of wild honeysuckles, azaleas, or the painted blossoms of Las Mariposas.

The men had suddenly awakened to the fact that there were beauty and significance in these trifles, which they had so long trodden carelessly beneath their feet. A flake of glittering mica, a fragment of variegated quartz, a bright pebble from the bed of the creek, became beautiful to eyes thus cleared and strengthened, and were invariably put aside for The Luck. It was wonderful how many treasures the woods and hillsides yielded that "would do for Tommy." Surrounded by playthings such as never child out of fairyland had before, it is to be hoped that Tommy was content. He appeared to be serenely happy, albeit there was an infantine gravity about him, a contemplative light in his round gray eyes, that sometimes worried Stumpy.

He was always tractable and quiet, and it is recorded that once, having crept beyond his corral—a hedge of tessellated pine boughs, which surrounded his bed—he dropped over the bank on his head in the soft earth, and remained with his mottled legs in the air in that position for at least five minutes with unflinching gravity. He was extricated without a murmur. I hesitate to record the many other instances of his sagacity, which rest, unfortunately, upon the statements of prejudiced friends. Some of them were not without a tinge of superstition.

"I crep' up the bank just now," said Kentuck one day, in a breathless state of excitement, "and dern my skin if he wasn't a-talking to a jaybird as was a-sittin' on his lap. There they was, just as free and sociable as anything you please, a-jawin' at each other just like two cherrybums."

Howbeit, whether creeping over the pine boughs or lying lazily on his back blinking at the leaves above him, to him the birds sang, the squirrels chattered, and the flowers bloomed. Nature was his nurse and playfellow. For him she would let slip between the leaves golden shafts of sunlight that fell just within his grasp; she would send wandering breezes to visit him with the balm of bay and resinous gum; to him the tall redwoods nodded familiarly and sleepily, the bumblebees buzzed, and the rooks cawed a slumbrous accompaniment.

Such was the golden summer of Roaring Camp. They were "flush times," and the luck was with them. The claims had yielded enormously. The camp was jealous of its privileges and looked suspiciously on strangers. No encouragement was given to immigration, and, to make their seclusion more perfect, the land on either side of the mountain wall that surrounded the camp they duly pre-empted.

This, and a reputation for singular proficiency with the revolver, kept the reserve of Roaring Camp inviolate. The expressman—their only connecting link with the surrounding world—sometimes told wonderful stories of the camp. He would say, "They've a street up there in 'Roaring' that would lay over any street in Red Dog. They've got vines and flowers round their houses, and they wash themselves twice a day. But they're mighty rough on strangers, and they worship an Injin baby."

With the prosperity of the camp came a desire for further improvement. It was proposed to build a hotel in the following spring, and to invite one or two decent families to reside there for the sake of The Luck, who might perhaps profit by female companionship. The sacrifice that this concession to the sex cost these men, who were fiercely skeptical in regard to its general virtue and usefulness, can only be accounted for by their affection for Tommy. A few still held out. But the resolve could not be carried into effect for three months, and the minority meekly yielded in the hope that something might turn up to prevent it. And it did.

The winter of 1851 will long be remembered in the foothills. The snow lay deep on the Sierras, and every mountain creek became a river, and every river a lake. Each gorge and gulch was transformed into a tumultuous watercourse that descended the hillsides, tearing down giant trees and scattering its drift and débris along the plain. Red Dog had been twice under water, and Roaring Camp had been forewarned.

"Water put the gold into them gulches," said Stumpy. "It's been here once and will be here again!" And that night the North Fork suddenly leaped over its banks and swept up the triangular valley of Roaring Camp.

In the confusion of rushing water, crashing trees, and crackling timber, and the darkness which seemed to flow with the water and blot out the fair valley, but little could be done to collect the scattered camp.

When the morning broke, the cabin of Stumpy, nearest the riverbank, was gone. Higher up the gulch they found the body of its unlucky owner; but the pride, the hope, the joy, The Luck, of Roaring Camp had disappeared. They were returning with sad hearts when a shout from the bank recalled them.

It was a relief-boat from down the river. They had picked up, they said, a man and an infant, nearly exhausted, about two miles below. Did anybody know them, and did they belong here?

It needed but a glance to show them Kentuck lying there, cruelly crushed and bruised, but still holding The Luck of Roaring Camp in his arms. As they bent over the strangely assorted pair, they saw that the child was cold and pulseless. "He is dead," said one.

Kentuck opened his eyes. "Dead?" he repeated feebly.

"Yes, my man, and you are dying too."

A smile lit the eyes of the expiring Kentuck. "Dying!" he repeated; "he's a-taking me with him. Tell the boys I've got The Luck with me now"; and the strong man, clinging to the frail babe as a drowning man is said to cling to a straw, drifted away into the shadowy river that flows forever to the unknown sea.

THE OUTCASTS
OF POKER FLAT

A s Mr. John Oakhurst, gambler, stepped into the main street of Poker Flat on the morning of the 23d of November, 1850, he was conscious of a change in its moral atmosphere since the preceding night. Two or three men, conversing earnestly together, ceased as he approached, and exchanged significant glances. There was a Sabbath lull in the air, which, in a settlement unused to Sabbath influences, looked ominous.

Mr. Oakhurst's calm, handsome face betrayed small concern in these indications. Whether he was conscious of any predisposing cause was another question. "I reckon they're after somebody," he reflected; "likely it's me." He returned to his pocket the handkerchief with which he had been whipping away the red dust of Poker Flat from his neat boots, and quietly discharged his mind of any further conjecture.

In point of fact, Poker Flat was "after somebody." It had lately suffered the loss of several thousand dollars, two valuable horses, and a prominent citizen. It was experiencing a spasm of virtuous reaction, quite as lawless and ungovernable as any of the acts that had provoked it. A secret committee had determined to rid the town of all improper persons. This was done permanently in regard of two men who were then hanging from the boughs of a sycamore in the gulch, and temporarily in the banishment of certain other objectionable characters. I regret to say that some of these were ladies. It is but due to the sex, however, to state that their impropriety was professional, and it was only in such easily established standards of evil that Poker Flat ventured to sit in judgment.

Mr. Oakhurst was right in supposing that he was included in this category. A few of the committee had urged hanging him as a possible example and a sure method of reimbursing themselves from his pockets of the sums he had won from them. "It's agin justice," said Jim Wheeler, "to let this yer young man from Roaring Camp—an entire stranger—carry away our money." But a crude sentiment of equity residing in the breasts of those who had been fortunate enough to win from Mr. Oakhurst overruled this narrower local prejudice.

Mr. Oakhurst received his sentence with philosophic calmness, none the less coolly that he was aware of the hesitation of his judges. He was too much of a gambler not to accept fate. With him life was at best an uncertain game, and he recognized the usual percentage in favor of the dealer.

A body of armed men accompanied the deported wickedness of Poker Flat to the outskirts of the settlement. Besides Mr. Oakhurst, who was known to be a coolly desperate man, and for whose intimidation the armed escort was intended, the expatriated party consisted of a young woman familiarly known as "The Duchess"; another who had won the title of "Mother Shipton"; and "Uncle Billy," a suspected sluice-robber and confirmed drunkard.

The cavalcade provoked no comments from the spectators, nor was any word uttered by the escort. Only when the gulch which marked the uttermost limit of Poker Flat was reached, the leader spoke briefly and to the point. The exiles were forbidden to return at the peril of their lives.

As the escort disappeared, their pent-up feelings found vent in a few hysterical tears from the Duchess, some bad language from Mother Shipton, and a Parthian volley of expletives from Uncle Billy. The philosophic Oakhurst alone remained silent. He listened calmly to Mother Shipton's desire to cut somebody's heart out, to the repeated statements of the Duchess that she would die in the road, and to the alarming oaths that seemed to be bumped out of Uncle Billy as he rode forward.

With the easy good humor characteristic of his class, he insisted upon exchanging his own riding-horse, "Five-Spot," for the sorry mule which the Duchess rode. But even this act did not draw the party into any closer sympathy. The young woman readjusted her somewhat draggled plumes with a feeble, faded coquetry; Mother Shipton eyed the possessor of "Five-Spot" with malevolence, and Uncle Billy included the whole party in one sweeping anathema.

The road to Sandy Bar—a camp that, not having as yet experienced the regenerating influences of Poker Flat, consequently seemed to offer some invitation to the emigrants—lay over a steep mountain range. It was distant a day's severe travel. In that advanced season the party soon passed out of the moist, temperate regions of the foothills into the dry, cold, bracing air of the Sierras. The trail was narrow and difficult. At noon the Duchess, rolling out of her saddle upon the ground, declared her intention of going no farther, and the party halted.

The spot was singularly wild and impressive. A wooded amphitheatre, surrounded on three sides by precipitous cliffs of naked granite, sloped gently toward the crest of another precipice that overlooked the valley. It was, undoubtedly, the most suitable spot for a camp, had camping been advisable. But Mr. Oakhurst knew that scarcely half the journey to Sandy Bar was accomplished, and the party were not equipped or provisioned for delay. This fact he pointed out to his companions curtly, with a philosophic commentary on the folly of throwing up their hand before the game was played out.

But they were furnished with liquor, which in this emergency stood them in place of food, fuel, rest, and prescience. In spite of his remonstrances, it was not long before they were more or less under its influence. Uncle Billy passed rapidly from a bellicose state into one of stupor, the Duchess became maudlin, and Mother Shipton snored. Mr. Oakhurst alone remained erect, leaning against a rock, calmly surveying them.

Mr. Oakhurst did not drink. It interfered with a profession which required coolness, impassiveness, and presence of mind, and, in his own language, he "couldn't afford it." As he gazed at his recumbent fellow exiles, the loneliness begotten of his pariah trade, his habits of life, his very vices, for the first time seriously oppressed him. He bestirred himself in dusting his black clothes, washing his hands and face, and other acts characteristic of his studiously neat habits, and for a moment forgot his annoyance.

The thought of deserting his weaker and more pitiable companions never perhaps occurred to him. Yet he could not help feeling the want of that excitement which, singularly enough, was most conducive to that calm equanimity for which he was notorious. He looked at the gloomy walls that rose a thousand feet sheer above the circling pines around him, at the sky ominously clouded, at the valley below, already deepening into shadow; and, doing so, suddenly he heard his own name called.

A horseman slowly ascended the trail. In the fresh, open face of the newcomer Mr. Oakhurst recognized Tom Simson, otherwise known as "The Innocent," of Sandy Bar. He had met him some months before over a "little game," and had, with perfect equanimity, won the entire fortune—amounting to some forty dollars—of that guileless youth. After the game was finished, Mr. Oakhurst drew the youthful speculator behind the door and thus addressed him: "Tommy, you're a good little man, but you can't gamble worth a cent. Don't try it over again." He then handed him his money back, pushed him gently from the room, and so made a devoted slave of Tom Simson.

THERE WAS A REMEMBRANCE of this in his boyish and enthusiastic greeting of Mr. Oakhurst. He had started, he said, to go to Poker Flat to seek his fortune. "Alone?" No, not exactly alone; in fact (a giggle), he had run away with Piney Woods. Didn't Mr. Oakhurst remember Piney? She that used to wait on the table at the Temperance House? They had been engaged a long time, but old Jake Woods had objected, and so they had run away, and were going to Poker Flat to be married, and here they were. And they were tired out, and how lucky it was they had found a place to camp, and company.

All this the Innocent delivered rapidly, while Piney, a stout, comely damsel of fifteen, emerged from behind the pine-tree, where she had been blushing unseen, and rode to the side of her lover.

Mr. Oakhurst seldom troubled himself with sentiment, still less with propriety; but he had a vague idea that the situation was not fortunate. He retained, however, his presence of mind sufficiently to kick Uncle Billy, who was about to say something, and Uncle Billy was sober enough to recognize in Mr. Oakhurst's kick a superior power that would not bear trifling.

He then endeavored to dissuade Tom Simson from delaying further, but in vain. He even pointed out the fact that there was no provision, nor means of making a camp. But, unluckily, the Innocent met this objection by assuring the party that he was provided with an extra mule loaded with provisions, and by the discovery of a rude attempt at a log house near the trail. "Piney can stay with Mrs.

Oakhurst," said the Innocent, pointing to the Duchess, "and I can shift for myself."

Nothing but Mr. Oakhurst's admonishing foot saved Uncle Billy from bursting into a roar of laughter. As it was, he felt compelled to retire up the cañon until he could recover his gravity. There he confided the joke to the tall pine-trees, with many slaps of his leg, contortions of his face, and the usual profanity. But when he returned to the party, he found them seated by a fire—for the air had grown strangely chill and the sky overcast—in apparently amicable conversation.

Piney was actually talking in an impulsive girlish fashion to the Duchess, who was listening with an interest and animation she had not shown for many days. The Innocent was holding forth, apparently with equal effect, to Mr. Oakhurst and Mother Shipton, who was actually relaxing into amiability.

"Is this yer a d——d picnic?" said Uncle Billy, with inward scorn, as he surveyed the sylvan group, the glancing firelight, and the tethered animals in the foreground.

Suddenly an idea mingled with the alcoholic fumes that disturbed his brain. It was apparently of a jocular nature, for he felt impelled to slap his leg again and cram his fist into his mouth.

As the shadows crept slowly up the mountain, a slight breeze rocked the tops of the pine-trees and moaned through their long and gloomy aisles. The ruined cabin, patched and covered with pine boughs, was set apart for the ladies. As the lovers parted, they unaffectedly exchanged a kiss, so honest and sincere that it might have been heard above the swaying pines. The frail Duchess and the malevolent Mother Shipton were probably too stunned to remark upon this last evidence of simplicity, and so turned without a word to the hut. The fire was replenished, the men lay down before the door, and in a few minutes were asleep.

Mr. Oakhurst was a light sleeper. Toward morning he awoke benumbed and cold. As he stirred the dying fire, the wind, which was now blowing strongly, brought to his cheek that which caused the blood to leave it—snow!

He started to his feet with the intention of awakening the sleepers, for there was no time to lose. But turning to where Uncle Billy had been lying, he found him gone. A suspicion leaped to his brain, and a curse to his lips. He ran to the spot where the mules had been tethered—they were no longer there. The tracks were already rapidly disappearing in the snow.

The momentary excitement brought Mr. Oakhurst back to the fire with his usual calm. He did not waken the sleepers. The Innocent slumbered peacefully, with a smile on his good-humored, freckled face; the virgin Piney slept beside her frailer sisters as sweetly as though attended by celestial guardians; and Mr. Oakhurst, drawing his blanket over his shoulders, stroked his mustaches and waited for the dawn. It came slowly in a whirling mist of snowflakes that dazzled and confused the eye. What could be seen of the landscape appeared magically changed. He looked over the valley, and summed up the present and future in two words, "Snowed in!"

A careful inventory of the provisions, which, fortunately for the party, had been stored within the hut, and so escaped the felonious fingers of Uncle Billy, disclosed the fact that with care and prudence they might last ten days longer.

"That is," said Mr. Oakhurst *sotto voce* to the Innocent, "if you're willing to board us. If you ain't—and perhaps you'd better not—you can wait till Uncle Billy gets back with provisions."

For some occult reason, Mr. Oakhurst could not bring himself to disclose Uncle Billy's rascality, and so offered the hypothesis that he had wandered from the camp and had accidentally stampeded the animals. He dropped a warning to the Duchess and Mother Shipton, who of course knew the facts of their associate's defection.

"They'll find out the truth about us *all* when they find out anything," he added significantly, "and there's no good frightening them now."

Tom Simson not only put all his worldly store at the disposal of Mr. Oakhurst, but seemed to enjoy the prospect of their enforced seclusion. "We'll have a good camp for a week, and then the snow'll melt, and we'll all go back together."

The cheerful gayety of the young man and Mr. Oakhurst's calm infected the others. The Innocent, with the aid of pine boughs, extemporized a thatch for the roofless cabin, and the Duchess directed Piney in the rearrangement of the interior with a taste and tact that opened the blue eyes of that provincial maiden to their fullest extent.

"I reckon now you're used to fine things at Poker Flat," said Piney.

The Duchess turned away sharply to conceal something that reddened her cheeks through their professional tint, and Mother Shipton requested Piney not to "chatter." But when Mr. Oakhurst returned from a weary search for the trail, he heard the sound of happy laughter echoed from the rocks. He stopped in some alarm, and his thoughts first naturally reverted to the whiskey, which he had prudently cached. "And yet it don't somehow sound like whiskey," said the gambler. It was not until he caught sight of the blazing fire through the still blinding storm, and the group around it, that he settled to the conviction that it was "square fun."

Whether Mr. Oakhurst had cached his cards with the whiskey as something debarred the free access of the community, I cannot say. It was certain that, in Mother Shipton's words, he "didn't say 'cards' once" during that evening. Haply the time was beguiled by an accordion, produced somewhat ostentatiously by Tom Simson from his pack. Notwithstanding some difficulties attending the manipulation of this instrument, Piney Woods managed to pluck several reluctant melodies from its keys, to an accompaniment by the Innocent on a pair of bone castanets.

But the crowning festivity of the evening was reached in a rude camp-meeting hymn, which the lovers, joining hands, sang with great earnestness and vociferation. I fear that a certain defiant tone and Covenanter's swing to its chorus, rather than any devotional quality, caused it speedily to infect the others, who at last joined in the refrain:

> "I'm proud to live in the service of the Lord,
> And I'm bound to die in His army."

The pines rocked, the storm eddied and whirled above the miserable group, and the flames of their altar leaped heavenward, as if in token of the vow.

At midnight the storm abated, the rolling clouds parted, and the stars glittered keenly above the sleeping camp. Mr. Oakhurst, whose professional habits had enabled him to live on the smallest possible amount of sleep, in dividing the watch with Tom Simson somehow managed to take upon himself the greater part of that duty. He excused himself to the Innocent by saying that he had "often been a week without sleep."

"Doing what ?" asked Tom.

"Poker!" replied Oakhurst sententiously. "When a man gets a streak of luck—nigger-luck—he don't get tired. The luck gives in first. Luck," continued the gambler reflectively, "is a mighty queer thing. All you

{18}

know about it for certain is that it's bound to change. And it's finding out when it's going to change that makes you. We've had a streak of bad luck since we left Poker Flat—you come along, and slap you get into it, too. If you can hold your cards right along you're all right. For," added the gambler, with cheerful irrelevance,

> "'I'm proud to live in the service of the Lord,
> And I'm bound to die in His army.'"

The third day came, and the sun, looking through the white-curtained valley, saw the outcasts divide their slowly decreasing store of provisions for the morning meal. It was one of the peculiarities of that mountain climate that its rays diffused a kindly warmth over the wintry landscape, as if in regretful commiseration of the past. But it revealed drift on drift of snow piled high around the hut—a hopeless, uncharted, trackless sea of white lying below the rocky shores to which the castaways still clung.

Through the marvelously clear air the smoke of the pastoral village of Poker Flat rose miles away. Mother Shipton saw it, and from a remote pinnacle of her rocky fastness hurled in that direction a final malediction. It was her last vituperative attempt, and perhaps for that reason was invested with a certain degree of sublimity. It did her good, she privately informed the Duchess. "Just you go out there and cuss, and see."

She then set herself to the task of amusing "the child," as she and the Duchess were pleased to call Piney. Piney was no chicken, but it was a soothing and original theory of the pair thus to account for the fact that she didn't swear and wasn't improper.

When night crept up again through the gorges, the reedy notes of the accordion rose and fell in fitful spasms and long-drawn gasps by the flickering campfire. But music failed to fill entirely the aching void left by insufficient food, and a new diversion was proposed by Piney—story-telling. Neither Mr. Oakhurst nor his female companions caring to relate their personal experiences, this plan would have failed too, but for the Innocent.

Some months before he had chanced upon a stray copy of Mr. Pope's ingenious translation of the Iliad. He now proposed to narrate the principal incidents of that poem—having thoroughly mastered the argument and fairly forgotten the words—in the current vernacular of Sandy Bar. And so for the rest of that night the Homeric demigods again walked the earth. Trojan bully and wily Greek wrestled in the winds, and the great pines in the cañon seemed to bow to the wrath of the son of Peleus.

Mr. Oakhurst listened with quiet satisfaction. Most especially was he interested in the fate of "Ash-heels," as the Innocent persisted in denominating the "swift-footed Achilles."

So, with small food and much of Homer and the accordion, a week passed over the heads of the outcasts. The sun again forsook them, and again from leaden skies the snowflakes were sifted over the land. Day by day closer around them drew the snowy circle, until at last they looked from their prison over drifted walls of dazzling white, that towered twenty feet above their heads. It became more and more difficult to replenish their fires, even from the fallen trees beside them, now half hidden in the drifts. And yet no one complained.

The lovers turned from the dreary prospect and looked into each other's eyes, and were happy. Mr. Oakhurst settled himself coolly to the losing game before him. The Duchess, more cheerful than she had been, assumed the care of Piney.

Only Mother Shipton—once the strongest of the party—seemed to sicken and fade. At midnight on the tenth day she called Oakhurst to her side. "I'm going," she said, in a voice of querulous weakness, "but don't say anything about it. Don't waken the kids. Take the bundle from under my head, and open it."

Mr. Oakhurst did so. It contained Mother Shipton's rations for the last week, untouched. "Give 'em to the child," she said, pointing to the sleeping Piney.

"You've starved yourself," said the gambler.

"That's what they call it," said the woman querulously, as she lay down again, and, turning her face to the wall, passed quietly away.

The accordion and the bones were put aside that day, and Homer was forgotten. When the body of Mother Shipton had been committed to the snow, Mr. Oakhurst took the Innocent aside, and showed him a pair of snowshoes, which he had fashioned from the old pack-saddle.

"There's one chance in a hundred to save her yet," he said, pointing to Piney; "but it's there," he added, pointing toward Poker Flat. "If you can reach there in two days she's safe." "And you?" asked Tom Simson.

"I'll stay here," was the curt reply.

The lovers parted with a long embrace. "You are not going, too?" said the Duchess, as she saw Mr. Oakhurst apparently waiting to accompany him.

"As far as the cañon," he replied. He turned suddenly and kissed the Duchess, leaving her pallid face aflame, and her trembling limbs rigid with amazement.

Night came, but not Mr. Oakhurst. It brought the storm again and the whirling snow. Then the Duchess, feeding the fire, found that someone had quietly piled beside the hut enough fuel to last a few days longer. The tears rose to her eyes, but she hid them from Piney.

The women slept but little. In the morning, looking into each other's faces, they read their fate. Neither spoke, but Piney, accepting the position of the stronger, drew near and placed her arm around the Duchess's waist. They kept this attitude for the rest of the day. That night the storm reached its greatest fury, and, rending asunder the protecting vines, invaded the very hut.

Toward morning they found themselves unable to feed the fire, which gradually died away. As the embers slowly blackened, the Duchess crept closer to Piney, and broke the silence of many hours: "Piney, can you pray?" "No, dear," said Piney simply. The Duchess, without knowing exactly why, felt relieved, and, putting her head upon Piney's shoulder, spoke no more. And so reclining, the younger and purer pillowing the head of her soiled sister upon her virgin breast, they fell asleep.

The wind lulled as if it feared to waken them. Feathery drifts of snow, shaken from the long pine boughs, flew like white winged birds, and settled about them as they slept. The moon through the rifted clouds looked down upon what had been the camp. But all human stain, all trace of earthly travail, was hidden beneath the spotless mantle mercifully flung from above.

They slept all that day and the next, nor did they waken when voices and footsteps broke the silence of the camp. And when pitying fingers brushed the snow from their wan faces, you could scarcely have told from the equal peace that dwelt upon them which was she that had sinned. Even the law of Poker Flat recognized this, and turned away, leaving them still locked in each other's arms.

But at the head of the gulch, on one of the largest pine-trees, they found the deuce of clubs pinned to the bark with a bowie-knife. It bore the following, written in pencil in a firm hand:

†

BENEATH THIS TREE
LIES THE BODY
OF

JOHN OAKHURST,

WHO STRUCK A STREAK OF BAD LUCK
ON THE 23D OF NOVEMBER 1850,
AND
HANDED IN HIS CHECKS
ON THE 7TH DECEMBER, 1850.

†

And pulseless and cold, with a derringer by his side and a bullet in his heart, though still calm as in life, beneath the snow lay he who was at once the strongest and yet the weakest of the outcasts of Poker Flat.

MIGGLES

We were eight including the driver. We had not spoken during the passage of the last six miles, since the jolting of the heavy vehicle over the roughening road had spoiled the Judge's last poetical quotation. The tall man beside the Judge was asleep, his arm passed through the swaying strap and his head resting upon it—altogether a limp, helpless looking object, as if he had hanged himself and been cut down too late.

The French lady on the back seat was asleep too, yet in a half-conscious propriety of attitude, shown even in the disposition of the handkerchief which she held to her forehead and which partially veiled her face. The lady from Virginia City, traveling with her husband, had long since lost all individuality in a wild confusion of ribbons, veils, furs, and shawls. There was no sound but the rattling of wheels and the dash of rain upon the roof.

Suddenly the stage stopped and we became dimly aware of voices. The driver was evidently in the midst of an exciting colloquy with some one in the road—a colloquy of which such fragments as "bridge gone," "twenty feet of water," "can't pass," were occasionally distinguishable above the storm. Then came a lull, and a mysterious voice from the road shouted the parting adjuration:

"Try Miggles's."

We caught a glimpse of our leaders as the vehicle slowly turned, of a horseman vanishing through the rain, and we were evidently on our way to Miggles's.

Who and where was Miggles? The Judge, our authority, did not remember the name, and he knew the country thoroughly. The Washoe traveler thought Miggles must keep a hotel. We only knew that we were stopped by high water in front and rear, and that Miggles was our rock of refuge. A ten minutes' splashing through a tangled byroad, scarcely wide enough for the stage, and we drew up before a barred and boarded gate in a wide stone wall or fence about eight feet high. Evidently Miggles's, and evidently Miggles did not keep a hotel.

The driver got down and tried the gate. It was securely locked.

"Miggles! O Miggles!"

No answer.

"Migg-ells! You Miggles!" continued the driver, with rising wrath.

"Migglesy!" joined in the expressman persuasively. "O Miggy! Mig!"

But no reply came from the apparently insensate Miggles. The Judge, who had finally got the window down, put his head out and propounded a series of questions, which if answered categorically would have undoubtedly elucidated the whole mystery, but which the driver evaded by replying that "if we didn't want to sit in the coach all night we had better rise up and sing out for Miggles."

So we rose up and called on Miggles in chorus, then separately. And when we had finished, a Hibernian fellow passenger from the roof called for "Maygells!" whereat we all laughed. While we were laughing the driver cried, "Shoo!"

We listened. To our infinite amazement the chorus of "Miggles" was repeated from the other side of the wall, even to the final and supplemental "Maygells."

"Extraordinary echo!" said the Judge.

"Extraordinary d——d skunk!" roared the driver contemptuously. "Come out of that, Miggles, and show yourself! Be a man, Miggles! Don't hide in the dark; I wouldn't if I were you, Miggles," continued Yuba Bill, now dancing about in an excess of fury.

"Miggles!" continued the voice, "O Miggles!"

"My good man! Mr. Myghail!" said the Judge, softening the asperities of the name as much as possible. "Consider the inhospitality of refusing shelter from the inclemency of the weather to helpless females. Really, my dear sir——" But a succession of "Miggles," ending in a burst of laughter, drowned his voice.

Yuba Bill hesitated no longer. Taking a heavy stone from the road, he battered down the gate, and with the expressman entered the inclosure. We followed. Nobody was to be seen. In the gathering darkness all that we could distinguish was that we were in a garden—from the rose bushes that scattered over us a minute spray from their dripping leaves—and before a long, rambling wooden building.

"Do you know this Miggles?" asked the Judge of Yuba Bill.

"No, nor don't want to," said Bill shortly, who felt the Pioneer Stage Company insulted in his person by the contumacious Miggles.

"But, my dear sir," expostulated the Judge, as he thought of the barred gate.

"Lookee here," said Yuba Bill, with fine irony, "hadn't you better go back and sit in the coach till yer introduced? I'm going in," and he pushed open the door of the building.

A long room, lighted only by the embers of a fire that was dying on the large hearth at its farther extremity; the walls curiously papered, and the flickering firelight bringing out its grotesque pattern; somebody sitting in a large armchair by the fireplace. All this we saw as we crowded together into the room after the driver and expressman.

"Hello! be you Miggles?" said Yuba Bill to the solitary occupant.

The figure neither spoke nor stirred. Yuba Bill walked wrathfully toward it and turned the eye of his coach-lantern upon its face. It was a man's face, prematurely old and wrinkled, with very large eyes, in which there was that expression of perfectly gratuitous solemnity which I had sometimes seen in an owl's. The large eyes wandered from Bill's face to the lantern, and finally fixed their gaze on that luminous object without further recognition.

Bill restrained himself with an effort.

"Miggles! be you deaf? You ain't dumb anyhow, you know," and Yuba Bill shook the insensate figure by the shoulder.

To our great dismay, as Bill removed his hand, the venerable stranger apparently collapsed, sinking into half his size and an undistinguishable heap of clothing.

"Well, dern my skin," said Bill, looking appealingly at us, and hopelessly retiring from the contest.

The Judge now stepped forward, and we lifted the mysterious invertebrate back into his original position. Bill was dismissed with the lantern to reconnoitre outside, for it was evident that, from the helplessness of this solitary man, there must be attendants near at hand, and we all drew around the fire. The Judge, who had regained his authority, and had never lost his conversational amiability—standing before us with his back to the hearth—charged us, as an imaginary jury, as follows:

"It is evident that either our distinguished friend here has reached that condition described by Shakespeare as 'the sere and yellow leaf,' or has suffered some premature abatement of his mental and physical faculties. Whether he is really the Miggles——"

Here he was interrupted by "Miggles! O Miggles! Migglesy! Mig!" and, in fact, the whole chorus of Miggles in very much the same key as it had once before been delivered unto us.

We gazed at each other for a moment in some alarm. The Judge, in particular, vacated his position quickly, as the voice seemed to come directly over his shoulder. The cause, however, was soon discovered in a large magpie who was perched upon a shelf over the fireplace, and who immediately relapsed into a sepulchral silence, which contrasted singularly with his previous volubility. It was, undoubtedly, his voice which we had heard in the road, and our friend in the chair was not responsible for the discourtesy.

Yuba Bill, who re-entered the room after an unsuccessful search, was loth to accept the explanation, and still eyed the helpless sitter with suspicion. He had found a shed in which he had put up his horses, but he came back dripping and skeptical. "Thar ain't nobody but him within ten mile of the shanty, and that ar d——d old skeesicks knows it."

But the faith of the majority proved to be securely based. Bill had scarcely ceased growling before we heard a quick step upon the porch, the trailing of a wet skirt, the door was flung open, and with a flash of white teeth, a sparkle of dark eyes, and an utter absence of ceremony or diffidence, a young woman entered, shut the door, and, panting, leaned back against it.

"Oh, if you please, I'm Miggles!"

And this was Miggles—this bright-eyed, full-throated young woman, whose wet gown of coarse blue stuff could not hide the beauty of the feminine curves to which it clung; from the chestnut crown of whose head, topped by a man's oil-skin sou'wester, to the little feet and ankles, hidden somewhere in the recesses of her boy's brogans, all was grace—this was Miggles, laughing at us, too, in the most airy, frank, off-hand manner imaginable.

"You see, boys," said she, quite out of breath, and holding one little hand against her side, quite unheeding the speechless discomfiture of our party or the complete demoralization of Yuba Bill, whose features had relaxed into an expression of gratuitous and imbecile cheerfulness—"you see, boys, I was mor'n two miles away when you passed down the road. I thought you might pull up here, and so I ran

the whole way, knowing nobody was home but Jim—and—and—
I'm out of breath—and—that lets me out."

And here Miggles caught her dripping oilskin hat from her head,
with a mischievous swirl that scattered a shower of raindrops over
us; attempted to put back her hair; dropped two hairpins in the attempt; laughed, and sat down beside Yuba Bill, with her hands crossed
lightly on her lap.

The Judge recovered himself first and essayed an extravagant com-
pliment.

"I'll trouble you for that ha'rpin," said Miggles gravely. Half a dozen
hands were eagerly stretched forward; the missing hairpin was restored to its fair owner; and Miggles, crossing the room, looked keenly
in the face of the invalid. The solemn eyes looked back at hers with
an expression we had never seen before. Life and intelligence seemed
to struggle back into the rugged face. Miggles laughed again—it was
a singularly eloquent laugh—and turned her black eyes and white
teeth once more towards us.

"This afflicted person is—" hesitated the Judge.

"Jim!" said Miggles.

"Your father?"

"No!"

"Brother?"

"No!"

"Husband?"

Miggles darted a quick, half-defiant glance at the two lady passengers, who I had noticed did not participate in the general masculine
admiration of Miggles, and said gravely, "No; it's Jim!"

There was an awkward pause. The lady passengers moved closer
to each other; the Washoe husband looked abstractedly at the fire,
and the tall man apparently turned his eyes inward for self-support
at this emergency. But Miggles's laugh, which was very infectious,
broke the silence.

"Come," she said briskly, "you must be hungry. Who'll bear a hand
to help me get tea?"

She had no lack of volunteers. In a few moments Yuba Bill was
engaged like Caliban in bearing logs for this Miranda; the expressman was grinding coffee on the veranda; to myself the arduous duty
of slicing bacon was assigned; and the Judge lent each man his good-
humored and voluble counsel. And when Miggles, assisted by the

Judge and our Hibernian "deck-passenger," set the table with all the available crockery, we had become quite joyous, in spite of the rain that beat against the windows, the wind that whirled down the chimney, the two ladies who whispered together in the corner, or the magpie, who uttered a satirical and croaking commentary on their conversation from his perch above.

In the now bright, blazing fire we could see that the walls were papered with illustrated journals, arranged with feminine taste and discrimination. The furniture was extemporized and adapted from candle-boxes and packing-cases, and covered with gay calico or the skin of some animal. The armchair of the helpless Jim was an ingenious variation of a flour-barrel. There was neatness, and even a taste for the picturesque, to be seen in the few details of the long, low room.

The meal was a culinary success. But more, it was a social triumph—chiefly, I think, owing to the rare tact of Miggles in guiding the conversation, asking all the questions herself, yet bearing throughout a frankness that rejected the idea of any concealment on her own part, so that we talked of ourselves, of our prospects, of the journey, of the weather, of each other—of everything but our host and hostess.

It must be confessed that Miggles's conversation was never elegant, rarely grammatical, and that at times she employed expletives the use of which had generally been yielded to our sex. But they were delivered with such a lighting up of teeth and eyes, and were usually followed by a laugh—a laugh peculiar to Miggles—so frank and honest that it seemed to clear the moral atmosphere.

Once during the meal we heard a noise like the rubbing of a heavy body against the outer walls of the house. This was shortly followed by a scratching and sniffling at the door. "That's Joaquin," said Miggles, in reply to our questioning glances; "would you like to see him?"

Before we could answer she had opened the door, and disclosed a half-grown grizzly, who instantly raised himself on his haunches, with his fore paws hanging down in the popular attitude of mendicancy, and looked admiringly at Miggles, with a very singular resemblance in his manner to Yuba Bill.

"That's my watch-dog," said Miggles, in explanation. "Oh, he don't bite," she added, as the two lady passengers fluttered into a corner. "Does he, old Toppy?" the latter remark being addressed directly to the sagacious Joaquin.

"I tell you what, boys," continued Miggles, after she had fed and closed the door on Ursa Minor, "you were in big luck that Joaquin wasn't hanging round when you dropped in tonight."

"Where was he?" asked the Judge.

"With me," said Miggles. "Lord love you! he trots round with me nights like as if he was a man."

We were silent for a few moments, and listened to the wind. Perhaps we all had the same picture before us—of Miggles walking through the rainy woods with her savage guardian at her side. The Judge, I remember, said something about Una and her lion; but Miggles received it, as she did other compliments, with quiet gravity. Whether she was altogether unconscious of the admiration she excited—she could hardly have been oblivious of Yuba Bill's adoration—I know not; but her very frankness suggested a perfect sexual equality that was cruelly humiliating to the younger members of our party.

The incident of the bear did not add anything in Miggles's favor to the opinions of those of her own sex who were present. In fact, the repast over, a chillness radiated from the two lady passengers that no pine boughs brought in by Yuba Bill and cast as a sacrifice upon the hearth could wholly overcome. Miggles felt it; and suddenly declaring that it was time to "turn in," offered to show the ladies to their bed in an adjoining room. "You, boys, will have to camp out here by the fire as well as you can," she added, "for thar ain't but the one room."

Our sex—by which, my dear sir, I allude of course to the stronger portion of humanity—has been generally relieved from the imputation of curiosity or a fondness for gossip. Yet I am constrained to say, that hardly had the door closed on Miggles than we crowded together, whispering, snickering, smiling, and exchanging suspicions, surmises, and a thousand speculations in regard to our pretty hostess and her singular companion. I fear that we even hustled that imbecile paralytic, who sat like a voiceless Memnon in our midst, gazing with the serene indifference of the Past in his passionless eyes upon our wordy counsels. In the midst of an exciting discussion the door opened again and Miggles re-entered.

But not, apparently, the same Miggles who a few hours before had flashed upon us. Her eyes were downcast, and as she hesitated for a moment on the threshold, with a blanket on her arm, she seemed to have left behind her the frank fearlessness which had charmed us a moment before.

Coming into the room, she drew a low stool beside the paralytic's chair, sat down, drew the blanket over her shoulders, and saying, "If it's all the same to you, boys, as we're rather crowded, I'll stop here tonight," took the invalid's withered hand in her own, and turned her eyes upon the dying fire. An instinctive feeling that this was only premonitory to more confidential relations, and perhaps some shame at our previous curiosity, kept us silent.

The rain still beat upon the roof, wandering gusts of wind stirred the embers into momentary brightness, until, in a lull of the elements, Miggles suddenly lifted up her head, and, throwing her hair over her shoulder, turned her face upon the group and asked:

"Is there any of you that knows me?"

There was no reply.

"Think again! I lived at Marysville in '53. Everybody knew me there, and everybody had the right to know me. I kept the Polka Saloon until I came to live with Jim. That's six years ago. Perhaps I've changed some."

The absence of recognition may have disconcerted her. She turned her head to the fire again, and it was some seconds before she again spoke, and then more rapidly:

"Well, you see I thought some of you must have known me. There's no great harm done anyway. What I was going to say was this: Jim here"—she took his hand in both of hers as she spoke—"used to know me, if you didn't, and spent a heap of money upon me. I reckon he spent all he had. And one day—it's six years ago this winter—Jim came into my back room, sat down on my sofy, like as you see him in that chair, and never moved again without help.

"He was struck all of a heap, and never seemed to know what ailed him. The doctors came and said as how it was caused all along of his way of life—for Jim was mighty free and wild-like—and that he would never get better, and couldn't last long anyway.

"They advised me to send him to Frisco to the hospital, for he was no good to anyone and would be a baby all his life. Perhaps it was something in Jim's eye, perhaps it was that I never had a baby, but I said 'No.' I was rich then, for I was popular with everybody—gentlemen like yourself, sir, came to see me—and I sold out my business and bought this yer place, because it was sort of out of the way of travel, you see, and I brought my baby here."

With a woman's intuitive tact and poetry, she had, as she spoke, slowly shifted her position so as to bring the mute figure of the ruined man between her and her audience, hiding in the shadow behind it, as if she offered it as a tacit apology for her actions. Silent and expressionless, it yet spoke for her; helpless, crushed, and smitten with the Divine thunderbolt, it still stretched an invisible arm around her.

Hidden in the darkness, but still holding his hand, she went on:

"It was a long time before I could get the hang of things about yer, for I was used to company and excitement. I couldn't get any woman to help me, and a man I dursn't trust; but what with the Indians hereabout, who'd do odd jobs for me, and having everything sent from the North Fork, Jim and I managed to worry through. The Doctor would run up from Sacramento once in a while. He'd ask to see 'Miggles's baby,' as he called Jim, and when he'd go away, he'd say, 'Miggles, you're a trump—God bless you,' and it didn't seem so lonely after that.

"But the last time he was here he said, as he opened the door to go, 'Do you know, Miggles, your baby will grow up to be a man yet and an honor to his mother; but not here, Miggles, not here!' And I thought he went away sad—and——and" And here Miggles's voice and head were somehow both lost completely in the shadow.

"The folks about here are very kind," said Miggles, after a pause, coming a little into the light again. "The men from the Fork used to hang around here, until they found they wasn't wanted, and the women are kind, and don't call.

"I was pretty lonely until I picked up Joaquin in the woods yonder one day, when he wasn't so high, and taught him to beg for his dinner; and then thar's Polly—that's the magpie—she knows no end of tricks, and makes it quite sociable of evenings with her talk, and so I don't feel like as I was the only living being about the ranch.

"And Jim here," said Miggles, with her old laugh again, and coming out quite into the firelight—'Jim—Why, boys, you would admire to see how much he knows for a man like him. Sometimes I bring him flowers, and he looks at 'em just as natural as if he knew 'em; and times, when we're sitting alone, I read him those things on the wall. Why, Lord!" said Miggles, with her frank laugh, "I've read him that whole side of the house this winter. There never was such a man for reading as Jim."

"Why," asked the Judge, "do you not marry this man to whom you have devoted your youthful life?"

"Well, you see," said Miggles, "it would be playing it rather low down on Jim to take advantage of his being so helpless. And then, too, if we were man and wife, now, we'd both know that I was bound to do what I do now of my own accord."

"But you are young yet and attractive——"

"It's getting late," said Miggles gravely, "and you'd better all turn in. Goodnight, boys." And throwing the blanket over her head, Miggles laid herself down beside Jim's chair, her head pillowed on the low stool that held his feet, and spoke no more. The fire slowly faded from the hearth, we each sought our blankets in silence; and presently there was no sound in the long room but the pattering of the rain upon the roof and the heavy breathing of the sleepers.

It was nearly morning when I awoke from a troubled dream. The storm had passed, the stars were shining, and through the shutterless window the full moon, lifting itself over the solemn pines without, looked into the room. It touched the lonely figure in the chair with an infinite compassion, and seemed to baptize with a shining flood the lowly head of the woman whose hair, as in the sweet old story, bathed the feet of him she loved. It even lent a kindly poetry to the rugged outline of Yuba Bill, half reclining on his elbow between them and his passengers, with savagely patient eyes keeping watch and ward. And then I fell asleep and only woke at broad day, with Yuba Bill standing over me, and "All aboard" ringing in my ears.

Coffee was waiting for us on the table, but Miggles was gone. We wandered about the house and lingered long after the horses were harnessed, but she did not return. It was evident that she wished to avoid a formal leave-taking, and had so left us to depart as we had come. After we had helped the ladies into the coach, we returned to the house and solemnly shook hands with the paralytic Jim, as solemnly setting him back into position after each handshake. Then we looked for the last time around the long low room, at the stool where Miggles had sat, and slowly took our seats in the waiting coach. The whip cracked, and we were off!

But as we reached the highroad, Bill's dexterous hand laid the six horses back on their haunches, and the stage stopped with a jerk. For there, on a little eminence beside the road, stood Miggles, her hair flying, her eyes sparkling, her white handkerchief waving, and her white teeth flashing a last "good-bye." We waved our hats in return.

And then Yuba Bill, as if fearful of further fascination, madly lashed his horses forward, and we sank back in our seats.

We exchanged not a word until we reached the North Fork and the stage drew up at the Independence House. Then, the Judge leading, we walked into the bar-room and took our places gravely at the bar.

"Are your glasses charged, gentlemen?" said the Judge, solemnly taking off his white hat.

They were.

"Well, then, here's to Miggles—GOD BLESS HER!"

Perhaps He had. Who knows?

TENNESSEE'S PARTNER

I do not think that we ever knew his real name. Our ignorance of it certainly never gave us any social inconvenience, for at Sandy Bar in 1854 most men were christened anew.

Sometimes these appellatives were derived from some distinctiveness of dress, as in the case of "Dungaree Jack"; or from some peculiarity of habit, as shown in "Saleratus Bill," so called from an undue proportion of that chemical in his daily bread; or from some unlucky slip, as exhibited in "The Iron Pirate," a mild, inoffensive man, who earned that baleful title by his unfortunate mispronunciation of the term "iron pyrites."

Perhaps this may have been the beginning of a rude heraldry; but I am constrained to think that it was because a man's real name in that day rested solely upon his own unsupported statement.

"Call yourself Clifford, do you?" said Boston, addressing a timid newcomer with infinite scorn; "Hell is full of such Cliffords!" He then introduced the unfortunate man, whose name happened to be really Clifford, as "Jaybird Charley"—an unhallowed inspiration of the moment that clung to him ever after.

But to return to Tennessee's Partner, whom we never knew by any other than this relative title. That he had ever existed as a separate and distinct individuality we only learned later.

It seems that in 1853 he left Poker Flat to go to San Francisco, ostensibly to procure a wife. He never got any farther than Stockton. At that place he was attracted by a young person who waited upon the table at the hotel where he took his meals. One morning he said something to her which caused her to smile not unkindly, to somewhat coquettishly break a plate of toast over his upturned, serious, simple face, and to retreat to the kitchen. He followed her, and emerged a few moments later, covered with more toast and victory.

That day week they were married by a justice of the peace, and returned to Poker Flat. I am aware that something more might be made of this episode, but I prefer to tell it as it was current at Sandy Bar—in the gulches and barrooms—where all sentiment was modified by a strong sense of humor.

Of their married felicity but little is known, perhaps for the reason that Tennessee, then living with his partner, one day took occasion to say something to the bride on his own account, at which, it is said, she smiled not unkindly and chastely retreated—this time as far as Marysville, where Tennessee followed her, and where they went to housekeeping without the aid of a justice of the peace.

Tennessee's Partner took the loss of his wife simply and seriously, as was his fashion. But to everybody's surprise, when Tennessee one day returned from Marysville, without his partner's wife—she having smiled and retreated with somebody else—Tennessee's Partner was the first man to shake his hand and greet him with affection.

The boys who had gathered in the cañon to see the shooting were naturally indignant. Their indignation might have found vent in sarcasm but for a certain look in Tennessee's Partner's eye that indicated a lack of humorous appreciation. In fact, he was a grave man, with a steady application to practical detail which was unpleasant in a difficulty.

Meanwhile a popular feeling against Tennessee had grown up on the Bar. He was known to be a gambler; he was suspected to be a thief. In these suspicions Tennessee's Partner was equally compromised; his continued intimacy with Tennessee after the affair above quoted could only be accounted for on the hypothesis of a copartnership of crime.

At last Tennessee's guilt became flagrant. One day he overtook a stranger on his way to Red Dog. The stranger afterward related that Tennessee beguiled the time with interesting anecdote and reminiscence, but illogically concluded the interview in the following words: "And now, young man, I'll trouble you for your knife, your pistols, and your money. You see your weppings might get you into trouble at Red Dog, and your money's a temptation to the evilly disposed. I think you said your address was San Francisco. I shall endeavor to call."

It may be stated here that Tennessee had a fine flow of humor, which no business preoccupation could wholly subdue.

This exploit was his last. Red Dog and Sandy Bar made common cause against the highwayman. Tennessee was hunted in very much the same fashion as his prototype, the grizzly. As the toils closed around him, he made a desperate dash through the Bar, emptying his revolver at the crowd before the Arcade Saloon, and so on up Grizzly Cañon; but at its farther extremity he was stopped by a small man on a gray horse. The men looked at each other a moment in silence. Both were fearless, both self-possessed and independent, and both types of a civilization that in the seventeenth century would have been called heroic, but in the nineteenth simply "reckless."

"What have you got there?—I call," said Tennessee quietly.

"Two bowers and an ace," said the stranger as quietly, showing two revolvers and a bowie-knife.

"That takes me," returned Tennessee; and, with this gambler's epigram, he threw away his useless pistol and rode back with his captor.

It was a warm night. The cool breeze which usually sprang up with the going down of the sun behind the chaparral-crested mountain was that evening withheld from Sandy Bar. The little cañon was stifling with heated resinous odors, and the decaying driftwood on the Bar sent forth faint sickening exhalations. The feverishness of day and its fierce passions still filled the camp. Lights moved restlessly along the bank of the river, striking no answering reflection from its tawny current.

Against the blackness of the pines the windows of the old loft above the express-office stood out staringly bright; and through their curtainless panes the loungers below could see the forms of those who were even then deciding the fate of Tennessee. And above all this, etched on the dark firmament, rose the Sierra, remote and passionless, crowned with remoter passionless stars.

The trial of Tennessee was conducted as fairly as was consistent with a judge and jury who felt themselves to some extent obliged to justify, in their verdict, the previous irregularities of arrest and indictment. The law of Sandy Bar was implacable, but not vengeful. The excitement and personal feeling of the chase were over; with Tennessee safe in their hands, they were ready to listen patiently to any defense, which they were already satisfied was insufficient.

There being no doubt in their own minds, they were willing to give the prisoner the benefit of any that might exist. Secure in the hypothesis that he ought to be hanged on general principles, they indulged him with more latitude of defense than his reckless hardihood seemed to ask.

The Judge appeared to be more anxious than the prisoner, who, otherwise unconcerned, evidently took a grim pleasure in the responsibility he had created. "I don't take any hand in this yer game," had been his invariable but good-humored reply to all questions. The Judge—who was also his captor—for a moment vaguely regretted that he had not shot him "on sight" that morning, but presently dismissed this human weakness as unworthy of the judicial mind.

Nevertheless, when there was a tap at the door, and it was said that Tennessee's Partner was there on behalf of the prisoner, he was admitted at once without question. Perhaps the younger members of the jury, to whom the proceedings were becoming irksomely thoughtful, hailed him as a relief.

For he was not, certainly, an imposing figure. Short and stout, with a square face, sunburned into a preternatural redness, clad in a loose duck "jumper" and trousers streaked and splashed with red soil, his aspect under any circumstances would have been quaint, and was now even ridiculous.

As he stooped to deposit at his feet a heavy carpetbag he was carrying, it became obvious, from partially developed legends and inscriptions, that the material with which his trousers had been patched had been originally intended for a less ambitious covering. Yet he advanced with great gravity, and after shaking the hand of each person in the room with labored cordiality, he wiped his serious perplexed face on a red bandana handkerchief, a shade lighter than his complexion, laid his powerful hand upon the table to steady himself, and thus addressed the Judge:

"I was passin' by," he began, by way of apology, "and I thought I'd just step in and see how things was gittin' on with Tennessee thar— my pardner. It's a hot night. I disremember any sich weather before on the Bar."

He paused a moment, but nobody volunteering any other meteorological recollection, he again had recourse to his pocket-handkerchief, and for some moments mopped his face diligently.

"Have you anything to say on behalf of the prisoner?" said the Judge finally.

"Thet's it," said Tennessee's Partner, in a tone of relief. "I come yar as Tennessee's pardner—knowing him nigh on four year, off and on, wet and dry, in luck and out o' luck. His ways ain't aller my ways, but thar ain't any p'ints in that young man, thar ain't any liveliness as he's been up to, as I don't know. And you sez to me, sez you—confidential-like, and between man and man—sez you, 'Do you know anything in his behalf?' and I sez to you, sez I—confidential like, as between man and man—'What should a man know of his pardner?'"

"Is this all you have to say?" asked the Judge impatiently, feeling, perhaps, that a dangerous sympathy of humor was beginning to humanize the court.

"Thet's so," continued Tennessee's Partner. "It ain't for me to say anything agin' him. And now, what's the case? Here's Tennessee wants money, wants it bad, and doesn't like to ask it of his old pardner. Well, what does Tennessee do? He lays for a stranger, and he fetches that stranger; and you lays for *him*, and you fetches *him*; and the honors is easy. And I put it to you, bein' a fa'r-minded man, and to you, gentlemen all, as fa'r-minded men, ef this isn't so."

"Prisoner," said the Judge, interrupting, "have you any questions to ask this man?"

"No! no!" continued Tennessee's Partner hastily. "I play this yer hand alone. To come down to the bed-rock, it's just this: Tennessee, thar, has played it pretty rough and expensive-like on a stranger, and on this yer camp. And now, what's the fair thing? Some would say more, some would say less. Here's seventeen hundred dollars in coarse gold and a watch—it's about all my pile—and call it square!" And before a hand could be raised to prevent him, he had emptied the contents of the carpetbag upon the table.

For a moment his life was in jeopardy. One or two men sprang to their feet, several hands groped for hidden weapons, and a suggestion to throw him from the window was only overridden by a gesture from the Judge.

Tennessee laughed. And apparently oblivious of the excitement, Tennessee's Partner improved the opportunity to mop his face again with his handkerchief.

When order was restored, and the man was made to understand, by the use of forcible figures and rhetoric, that Tennessee's offense could not be condoned by money, his face took a more serious and sanguinary hue, and those who were nearest to him noticed that his rough hand trembled slightly on the table.

He hesitated a moment as he slowly returned the gold to the carpetbag, as if he had not yet entirely caught the elevated sense of justice which swayed the tribunal, and was perplexed with the belief that he had not offered enough.

Then he turned to the Judge, and saying, "This yer is a lone hand, played alone, and without my pardner," he bowed to the jury and was about to withdraw, when the Judge called him back:

"If you have anything to say to Tennessee, you had better say it now."

For the first time that evening the eyes of the prisoner and his strange advocate met.

Tennessee smiled, showed his white teeth, and saying, "Euchred, old man!" held out his hand.

Tennessee's Partner took it in his own, and saying, "I just dropped in as I was passin' to see how things was gettin' on," let the hand passively fall, and adding that "it was a warm night," again mopped his face with his handkerchief, and without another word withdrew.

The two men never again met each other alive. For the unparalleled insult of a bribe offered to Judge Lynch—who, whether bigoted, weak, or narrow, was at least incorruptible—firmly fixed in the mind of that mythical personage any wavering determination of Tennessee's fate; and at the break of day he was marched, closely guarded, to meet it at the top of Marley's Hill.

How he met it, how cool he was, how he refused to say anything, how perfect were the arrangements of the committee, were all duly reported, with the addition of a warning moral and example to all future evil-doers, in the *Red Dog Clarion*, by its editor, who was present.

But the beauty of that midsummer morning, the blessed amity of earth and air and sky, the awakened life of the free woods and hills, the joyous renewal and promise of Nature, and above all, the infinite serenity that thrilled through each, was not reported, as not being a part of the social lesson.

And yet, when the weak and foolish deed was done, and a life, with its possibilities and responsibilities, had passed out of the misshapen thing that dangled between earth and sky, the birds sang, the flowers bloomed, the sun shone, as cheerily as before; and possibly the *Red Dog Clarion* was right.

Tennessee's Partner was not in the group that surrounded the ominous tree. But as they turned to disperse, attention was drawn to the singular appearance of a motionless donkey-cart halted at the side of the road.

As they approached, they at once recognized the venerable "Jenny" and the two-wheeled cart as the property of Tennessee's Partner, used by him in carrying dirt from his claim; and a few paces distant the owner of the equipage himself, sitting under a buckeye-tree, wiping the perspiration from his glowing face.

In answer to an inquiry, he said he had come for the body of the "diseased," "if it was all the same to the committee." He didn't wish to "hurry anything"; he could "wait." He was not working that day; and when the gentlemen were done with the "diseased," he would take him. "Ef thar is any present," he added, in his simple, serious way, "as would care to jine in the fun'l, they kin come."

Perhaps it was from a sense of humor, which I have already intimated was a feature of Sandy Bar—perhaps it was from something even better than that, but two thirds of the loungers accepted the invitation at once.

It was noon when the body of Tennessee was delivered into the hands of his partner. As the cart drew up to the fatal tree, we noticed that it contained a rough oblong box—apparently made from a section of sluicing—and half filled with bark and the tassels of pine. The cart was further decorated with slips of willow and made fragrant with buckeye-blossoms. When the body was deposited in the box, Tennessee's Partner drew over it a piece of tarred canvas, and gravely mounting the narrow seat in front, with his feet upon the shafts, urged the little donkey forward.

The equipage moved slowly on, at that decorous pace which was habitual with Jenny even under less solemn circumstances. The men—half curiously, half jestingly, but all good-humoredly—strolled along beside the cart, some in advance, some a little in the rear of the homely catafalque.

But whether from the narrowing of the road or some present sense of decorum, as the cart passed on, the company fell to the rear in couples, keeping step, and otherwise assuming the external show of a formal procession. Jack Folinsbee, who had at the outset played a funeral march in dumb show upon an imaginary trombone, desisted from a lack of sympathy and appreciation—not having, perhaps, your true humorist's capacity to be content with the enjoyment of his own fun.

The way led through Grizzly Cañon, by this time clothed in funereal drapery and shadows. The redwoods, burying their moccasined feet in the red soil, stood in Indian file along the track, trailing an uncouth benediction from their bending boughs upon the passing bier. A hare, surprised into helpless inactivity, sat upright and pulsating in the ferns by the roadside as the cortège went by. Squirrels hastened to gain a secure outlook from higher boughs; and the bluejays, spreading their wings, fluttered before them like outriders, until the outskirts of Sandy Bar were reached, and the solitary cabin of Tennessee's Partner.

Viewed under more favorable circumstances, it would not have been a cheerful place. The unpicturesque site, the rude and unlovely outlines, the unsavory details, which distinguish the nest-building of the California miner, were all here with the dreariness of decay superadded. A few paces from the cabin there was a rough inclosure, which, in the brief days of Tennessee's Partner's matrimonial felicity, had been used as a garden, but was now overgrown with fern. As we approached it, we were surprised to find that what we had taken for a recent attempt at cultivation was the broken soil about an open grave.

The cart was halted before the inclosure, and rejecting the offers of assistance with the same air of simple self-reliance he had displayed throughout, Tennessee's Partner lifted the rough coffin on his back, and deposited it unaided within the shallow grave. He then nailed down the board which served as a lid, and mounting the little mound of earth beside it, took off his hat and slowly mopped his face with his handkerchief. This the crowd felt was a preliminary to speech, and they disposed themselves variously on stumps and boulders, and sat expectant.

"When a man," began Tennessee's Partner slowly, "has been running free all day, what's the natural thing for him to do? Why, to come home. And if he ain't in a condition to go home, what can his best friend do? Why, bring him home. And here's Tennessee has been running free, and we brings him home from his wandering."

He paused and picked up a fragment of quartz, rubbed it thoughtfully on his sleeve, and went on: "It ain't the first time that I've packed him on my back, as you see'd me now. It ain't the first time that I brought him to this yer cabin when he couldn't help himself; it ain't the first time that I and Jinny have waited for him on yon hill, and picked him up and so fetched him home, when he couldn't speak and didn't know me. And now that it's the last time, why"—he paused and rubbed the quartz gently on his sleeve—"you see it's sort of rough on his pardner.

"And now, gentlemen," he added abruptly, picking up his long-handled shovel, "the fun'l's over; and my thanks, and Tennessee's thanks, to you for your trouble."

Resisting any proffers of assistance, he began to fill in the grave, turning his back upon the crowd, that after a few moments' hesitation gradually withdrew. As they crossed the little ridge that hid Sandy Bar from view, some, looking back, thought they could see Tennessee's Partner, his work done, sitting upon the grave, his shovel between his knees, and his face buried in his red bandana handkerchief. But it was argued by others that you couldn't tell his face from his handkerchief at that distance, and this point remained undecided.

In the reaction that followed the feverish excitement of that day, Tennessee's Partner was not forgotten. A secret investigation had cleared him of any complicity in Tennessee's guilt, and left only a suspicion of his general sanity. Sandy Bar made a point of calling on him, and proffering various uncouth but well-meant kindnesses. But from that day his rude health and great strength seemed visibly to decline; and when the rainy season fairly set in, and the tiny grass-blades were beginning to peep from the rocky mound above Tennessee's grave, he took to his bed.

One night, when the pines beside the cabin were swaying in the storm and trailing their slender fingers over the roof, and the roar and rush of the swollen river were heard below, Tennessee's Partner lifted his head from the pillow, saying, "It is time to go for Tennessee; I must put Jinny in the cart"; and would have risen from his bed but for the restraint of his attendant.

Struggling, he still pursued his singular fancy: "There, now, steady, Jinny—steady, old girl. How dark it is! Look out for the ruts—and look out for him, too, old gal. Sometimes, you know, when he's blind drunk, he drops down right in the trail. Keep on straight up to the pine on the top of the hill. Thar! I told you so!—thar he is—coming this way, too—all by himself, sober, and his face a-shining. Tennessee! Pardner!"

And so they met.

HIGH-WATER MARK

When the tide was out on the Dedlow Marsh, its extended dreariness was patent. Its spongy, low-lying surface, sluggish, inky pools, and tortuous sloughs, twisting their slimy way, eel-like, toward the open bay, were all hard facts. So were the few green tussocks, with their scant blades, their amphibious flavor, and unpleasant dampness.

And if you chose to indulge your fancy—although the flat monotony of the Dedlow Marsh was not inspiring—the wavy line of scattered drift gave an unpleasant consciousness of the spent waters, and made the dead certainty of the returning tide a gloomy reflection, which no present sunshine could dissipate. The greener meadowland seemed oppressed with this idea, and made no positive attempt at vegetation until the work of reclamation should be complete. In the bitter fruit of the low cranberry bushes one might fancy he detected a naturally sweet disposition curdled and soured by an injudicious course of too much regular cold water.

The vocal expression of the Dedlow Marsh was also melancholy and depressing. The sepulchral boom of the bittern, the shriek of the curlew, the scream of passing brant, the wrangling of quarrelsome teal, the sharp querulous protest of the startled crane, and syllabled complaint of the "killdeer" plover were beyond the power of written expression.

Nor was the aspect of these mournful fowls at all cheerful and inspiring. Certainly not the blue heron, standing midleg deep in the water, obviously catching cold in a reckless disregard of wet feet and consequences; nor the mournful curlew, the dejected plover, or the low-spirited snipe, who saw fit to join him in his suicidal contemplation; nor the impassive kingfisher—an ornithological Marius—reviewing the desolate expanse; nor the black raven that went to and fro over the face of the marsh continually, but evidently couldn't make up his mind whether the waters had subsided, and felt low-spirited in the reflection that after all this trouble he wouldn't be able to give a definite answer. On the contrary, it was evident at a glance that the dreary expanse of Dedlow Marsh told unpleasantly on the birds, and that the season of migration was looked forward to with a feeling of relief and satisfaction by the full grown, and of extravagant anticipation by the callow brood.

But if Dedlow Marsh was cheerless at the slack of the low tide, you should have seen it when the tide was strong and full. When the damp air blew chilly over the cold glittering expanse, and came to the faces of those who looked seaward like another tide; when a steel-like glint marked the low hollows and the sinuous line of slough; when the great shell-incrusted trunks of fallen trees arose again, and went forth on their dreary purposeless wanderings, drifting hither and thither, but getting no farther toward any goal at the falling tide or the day's decline than the cursed Hebrew in the legend. When the glossy ducks swung silently, making neither ripple nor furrow on the shimmering surface; when the fog came in with the tide and shut out the blue above, even as the green below had been obliterated; when boatmen, lost in that fog, paddling about in a hopeless way, started at what seemed the brushing of mermen's fingers on the boat's keel, or shrank from the tufts of grass spreading around like the floating hair of a corpse, and knew by these signs that they were lost upon Dedlow Marsh, and must make a night of it, and a gloomy one at that—then you might know something of Dedlow Marsh at high water.

Let me recall a story connected with this latter view which never failed to recur to my mind in my long gunning excursions upon Dedlow Marsh. Although the event was briefly recorded in the county paper, I had the story, in all its eloquent detail, from the lips of the principal actor. I cannot hope to catch the varying emphasis and peculiar coloring of feminine delineation, for my narrator was a woman; but I'll try to give at least its substance.

She lived midway of the great slough of Dedlow Marsh and a good-sized river, which debouched four miles beyond into an estuary formed by the Pacific Ocean, on the long sandy peninsula which constituted the southwestern boundary of a noble bay. The house in which she lived was a small frame cabin raised from the marsh a few feet by stout piles, and was three miles distant from the settlements upon the river. Her husband was a logger—a profitable business in a county where the principal occupation was the manufacture of lumber.

It was the season of early spring, when her husband left on the ebb of a high tide with a raft of logs for the usual transportation to the lower end of the bay. As she stood by the door of the little cabin when the voyagers departed, she noticed a cold look in the south-eastern sky, and she remembered hearing her husband say to his companions that they must endeavor to complete their voyage before the coming of the south-westerly gale which he saw brewing. And that night it began to storm and blow harder than she had ever before experienced, and some great trees fell in the forest by the river, and the house rocked like her baby's cradle.

But however the storm might roar about the little cabin, she knew that one she trusted had driven bolt and bar with his own strong hand, and that had he feared for her he would not have left her. This, and her domestic duties, and the care of her little sickly baby, helped to keep her mind from dwelling on the weather, except, of course, to hope that he was safely harbored with the logs at Utopia in the dreary distance. But she noticed that day, when she went out to feed the chickens and look after the cow, that the tide was up to the little fence of their garden patch, and the roar of the surf on the south beach, though miles away, she could hear distinctly.

And she began to think that she would like to have someone to talk with about matters, and she believed that if it had not been so far and so stormy, and the trail so impassable, she would have taken the baby and have gone over to Ryckman's, her nearest neighbor. But then, you see, he might have returned in the storm, all wet, with no one to see him; and it was a long exposure for baby, who was croupy and ailing.

But that night, she never could tell why, she didn't feel like sleeping or even lying down. The storm had somewhat abated, but she still "sat and sat," and even tried to read.

I don't know whether it was a Bible or some profane magazine that this poor woman read, but most probably the latter, for the words all ran together and made such sad nonsense that she was forced at last to put the book down and turn to that dearer volume which lay before her in the cradle, with its white initial leaf as yet unsoiled, and try to look forward to its mysterious future. And, rocking the cradle, she thought of everything and everybody, but still was wide awake as ever.

It was nearly twelve o'clock when she at last lay down in her clothes. How long she slept she could not remember, but she awoke with a dreadful choking in her throat, and found herself standing, trembling all over, in the middle of the room, with her baby clasped to her breast, and she was "saying something." The baby cried and sobbed, and she walked up and down trying to hush it, when she heard a scratching at the door. She opened it fearfully, and was glad to see it was only old Pete, their dog, who crawled, dripping with water, into the room.

She would have liked to look out, not in the faint hope of her husband's coming, but to see how things looked; but the wind shook the door so savagely that she could hardly hold it. Then she sat down a little while, and then walked up and down a little while, and then she lay down again a little while. Lying close by the wall of the little cabin, she thought she heard once or twice something scrape slowly against the clapboards, like the scraping of branches.

Then there was a little gurgling sound, like the baby made when it was swallowing, then something went "click-click" and "cluck-cluck," so that she sat up in bed. When she did so she was attracted by something else that seemed creeping from the back door toward the centre of the room. It wasn't much wider than her little finger, but soon it swelled to the width of her hand, and began spreading all over the floor. It was water!

She ran to the front door and threw it wide open, and saw nothing but water. She ran to the back door and threw it open, and saw nothing but water. She ran to the side window, and throwing that open, she saw nothing but water. Then she remembered hearing her husband once say that there was no danger in the tide, for that fell regularly, and people could calculate on it, and that he would rather live near the bay than the river, whose banks might overflow at any time. But was it the tide?

So she ran again to the back door, and threw out a stick of wood. It drifted away towards the bay. She scooped up some of the water and put it eagerly to her lips. It was fresh and sweet. It was the river, and not the tide!

It was then—oh, God be praised for his goodness! she did neither faint nor fall; it was then—blessed be the Savior, for it was his merciful

hand that touched and strengthened her in this awful moment—
that fear dropped from her like a garment, and her trembling ceased.
It was then and thereafter that she never lost her self-command,
through all the trials of that gloomy night.

She drew the bedstead toward the middle of the room, and placed
a table upon it, and on that she put the cradle. The water on the floor
was already over her ankles, and the house once or twice moved so
perceptibly, and seemed to be racked so, that the closet doors all
flew open.

Then she heard the same rasping and thumping against the wall,
and, looking out, saw that a large uprooted tree, which had lain near
the road at the upper end of the pasture, had floated down to the
house. Luckily its long roots dragged in the soil and kept it from
moving as rapidly as the current, for had it struck the house in its full
career, even the strong nails and bolts in the piles could not have
withstood the shock. The hound had leaped upon its knotty surface,
and crouched near the roots, shivering and whining.

A ray of hope flashed across her mind. She drew a heavy blanket
from the bed, and, wrapping it about the babe, waded in the deepening waters to the door. As the tree swung again, broadside on,
making the little cabin creak and tremble, she leaped on to its trunk.
By God's mercy she succeeded in obtaining a footing on its slippery
surface, and, twining an arm about its roots, she held in the other her
moaning child.

Then something cracked near the front porch, and the whole front
of the house she had just quitted fell forward— just as cattle fall on
their knees before they lie down—and at the same moment the great
redwood tree swung round and drifted away with its living cargo
into the black night.

For all the excitement and danger, for all her soothing of her crying babe, for all the whistling of the wind, for all the uncertainty of
her situation, she still turned to look at the deserted and water-swept
cabin. She remembered even then, and she wondered how foolish
she was to think of it at that time, that she wished she had put on
another dress and the baby's best clothes; and she kept praying that
the house would be spared so that he, when he returned, would
have something to come to, and it wouldn't be quite so desolate,
and—how could he ever know what had become of her and baby?
And at the thought she grew sick and faint. But she had something

else to do besides worrying, for whenever the long roots of her ark struck an obstacle the whole trunk made half a revolution, and twice dipped her in the black water.

The hound, who kept distracting her by running up and down the tree and howling, at last fell off at one of these collisions. He swam for some time beside her, and she tried to get the poor beast upon the tree, but he "acted silly" and wild, and at last she lost sight of him forever. Then she and her baby were left alone.

The light which had burned for a few minutes in the deserted cabin was quenched suddenly. She could not then tell whither she was drifting. The outline of the white dunes on the peninsula showed dimly ahead, and she judged the tree was moving in a line with the river. It must be about slack water, and she had probably reached the eddy formed by the confluence of the tide and the overflowing waters of the river.

Unless the tide fell soon, there was present danger of her drifting to its channel, and being carried out to sea or crushed in the floating drift. That peril averted, if she were carried out on the ebb toward the bay, she might hope to strike one of the wooded promontories of the peninsula, and rest till daylight.

Sometimes she thought she heard voices and shouts from the river, and the bellowing of cattle and bleating of sheep. Then again it was only the ringing in her ears and throbbing of her heart. She found at about this time that she was so chilled and stiffened in her cramped position that she could scarcely move, and the baby cried so when she put it to her breast that she noticed the milk refused to flow; and she was so frightened at that that she put her head under her shawl, and for the first time cried bitterly.

When she raised her head again the boom of the surf was behind her, and she knew that her ark had again swung round. She dipped up the water to cool her parched throat, and found that it was salt as her tears. There was a relief, though, for by this sign she knew that she was drifting with the tide. It was then the wind went down, and the great and awful silence oppressed her. There was scarcely a ripple against the furrowed sides of the great trunk on which she rested, and around her all was black gloom and quiet.

She spoke to the baby just to hear herself speak, and to know that she had not lost her voice. She thought then—it was queer, but she could not help thinking it—how awful must have been the night when the great ship swung over the Asiatic peak, and the sounds of creation were blotted out from the world. She thought, too, of mariners clinging to spars, and of poor women who were lashed to rafts and beaten to death by the cruel sea. She tried to thank God that she was thus spared, and lifted her eyes from the baby who had fallen into a fretful sleep.

Suddenly, away to the southward, a great light lifted itself out of the gloom, and flashed and flickered, and flickered and flashed again. Her heart fluttered quickly against the baby's cold cheek. It was the lighthouse at the entrance of the bay. As she was yet wondering the tree suddenly rolled a little, dragged a little, and then seemed to lie quiet and still. She put out her hand and the current gurgled against it. The tree was aground, and, by the position of the light and the noise of the surf, aground upon the Dedlow Marsh.

Had it not been for her baby, who was ailing and croupy, had it not been for the sudden drying up of that sensitive fountain, she would have felt safe and relieved. Perhaps it was this which tended to make all her impressions mournful and gloomy. As the tide rapidly fell, a great flock of black brant fluttered by her, screaming and crying. Then the plover flew up and piped mournfully as they wheeled around the trunk, and at last fearlessly lit upon it like a gray cloud. Then the heron flew over and around her, shrieking and protesting, and at last dropped its gaunt legs only a few yards from her.

But, strangest of all, a pretty white bird, larger than a dove—like a pelican, but not a pelican—circled around and around her. At last it lit upon a rootlet of the tree quite over her shoulder. She put out her hand and stroked its beautiful white neck, and it never appeared to move. It stayed there so long that she thought she would lift up the baby to see it and try to attract her attention. But when she did so, the child was so chilled and cold, and had such a blue look under the little lashes, which it didn't raise at all, that she screamed aloud, and the bird flew away, and she fainted.

Well, that was the worst of it, and perhaps it was not so much, after all, to any but herself. For when she recovered her senses it was bright sunlight and dead low water. There was a confused noise of guttural voices about her, and an old squaw, singing an Indian "hushaby," and rocking herself from side to side before a fire built on the marsh, before which she, the recovered wife and mother, lay weak and weary.

Her first thought was for her baby, and she was about to speak when a young squaw, who must have been a mother herself, fathomed her thought and brought her the "mowitch," pale but living, in such a queer little willow cradle, all bound up, just like the squaw's own young one, that she laughed and cried together, and the young squaw and the old squaw showed their big white teeth and glinted their black eyes, and said, "Plenty get well, skeena mowitch," "Wagee man come plenty soon," and she could have kissed their brown faces in her joy.

And then she found that they had been gathering berries on the marsh in their queer conical baskets, and saw the skirt of her gown fluttering on the tree from afar, and the old squaw couldn't resist the temptation of procuring a new garment, and came down and discovered the "wagee" woman and child.

And of course she gave the garment to the old squaw, as you may imagine, and when *he* came at last and rushed up to her, looking about ten years older in his anxiety, she felt so faint again that they had to carry her to the canoe. For, you see, he knew nothing about the flood until he met the Indians at Utopia, and knew by the signs that the poor woman was his wife. And at the next high tide he towed the tree away back home, although it wasn't worth the trouble, and built another house, using the old tree for the foundation and props, and called it after her, "Mary's Ark!"

But you may guess the next house was built above high-water mark. And that's all.

Not much, perhaps, considering the malevolent capacity of the Dedlow Marsh. But you must tramp over it at low water, or paddle over it at high tide, or get lost upon it once or twice in the fog, as I have, to understand properly Mary's adventure, or to appreciate duly the blessings of living beyond high-water mark.

THE IDYL OF RED GULCH

S andy was very drunk. He was lying under an azalea-bush, in pretty much the same attitude in which he had fallen some hours before. How long he had been lying there he could not tell, and didn't care; how long he should lie there was a matter equally indefinite and unconsidered. A tranquil philosophy, born of his physical condition, suffused and saturated his moral being.

The spectacle of a drunken man, and of this drunken man in particular, was not, I grieve to say, of sufficient novelty in Red Gulch to attract attention. Earlier in the day some local satirist had erected a temporary tombstone at Sandy's head, bearing the inscription, "Effects of McCorkle's whisky,—kills at forty rods," with a hand pointing to McCorkle's saloon. But this, I imagine, was, like most local satire, personal; and was a reflection upon the unfairness of the process rather than a commentary upon the impropriety of the result. With this facetious exception, Sandy had been undisturbed. A wandering mule, released from his pack, had cropped the scant herbage beside him, and sniffed curiously at the prostrate man; a vagabond dog, with that deep sympathy which the species have for drunken men, had licked his dusty boots, and curled himself up at his feet, and lay there, blinking one eye in the sunlight, with a simulation of dissipation that was ingenious and dog-like in its implied flattery of the unconscious man beside him.

Meanwhile the shadows of the pine-trees had slowly swung around until they crossed the road, and their trunks barred the open meadow with gigantic parallels of black and yellow. Little puffs of red dust, lifted by the plunging hoofs of passing teams, dispersed in a grimy shower upon the recumbent man. The sun sank and lower; and still Sandy stirred not. And then the repose of this philosopher was disturbed, as other philosophers have been, by the intrusion of an unphilosophical sex.

"Miss Mary," as she was known to the little flock that she had just dismissed from the log school-house beyond the pines, was taking her afternoon walk. Observing an unusually fine cluster of blossoms on the azalea bush opposite, she crossed the road to pluck it,—picking her way through the red dust, not without certain fierce little shivers of disgust, and some feline circumlocution. And then she came suddenly upon Sandy!

Of course she uttered the little *staccato* cry of her sex. But when she had paid that tribute to her physical weakness she became over-bold, and halted for a moment,—at least six feet from this prostrate monster,—with her white skirts gathered in her hand, ready for flight. But neither sound nor motion came from the bush. With one little foot she then overturned the satirical head-board, and muttered "Beasts!"—an epithet which probably, at that moment, conveniently classified in her mind the entire male population of Red Gulch. For Miss Mary, being possessed of certain rigid notions of her own, had not, perhaps, properly appreciated the demonstrative gallantry for which the Californian has been so justly celebrated by his brother Californians, and had, as a new-comer, perhaps, fairly earned the reputation of being "stuck-up."

As she stood there she noticed, also, that the slant sunbeams were heating Sandy's head to what she judged to be an unhealthy temperature, and that his hat was lying uselessly at his side. To pick it up and to place it over his face was a work requiring some courage, particularly as his eyes were open. Yet she did it and made good her retreat. But she was somewhat concerned, on looking back, to see that the hat was removed, and that Sandy was sitting up and saying something.

The truth was, that in the calm depths of Sandy's mind he was satisfied that the rays of the sun were beneficial and healthful; that from childhood he had objected to lying down in a hat; that no people but condemned fools, past redemption, ever wore hats; and that his right to dispense with them when he pleased was inalienable. This was the statement of his inner consciousness. Unfortunately, its outward expression was vague, being limited to a repetition of the following formula—"Su'shine all ri'! Wasser maär, eh? Wass up, su'shine?"

Miss Mary stopped, and, taking fresh courage from her vantage of distance, asked him if there was anything that he wanted.

"Wass up? Wasser maär?" continued Sandy, in a very high key.

"Get up, you horrid man!" said Miss Mary, now thoroughly incensed; "get up, and go home."

Sandy staggered to his feet. He was six feet high, and Miss Mary trembled. He started forward a few paces and then stopped.

"Wass I go home for?" he suddenly asked, with great gravity.

"Go and take a bath," replied Miss Mary, eyeing his grimy person with great disfavor.

To her infinite dismay, Sandy suddenly pulled off his coat and vest, threw them on the ground, kicked off his boots, and, plunging wildly forward, darted headlong over the hill, in the direction of the river.

"Goodness Heavens!—the man will be drowned!" said Miss Mary; and then, with feminine inconsistency, she ran back to the schoolhouse, and locked herself in.

That night, while seated at supper with her hostess, the blacksmith's wife, it came to Miss Mary to ask, demurely, if her husband ever got drunk. "Abner," responded Mrs. Stidger, reflectively, "let's see: Abner hasn't been tight since last 'lection." Miss Mary would have liked to ask if he preferred lying in the sun on these occasions, and if a cold bath would have hurt him; but this would have involved an explanation, which she did not then care to give. So she contented herself with opening her gray eyes widely at the red-cheeked Mrs. Stidger,—a fine specimen of South-western efflorescence,—and then dismissed the subject altogether. The next day she wrote to her dearest friend, in Boston: "I think I find the intoxicated portion of this community the least objectionable. I refer, my dear, to the men, of course. I do not know anything that could make the women tolerable."

In less than a week Miss Mary had forgotten this episode, except that her afternoon walks took thereafter, almost unconsciously, another direction. She noticed, however, that every morning a fresh cluster of azalea-blossoms appeared among the flowers on her desk. This was not strange, as her little flock were aware of her fondness for flowers, and invariably kept her desk bright with anemones, syringes, and lupines; but, on questioning them, they, one and all, professed ignorance of the azaleas. A few days later, Master Johnny Stidger, whose desk was nearest to the window, was suddenly taken with spasms of apparently gratuitous laughter, that threatened the discipline of the school. All that Miss Mary could get from him was, that some one had been "looking in the winder." Irate and indignant, she sallied from her hive to do battle with the intruder. As she turned the corner of the school-house she came plump upon the quondam drunkard,—now perfectly sober, and inexpressibly sheepish and guilty-looking.

These facts Miss Mary was not slow to take a feminine advantage of, in her present humor. But it was somewhat confusing to observe, also, that the beast, despite some faint signs of past dissipation, was amiable-looking,—in fact, a kind of blond Samson, whose corn-colored, silken beard apparently had never yet known the touch of barber's razor or Delilah's shears. So that the cutting speech which quivered on her ready tongue died upon her lips, and she contented herself with receiving his stammering apology with supercilious eyelids and the gathered skirts of uncontamination. When she re-entered the school-room, her eyes fell upon the azaleas with a new sense of revelation. And then she laughed, and the little people all laughed, and they were all unconsciously very happy.

It was on a hot day—and not long after this—that two short-legged boys came to grief on the threshold of the school with a pail of water, which they had laboriously brought from the spring, and that Miss Mary compassionately seized the pail and started for the spring herself. At the foot of the hill a shadow crossed her path, and a blue-shirted arm dexterously, but gently, relieved her of her burden. Miss Mary was both embarrassed and angry. "If you carried more of that for yourself," she said, spitefully, to the blue arm, without deigning to raise her lashes to its owner, "you'd do better." In the submissive silence that followed she regretted the speech, and thanked him so sweetly at the door that he stumbled. Which caused the children to laugh again,—a laugh in which Miss Mary joined, until the color came faintly into her pale cheek. The next day a barrel was mysteriously placed beside the door, and as mysteriously filled with fresh spring-water every morning.

Nor was this superior young person without other quiet attentions. "Profane Bill," driver of the Slumgullion Stage, widely known in the newspapers for his "gallantry" in invariably offering the box-seat to the fair sex, had excepted Miss Mary from this attention, on the ground that he had a habit of "cussin' on up grades," and gave her half the coach to herself. Jack Hamlin, a gambler, having once silently ridden with her in the same coach, afterward threw a decanter at the head of a confederate for mentioning her name in a bar-room. The over-dressed mother of a pupil whose paternity was doubtful had often lingered near this astute Vestal's temple, never daring to enter its sacred precincts, but content to worship the priestess from afar.

With such unconscious intervals the monotonous procession of blue skies, glittering sunshine, brief twilights, and starlit nights passed over Red Gulch. Miss Mary grew fond of walking in the sedate and proper woods. Perhaps she believed, with Mrs. Stidger, that the balsamic odors of the firs "did her chest good," for certainly her slight cough was less frequent and her step was firmer; perhaps she had learned the unending lesson which the patient pines are never weary of repeating to heedful or listless ears. And so, one day, she planned a picnic on Buckeye Hill, and took the children with her. Away from the dusty road, the straggling shanties, the yellow ditches, the clamor of restless engines, the cheap finery of shop-windows, the deeper glitter of paint and colored glass, and the thin veneering which barbarism takes upon itself such localities,—what infinite relief was theirs! The last heap of ragged rock and clay passed, the last unsightly chasm crossed,—how the waiting woods opened their long files to receive them! How the children—perhaps because they had not yet grown quite away from the breast of the bounteous Mother— threw themselves face downward on her brown bosom with uncouth caresses, filling the air with their laughter; and how Miss Mary herself—felinely fastidious and intrenched as she was in the purity of spotless skirts, collar, and cuffs—forgot all, and ran like a crested quail at the head of her brood, until, romping, laughing, and panting, with a loosened braid of brown hair, a hat hanging by a knotted ribbon from her throat, she suddenly and violently, in the heart of the forest, upon—the luckless Sandy!

The explanations, apologies, and not overwise conversation that ensued, need not be indicated here. It would seem, however, that Miss Mary had already established some acquaintance with this ex-drunkard. Enough that he was soon accepted as one of the party; that the children, with that quick intelligence which Providence gives the helpless, recognized a friend, and played with his blond beard, and long silken mustache and took other liberties,—as the helpless are apt to do. And when he had built a fire against a tree, and had shown them other mysteries of wood-craft, their admiration knew no bounds. At the close of two such foolish idle, happy hours he found himself lying at the feet of the schoolmistress, gazing dreamily in her face, as she sat upon the sloping hill-side, weaving wreaths of laurel and syringa, in very much the same attitude as he had lain when first they met. Nor was the similitude greatly forced. The weakness of an easy, sensuous nature, that had found a dreamy exaltation in liquor, it is to be feared was now finding an equal intoxication in love.

I think that Sandy was dimly conscious of this himself. I know that he longed to be doing something,—slaying a grizzly, scalping a savage, or sacrificing himself in some way for the sake of this sallow-faced, gray-eyed schoolmistress. As I should like to present him in a heroic attitude, I stay my hand with great difficulty at this moment, being only withheld from introducing such an episode by a strong conviction that it does not usually occur at such times. And I trust that my fairest reader, who remembers that, in a real crisis, it is always some uninteresting stranger or unromantic policeman, and not Adolphus, who rescues, will forgive the omission.

So they sat there, undisturbed,—the woodpeckers chattering overhead, and the voices of the children coming pleasantly from the hollow below. What they said matters little. What they thought—which might have been interesting—did not transpire. The woodpeckers only learned how Miss Mary was an orphan; how she left her uncle's house, to come to California, for the sake of health and independence; how Sandy was an orphan, too; how he came to California for excitement; how he had lived a wild life, and how he was trying to reform; and other details, which, from a woodpecker's view-point, undoubtedly must have seemed stupid, and a waste of time. But even in such trifles was the afternoon spent; and when the children were again gathered, and Sandy, with a delicacy which the schoolmistress well understood, took leave of them quietly at the outskirts of the settlement, it had seemed the shortest day of her weary life.

As the long, dry summer withered to its roots, the school term of Red Gulch—to use a local euphuism "dried up" also. In another day Miss Mary would be free; and for a season, at least, Red Gulch would know her no more. She was seated alone in the schoolhouse, her cheek resting on her hand, her eyes half closed in one of those daydreams in which Miss Mary—I fear, to the danger of school discipline—was lately in the habit of indulging. Her lap was full of mosses, ferns, and other woodland memories. She was so preoccupied with these and her own thoughts that a gentle tapping at the door passed unheard, or translated itself into the remembrance of far-off woodpeckers. When at last it asserted itself more distinctly, she started up with a flushed cheek and opened the door. On the threshold stood a woman, the self-assertion and audacity of whose dress were in singular contrast to her timid, irresolute bearing.

Miss Mary recognized at a glance the dubious mother of her anonymous pupil. Perhaps she was disappointed, perhaps she was only fastidious; but as she coldly invited her to enter, she half unconsciously settled her white cuffs and collar, and gathered closer her own chaste skirts. It was, perhaps, for this reason that the embarrassed stranger, after a moment's hesitation, left her gorgeous parasol open and sticking in the dust beside the door and then sat down at the farther end of a long bench. Her voice was husky as she began,—

"I heerd tell that you were goin' down to the Bay to-morrow, and I couldn't let you go until I came to thank you for your kindness to my Tommy."

Tommy, Miss Mary said, was a good boy, and deserved more than the poor attention she could give him

"Thank you, miss; thank ye!" cried the stranger, brightening even through the color which Red Gulch knew facetiously as her "war paint," and striving, in her embarrassment, to drag the long bench nearer the schoolmistress. "I thank you, miss, for that! and if I am his mother, there ain't a sweeter, dearer, better boy lives than him. And if I ain't much as says it, thar ain't a sweeter, dearer, angeler teacher lives than he's got."

Miss Mary, sitting primly behind her desk, with a ruler over her shoulder, opened her gray eyes widely at this, but said nothing.

"It ain't for you to be complimented by the like of me, I know," she went on, hurriedly. "It ain't for me to be comin' here, in broad day, to do it, either; but I come to ask a favor,—not for me, miss,— not for me, but for the darling boy."

Encouraged by a look in the young schoolmistress's eye, and putting her lilac-gloved hands together, the fingers downward, between her knees, she went on, in a low voice,—

"You see, miss, there's no one the boy has any claim on but me, and I ain't the proper person to bring him up. I thought some, last year, of sending him away to 'Frisco to school, but when they talked of bringing a schoolma'am here, I waited till I saw you, and then I knew it was all right, and I could keep my boy a little longer. And O, miss, he loves you so much; and if you could hear him talk about you, in his pretty way, and if he could ask you what I ask you now, you couldn't refuse him.

"It is natural," she went on rapidly, in a voice that trembled strangely between pride and humility,—"it's natural that he should take to you, miss, for his father, when I first knew him, was a gentleman,— and the boy must forget me, sooner or later,—and so I ain't a-goin' to cry about that. For I come to ask you to take my Tommy,—God bless him for the bestest, sweetest boy that lives!—to—to—take him with you."

She had risen and caught the young girl's hand in her own, and had fallen on her knees beside her.

"I've money plenty, and it's all yours and his. Put him in some good school, where you can go and see him, and help him to—to— to forget his mother. Do with him what you like. The worst you can do will be kindness to what he will learn with me. Only take him out of this wicked life, this cruel place, this home of shame and sorrow. You will; I know you will,—won't you? You will,—you must not, you cannot say no! You will make him as pure, as gentle as yourself; and when he has grown up, you will tell him his father's name,—the name that hasn't passed my lips for years,—the name of Alexander Morton, whom they call here Sandy! Miss Mary!—do not take your hand away! Miss Mary, speak to me! You will take my boy? Do not put your face from me. I know it ought not to look on such as me. Miss Mary!—my God, be merciful!—she is leaving me!"

Miss Mary had risen, and, in the gathering twilight, had felt her way to the open window. She stood there, leaning against the case-ment, her eyes fixed on the last rosy tints that were fading from the western sky. There was still some of its light on her pure young fore-head, on her white collar, on her clasped white hands, but all fading slowly away. The suppliant had dragged herself, still on her knees, beside her.

"I know it takes time to consider. I will wait here all night, but I cannot go until you speak. Do not deny me now. You will!—I see it in your sweet face,—such a face as I have seen in my dreams. I see it in your eyes, Miss Mary!—you will take my boy!"

The last red beam crept higher, suffused Miss Mary's eyes with something of its glory, flickered, and faded, and went out. The sun had set on Red Gulch. In the twilight and silence Miss Mary's voice sounded pleasantly.

"I will take the boy. Send him to me to-night."

The happy mother raised the hem of Miss Mary's shirts to her lips. She would have buried her hot face in its virgin folds, but she dared not. She rose to her feet.

"Does—this man—know of your intention?" asked Mary, suddenly.

"No, nor cares. He has never even seen the child to know it."

"Go to him at once,—to-night,—now! Tell him what you have done. Tell him I have taken his child, and tell him—he must never see—see—the child again. Wherever it may be, he must not come; wherever I may take it, he must not follow! There, go now, please—I'm weary, and—have much yet to do!"

They walked together to the door. On the threshold the woman turned.

"Good night."

She would have fallen at Miss Mary's feet. But at the same moment the young girl reached out her arms, caught the sinful woman to her own pure breast for one brief moment, and then closed and locked the door.

IT WAS WITH A SUDDEN sense of great responsibility that Profane Bill took the reins of the Slumgullion Stage the next morning, for the schoolmistress was one of his passengers, As he entered the high-road, in obedience to a pleasant voice from the "inside," he suddenly reined up his horses and respectfully waited, as "Tommy" hopped out at the command of Miss Mary.

"Not that bush, Tommy,—the next."

Tommy whipped out his new pocket-knife, and, cutting a branch from a tall azalea-bush, returned with it to Miss Mary.

"All right now?"

"All right."

And the stage-door closed on the Idyl of Red Gulch.

MR. THOMPSON'S PRODIGAL

W e all knew that Mr. Thompson was looking for his son, and a pretty bad one at that. That he was coming to California for this sole object was no secret to his fellow-passengers; and the physical peculiarities, as well as the moral weaknesses, of the missing prodigal were made equally plain to us through the frank volubility of the parent. "You was speaking of a young man which was hung at Red Dog for sluice-robbing," said Mr. Thompson to a steerage passenger one day; "be you aware of the color of his eyes?" "Black," responded the passenger. "Ah!" said Mr. Thompson, referring to some mental memoranda, "Char-les's eyes was blue." He then walked away. Perhaps it was from this unsympathetic mode of inquiry, perhaps it was from that Western predilection to take a humorous view of any principle or sentiment persistently brought before them, that Mr. Thompson's quest was the subject of some satire among the passengers. A gratuitous advertisement of the missing Charles, addressed to "Jailers and Guardians," circulated privately among them; everybody remembered to have met Charles under distressing circumstances. Yet it is but due to my countrymen to state that when it was known that Thompson had embarked some wealth in this visionary project, but little of this satire found its way to his ears, and nothing was uttered in his hearing that might bring a pang to a father's heart, or imperil a possible pecuniary advantage of the satirist. Indeed, Mr. Bracy Tibbets's jocular proposition to form a joint-stock company to "prospect" for the missing youth received at one time quite serious entertainment.

Perhaps to superficial criticism Mr. Thompson's nature was not picturesque nor lovable. His history, as imparted at dinner one day by himself, was practical even in its singularity. After a hard and wilful youth and maturity, in which he had buried a broken-spirited wife and driven his son to sea, he suddenly experienced religion. "I got it in New Orleans in '59," said Mr. Thompson, with the general suggestion of referring to an epidemic. "Enter ye the narrer gate. Parse me the beans." Perhaps this practical quality upheld him in his apparently hopeless search. He had no clue to the whereabouts of his runaway son; indeed, scarcely a proof of his present existence. From his indifferent recollection of the boy of twelve, he now expected to identify the man of twenty-five.

It would seem that he was successful. How he succeeded was one of the few things he did not tell. There are, I believe, two versions of the story. One, that Mr. Thompson, visiting a hospital, discovered his son by reason of a peculiar hymn, chanted by the sufferer in a delirious dream of his boyhood. This version, giving as it did wide range to the finer feelings of the heart, was quite popular; and as told by the Rev. Mr. Gushington on his return from his California tour, never failed to satisfy an audience. The other was less simple, and, as I shall adopt it here, deserves more elaboration.

It was after Mr. Thompson had given up searching for his son among the living, and had taken to the examination of cemeteries and a careful inspection of the "cold *hic jacets* of the dead." At this time he was a frequent visitor of "Lone Mountain," a dreary hill-top, bleak enough in its original isolation, and bleaker for the white-faced marbles by which San Francisco anchored her departed citizens, and kept them down in a shifting sand that refused to cover them, and against a fierce and persistent wind that strove to blow them utterly away. Against this wind the old man opposed a will quite as persistent, a grizzled hard face, and a tall crape-bound hat drawn tightly over his eyes,—and so spent days in reading the mortuary inscriptions audibly to himself. The frequency of Scriptural quotation pleased him, and he was fond of corroborating them by a pocket Bible. "That's from Psalms," he said one day to an adjacent gravedigger. The man made no reply. Not at all rebuffed, Mr. Thompson at once slid down into the open grave with a more practical inquiry, "Did you ever, in your profession, come across Char-les Thompson?" "Thompson be d—d!" said the gravedigger, with great directness. "Which, if he hadn't religion, I think he is," responded the old man, as he clambered out of the grave.

It was perhaps on this occasion that Mr. Thompson stayed later than usual. As he turned his face toward the city, lights were beginning to twinkle ahead, and a fierce wind, made visible by fog, drove him forward, or, lying in wait, charged him angrily from the corners of deserted suburban streets. It was on one of these corners that something else, quite as indistinct and malevolent, leaped upon him with an oath, a presented pistol, and a demand for money. But it was met by a will of iron and a grip of steel. The assailant and assailed rolled together on the ground. But the next moment the old man was erect, one hand grasping the captured pistol, the other clutching at arm's length the throat of a figure, surly, youthful, and savage.

"Young man," said Mr. Thompson, setting his thin lips together, "what might be your name?"

"Thompson!"

The old man's hand slid from the throat to the arm of his prisoner, without relaxing its firmness.

"Char-les Thompson, come with me," he said presently, and marched his captive to the hotel. What took place there has not transpired, but it was known the next morning that Mr. Thompson had found his son.

It is proper to add to the above improbable story, that there was nothing in the young man's appearance or manners to justify it. Grave, reticent, and handsome, devoted to his newly found parent, he assumed the emoluments and responsibilities of his new condition with a certain serious ease that more nearly approached that which San Francisco society lacked and—rejected. Some chose to despise this quality as a tendency to "psalm-singing"; others saw in it the inherited qualities of the parent, and were ready to prophesy for the son the same hard old age. But all agreed that it was not inconsistent with the habits of money-getting for which father and son were respected.

And yet the old man did not seem to be happy. Perhaps it was that the consummation of his wishes left him without a practical mission; perhaps—and it is the more probable—he had little love for the son he had regained. The obedience he exacted was freely given, the reform he had set his heart upon was complete; and yet somehow it did not seem to please him. In reclaiming his son he had fulfilled all the requirements that his religious duty required of him, and yet the act seemed to lack sanctification. In this perplexity he read again the parable of the Prodigal Son, which he had long ago adopted for his guidance, and found that he had omitted the final feast of reconciliation. This seemed to offer the proper quality of ceremoniousness in the sacrament between himself and his son; and so, a year after the appearance of Charles, he set about giving him a party. "Invite everybody, Char-les," he said dryly; "everybody who knows that I brought you out of the wine-husks of iniquity and the company of harlots; and bid them eat, drink, and be merry."

Perhaps the old man had another reason, not yet clearly analyzed. The fine house he had built on the sandhills sometimes seemed lonely and bare. He often found himself trying to reconstruct, from the grave features of Charles, the little boy whom he but dimly remembered in the past, and of whom lately he had been thinking a great deal. He believed this to be a sign of impending old age and childishness; but coming one day in his formal drawing-room, upon a child of one of the servants, who had strayed therein, he would have taken him in his arms, but the child fled from before his grizzled face. So that it seemed eminently proper to invite a number of people to his house, and, from the array of San Francisco maidenhood, to select a daughter-in-law. And then there would be a child—a boy, whom he could "rare up" from the beginning, and—love—as he did not love Charles.

We were all at the party. The Smiths, Joneses, Browns, and Robinsons also came, in that fine flow of animal spirits, unchecked by any respect for the entertainer, which most of us are apt to find so fascinating. The proceedings would have been somewhat riotous but for the social position of the actors. In fact, Mr. Bracy Tibbets, having naturally a fine appreciation of a humorous situation, but further impelled by the bright eyes of the Jones girls, conducted himself so remarkably as to attract the serious regard of Mr. Charles Thompson, who approached him, saying quietly, "You look ill, Mr. Tibbets; let me conduct you to your carriage. Resist, you hound, and I'll throw you through that window. This way, please; the room is close and distressing." It is hardly necessary to say that but a part of this speech was audible to the company, and that the rest was not divulged by Mr. Tibbets, who afterward regretted the sudden illness which kept him from witnessing a certain amusing incident, which the fastest Miss Jones characterized as the "richest part of the blow-out," and which I hasten to record.

It was at supper. It was evident that Mr. Thompson had overlooked much lawlessness in the conduct of the younger people, in his abstract contemplation of some impending event. When the cloth was removed, he rose to his feet and grimly tapped upon the table. A titter, that broke out among the Jones girls, became epidemic on one side of the board. Charles Thompson, from the foot of the table, looked up in tender perplexity. "He's going to sing a Doxology," "He's going to pray," "Silence for a speech," ran round the room.

"It's one year to-day, Christian brothers and sisters," said Mr. Thompson with grim deliberation,—"one year to-day since my son came home from eating of wine-husks and spending of his substance on harlots." (The tittering suddenly ceased.) "Look at him now. Char-les Thompson, stand up." (Charles Thompson stood up.) "One year ago to-day,—and look at him now."

He was certainly a handsome prodigal, standing there in his cheer-ful evening-dress,—a repentant prodigal, with sad obedient eyes turned upon the harsh and unsympathetic glance of his father. The youngest Miss Smith, from the pure depths of her foolish little heart, moved unconsciously toward him.

"It's fifteen years ago since he left my house," said Mr. Thompson, "a rovier and a prodigal. I was myself a man of sin, O Christian friends,—a man of wrath and bitterness" ("Amen," from the eldest Miss Smith)—"but praise be God, I've fled the wrath to come. It's five years ago since I got the peace that passeth understanding. Have you got it, friends?" (A general sub-chorus of "No, no," from the girls, and, "Pass the word for it," from Midshipman Coxe, of the U.S. sloop *Wethersfield.*) "Knock, and it shall be opened to you.

"And when I found the error of my ways, and the preciousness of grace," continued Mr. Thompson, "I came to give it to my son. By sea and land I sought him far, and fainted not. I did not wait for him to come to me, which the same I might have done, and justified myself by the Book of books, but I sought him out among his husks, and—" (the rest of the sentence was lost in the rustling withdrawal of the ladies). "Works, Christian friends, is my motto. By their works shall ye know them, and there is mine."

The particular and accepted work to which Mr. Thompson was alluding had turned quite pale, and was looking fixedly toward an open door leading to the veranda, lately filled by gaping servants, and now the scene of some vague tumult. As the noise continued, a man, shabbily dressed and evidently in liquor, broke through the opposing guardians, and staggered into the room. The transition from the fog and darkness without to the glare and heat within evidently dazzled and stupefied him. He removed his battered hat, and passed it once or twice before his eyes, as he steadied himself, but unsuccessfully, by the back of a chair. Suddenly his wandering glance fell upon the pale face of Charles Thompson; and with a gleam of childlike recognition, and a weak falsetto laugh, he darted forward, caught at the table, upset the glasses and literally fell upon the prodigal's breast.

"Sha'ly! yo' d—d ol' scoun'rel, hoo rar ye!"

"Hush!—sit down!—hush!" said Charles Thompson hurriedly endeavoring to extricate himself from the embrace of his unexpected guest.

"Look at 'm!" continued the stranger, unheeding the admonition, but suddenly holding the unfortunate Charles at arm's length, in loving and undisguised admiration of his festive appearance. "Look at 'm! Ain't he nasty? Sha'ls, I'm prow of yer!"

"Leave the house!" said Mr. Thompson, rising, with a dangerous look in his cold grey eye. "Char-les, how dare you?"

"Simmer down, ole man! Sha'ls, who's th' ol' bloat? Eh?"

"Hush, man; here, take this!" With nervous hands, Charles Thompson filled a glass with liquor. "Drink it and go—until to-morrow—any time, but—leave us!—go now!" But even then, ere the miserable wretch could drink, the old man, pale with passion, was upon him. Half carrying him in his powerful arms, half dragging him through the circling crowd of frightened guests, he had reached the door, swung open by the waiting servants, when Charles Thompson started from a seeming stupor, crying—

"Stop!"

The old man stopped. Through the open door the fog and wind drove chilly. "What does this mean?" he asked, turning a baleful face on Charles.

"Nothing—but stop—for God's sake. Wait till tomorrow, but not to-night. Do not, I implore you—do this thing."

There was something in the tone of the young man's voice, something, perhaps, in the contact of the struggling wretch he held in his powerful arms; but a dim, indefinite fear took possession of the old man's heart. "Who," he whispered hoarsely, "is this man?"

Charles did not answer.

"Stand back, there, all of you," thundered Mr. Thompson, to the

crowding guests around him. "Char-les come here! I command you—
I—I—I—beg you—tell me *who* is this man?"

Only two persons heard the answer that came faintly from the
lips of Charles Thompson—

"YOUR SON."

When day broke over the bleak sandhills, the guests had departed
from Mr. Thompson's banquet-halls. The lights still burned dimly
and coldly in the deserted rooms,—deserted by all but three figures,
that huddled together in the chill drawing-room, as if for warmth.
One lay in drunken slumber on a couch; at his feet sat he who had
been known as Charles Thompson; and beside them, haggard and
shrunken to half his size, bowed the figure of Mr. Thompson, his
grey eye fixed, his elbows upon his knees, and his hands clasped over
his ears, as if to shut out the sad, entreating voice that seemed to fill
the room.

"God knows I did not set about to wilfully deceive. The name I
gave that night was the first that came into my thought,—the name
of one whom I thought dead,— the dissolute companion of my shame.
And when you questioned further, I used the knowledge that I gained
from him to touch your heart to set me free; only, I swear, for that!
But when you told me who you were, and I first saw the opening of
another life before me—then—then— O, sir, if I was hungry, home-
less, and reckless, when I would have robbed you of your gold, I was
heartsick, helpless, and desperate, when I would have robbed you of
your love!"

The old man stirred not. From his luxurious couch the newly found
prodigal snored peacefully.

"I had no father I could claim. I never knew a home but this. I was
tempted. I have been happy,—very happy."

He rose and stood before the old man.

"Do not fear that I shall come between your son and his inherit-
ance. To-day I leave this place, never to return. The world is large, sir,
and, thanks to your kindness, I now see the way by which an honest
livelihood is gained. Good-bye. You will not take my hand? Well,
well! Good-bye."

He turned to go. But when he had reached the door he suddenly
came back, and, raising with both hands the grizzled head, he kissed
it once and twice.

"Char-les!"

There was no reply.

"Char-les!"

The old man rose with a frightened air, and tottered feebly to the door. It was open. There came to him the awakened tumult of a great city, in which the prodigal's footsteps were lost for ever.

THE ROMANCE
OF MADROÑO HOLLOW

T
he latch on the garden gate of the Folinsbee Ranch clicked twice. The gate itself was so much in shadow that lovely night, that "old man Folinsbee," sitting on his porch, could distinguish nothing but a tall white hat and beside it a few fluttering ribbons, under the pines that marked the entrance. Whether because of this fact, or that he considered a sufficient time had elapsed since the clicking of the latch for more positive disclosure, I do not know; but after a few moments' hesitation he quietly laid aside his pipe and walked slowly down the winding path toward the gate. At the Ceanothus hedge he stopped and listened.

There was not much to hear. The hat was saying to the ribbons that it was a fine night, and remarking generally upon the clear outline of the Sierras against the blue-black sky. The ribbons, it so appeared, had admired this all the way home, and asked the hat if it had ever seen anything half so lovely as the moonlight on the summit. The hat never had; it recalled some lovely nights in the South in Alabama ("in the South in Ahlabahm" was the way the old man heard it), but then there were other things that made this night seem so pleasant. The ribbons could not possibly conceive what the hat could be thinking about. At this point there was a pause, of which Mr. Folinsbee availed himself to walk very grimly and craunchingly down the gravel-walk toward the gate. Then the hat was lifted, and disappeared in the shadow, and Mr. Folinsbee confronted only the half-foolish, half-mischievous, but wholly pretty face of his daughter.

It was afterward known to Madroño Hollow that sharp words

passed between "Miss Jo" and the old man, and that the latter coupled the names of one Culpepper Starbottle and his uncle, Colonel Starbottle, with certain uncomplimentary epithets, and that Miss Jo retaliated sharply. "Her father's blood before her father's face boiled up and proved her truly of his race," quoted the blacksmith, who leaned toward the noble verse of Byron. "She saw the old man's bluff and raised him," was the direct comment of the college-bred Masters.

Meanwhile the subject of these animadversions proceeded slowly along the road to a point where the Folinsbee mansion came in view,— a long, narrow, white building unpretentious, yet superior to its neighbors, and bearing some evidences of taste and refinement in the vines that clambered over its porch, in its French windows, and the white muslin curtains that kept out the fierce California sun by day, and were now touched with silver in the gracious moonlight. Culpepper leaned against the low fence, and gazed long and earnestly at the building. Then the moonlight vanished ghostlike from one of the windows, a material glow took its place, and a girlish figure, holding a candle, drew the white curtains together. To Culpepper it was a vestal virgin standing before a hallowed shrine; to the prosaic observer I fear it was only a fair-haired young woman, whose wicked black eyes still shone with unfilial warmth. Howbeit, when the figure had disappeared he stepped out briskly into the moonlight of the high road. Here he took off his distinguishing hat to wipe his forehead, and the moon shone full upon his face.

It was not an unprepossessing one, albeit a trifle too thin and lank and bilious to be altogether pleasant. The cheek-bones were prominent, and the black eyes sunken in their orbits. Straight black hair fell slantwise off a high but narrow forehead, and swept part of a hollow cheek. A long black mustache followed the perpendicular curves of his mouth. It was on the whole a serious, even Quixotic face, but at times it was relieved by a rare smile of such tender and even pathetic sweetness, that Miss Jo is reported to have said that, if it would only last through the ceremony, she would have married its possessor on the spot. "I once told him so," added that shameless young woman; "but the man instantly fell into a settled melancholy, and hasn't smiled since."

A half-mile below the Folinsbee Ranch the white road dipped and was crossed by a trail that ran through Madroño Hollow. Perhaps because it was a near cut-off to the settlement, perhaps from some less practical reason, Culpepper took this trail, and in a few moments stood among the rarely beautiful trees that gave their name to the valley. Even in that uncertain light the weird beauty of these harlequin masqueraders was apparent; their red trunks—a blush in the moonlight, a deep blood-stain in the shadow—stood out against the silvery green foliage. It was as if Nature in some gracious moment had here caught and crystallized the gypsy memories of the transplanted Spaniard, to cheer him in his lonely exile.

As Culpepper entered the grove he heard loud voices. As he turned toward a clump of trees, a figure so bizarre and characteristic that it might have been a resident Daphne—a figure over-dressed in crimson silk and lace, with bare brown arms and shoulders, and a wreath of honeysuckle—stepped out of the shadow. It was followed by a man. Culpepper started. To come to the point briefly, he recognized in the man the features of his respected uncle, Colonel Starbottle; in the female, a lady who may be briefly described as one possessing absolutely no claim to an introduction to the polite reader. To hurry over equally unpleasant details, both were evidently under the influence of liquor.

From the excited conversation that ensued, Culpepper gathered that some insult had been put upon the lady at a public ball which she had attended that evening; that the Colonel, her escort, had failed to resent it with the sanguinary completeness that she desired. I regret that, even in a liberal age, I may not record the exact and even picturesque language in which this was conveyed to her hearers. Enough that at the close of a fiery peroration, with feminine inconsistency she flew at the gallant Colonel and would have visited her delayed vengeance upon his luckless head, but for the prompt interference of Culpepper. Thwarted in this, she threw herself upon the ground, and then into unpicturesque hysterics. There was a fine moral lesson, not only in this grotesque performance of a sex which cannot afford to be grotesque, but in the ludicrous concern with which it inspired the two men. Culpepper, to whom woman was more or less angelic, was pained and sympathetic; the Colonel, to whom she was more or less improper, was exceedingly terrified and embarrassed. Howbeit the storm was soon over, and after Mistress Dolores had returned a little dagger to its sheath (her garter), she quietly took herself out of Madroño Hollow, and happily out of these pages for ever. The two men, left to themselves, conversed in low tones. Dawn stole upon them before they separated: the Colonel quite sobered and in full possession of his usual jaunty self-assertion; Culpepper with a baleful glow in his hollow cheek, and in his dark eyes a rising fire.

THE NEXT MORNING the general ear of Madroño Hollow was filled with rumors of the Colonel's mishap. It was asserted that he had been invited to withdraw his female companion from the floor of the Assembly Ball at the Independence Hotel, and that, failing to do this, both were expelled. It is to be regretted that in 1854 public opinion was divided in regard to the propriety of this step, and that there was some discussion as to the comparative virtue of the ladies who were not expelled; but it was generally conceded that the real *casus belli* was political. "Is this a dashed Puritan meeting?" had asked the Colonel savagely. "It's no Pike County shindig," had responded the floor-manager, cheerfully. "You're a Yank!" had screamed the Colonel, profanely qualifying the noun. "Get! you border ruffian," was the reply. Such at least was the substance of the reports. As, at that sincere epoch, expressions like the above were usually followed by prompt action, a fracas was confidently looked for.

Nothing, however, occurred. Colonel Starbottle made his appearance next day upon the streets with somewhat of his usual pomposity, a little restrained by the presence of his nephew, who accompanied him, and who, as a universal favorite, also exercised some restraint upon the curious and impertinent. But Culpepper's face wore a look of anxiety quite at variance with his usual grave repose. "The Don don't seem to take the old man's set-back kindly," observed the sympathizing blacksmith. "P'r'aps he was sweet on Dolores himself," suggested the skeptical expressman.

It was a bright morning, a week after this occurrence, that Miss Jo Folinsbee stepped from her garden into the road. This time the latch did not click as she cautiously closed the gate behind her. After a moment's irresolution, which would have been awkward but that it was charmingly employed, after the manner of her sex, in adjusting a bow under a dimpled but rather prominent chin, and in pulling down the fingers of a neatly fitting glove, she tripped toward the settlement. Small wonder that a passing teamster drove his six mules into the wayside ditch and imperiled his load, to keep the dust from her spotless garments; small wonder that the "Lightning Express" withheld its speed and flash to let her pass, and that the expressman, who had never been known to exchange more than rapid monosyllables with his fellow man, gazed after her with breathless admiration. For she was certainly attractive. In a country where the ornamental sex followed the example of youthful Nature, and were prone to overdress and glaring efflorescence, Miss Jo's simple and tasteful raiment added much to the physical charm of, if it did not actually suggest a sentiment to, her presence. It is said that Euchre-deck Billy, working in the gulch at the crossing, never saw Miss Folinsbee pass but that he always remarked apologetically to his partner, that "he believed he *must* write a letter home." Even Bill Masters, who saw her in Paris presented to the favorable criticism of that most fastidious man, the late Emperor, said that she was stunning, but a big discount on what she was at Madroño Hollow.

It was still early morning, but the sun, with California extravagance, had already begun to beat hotly on the little chip hat and blue ribbons, and Miss Jo was obliged to seek the shade of a bypath. Here she received the timid advances of a vagabond yellow dog graciously, until, emboldened by his success, he insisted upon accompanying her, and, becoming slobberingly demonstrative, threatened her spotless skirt with his dusty paws, when she drove him from her with some slight acerbity, and a stone which haply fell within fifty feet of its destined mark. Having thus proved her ability to defend herself, with characteristic inconsistency she took a small panic, and, gathering her white skirts in one hand, and holding the brim of her hat over her eyes with the other, she ran swiftly at least a hundred yards before she stopped. Then she began picking some ferns and a few wild-flowers still spared to the withered fields, and then a sudden distrust of her small ankles seized her, and she inspected them narrowly for those burrs and bugs and snakes which are supposed to lie in wait for helpless womanhood. Then she plucked some golden heads of wild oats, and with a sudden inspiration placed them in her black hair, and then came quite unconsciously upon the trail leading to Madroño Hollow.

Here she hesitated. Before her ran the little trail, vanishing at last into the bosky depths below. The sun was very hot. She must be very far from home. Why should she not rest awhile under the shade of a madroño?

She answered these questions by going there at once. After thoroughly exploring the grove, and satisfying herself that it contained no other living human creature, she sat down under one of the largest trees, with a satisfactory little sigh. Miss Jo loved the madroño. It was a cleanly tree; no dust ever lay upon its varnished leaves; its immaculate shade never was known to harbor grub or insect.

She looked up at the rosy arms interlocked and arched above her head. She looked down at the delicate ferns and cryptogams at her feet. Something glittered at the root of the tree. She picked it up; it was a bracelet. She examined it carefully for cipher or inscription; there was none. She could not resist a natural desire to clasp it on her arm, and to survey it from that advantageous view-point. This absorbed her attention for some moments; and when she looked up again she beheld at a little distance Culpepper Starbottle.

He was standing where he had halted, with instinctive delicacy, on first discovering her. Indeed, he had even deliberated whether he ought not to go away without disturbing her. But some fascination held him to the spot. Wonderful power of humanity! Far beyond jutted an outlying spur of the Sierra, vast, compact, and silent. Scarcely a hundred yards away, a league-long chasm dropped its sheer walls of granite a thousand feet. On every side rose up the serried ranks of pine-trees, in whose close-set files centuries of storm and change had wrought no breach. Yet all this seemed to Culpepper to have been planned by an all-wise Providence as the natural background to the figure of a pretty girl in a yellow dress.

Although Miss Jo had confidently expected to meet Culpepper somewhere in her ramble, now that he came upon her suddenly, she felt disappointed and embarrassed. His manner, too, was more than usually grave and serious, and more than ever seemed to jar upon that audacious levity which was this giddy girl's power and security in a society where all feeling was dangerous. As he approached her she rose to her feet, but almost before she knew it he had taken her hand and drawn her to a seat beside him. This was not what Miss Jo had expected, but nothing is so difficult to predicate as the exact preliminaries of a declaration of love.

What did Culpepper say? Nothing, I fear, that will add anything to the wisdom of the reader; nothing, I fear, that Miss Jo had not heard substantially from other lips before. But there was a certain conviction, fire-speed, and fury in the manner that was deliciously novel to the young lady. It was certainly something to be courted in the nineteenth century with all the passion and extravagance of the sixteenth; it was something to hear, amid the slang of a frontier society, the language of knight-errantry poured into her ear by this lantern-jawed, dark-browed descendant of the Cavaliers.

I do not know that there was anything more in it. The facts, however, go to show that at a certain point Miss Jo dropped her glove, and that in recovering it Culpepper possessed himself first of her hand and then her lips. When they stood up to go, Culpepper had his arm around her waist, and her black hair, with its sheaf of golden oats, rested against the breast-pocket of his coat. But even then I do not think her fancy was entirely captive. She took a certain satisfaction in this demonstration of Culpepper's splendid height, and mentally compared it with a former flame, one Lieutenant McMirk, an active but under-sized Hector, who subsequently fell a victim to the incautiously composed and monotonous beverages of a frontier garrison. Nor was she so much preoccupied but that her quick eyes, even while absorbing Culpepper's glances, were yet able to detect, at a distance, the figure of a man approaching. In an instant she slipped out of Culpepper's arm, and, whipping her hands behind her said, "There's that horrid man!"

Culpepper looked up and beheld his respected uncle panting and blowing over the hill. His brow contracted as he turned to Miss Jo: "You don't like my uncle!"

"I hate him!" Miss Jo was recovering her ready tongue.

Culpepper blushed. He would have liked to enter upon some details of the Colonel's pedigree and exploits, but there was not time. He only smiled sadly. The smile melted Miss Jo. She held out her hand quickly, and said with even more than her usual effrontery, "Don't let that man get you into any trouble. Take care of yourself, dear, and don't let anything happen to you."

Miss Jo intended this speech to be pathetic; the tenure of life among her lovers had hitherto been very uncertain. Culpepper turned toward her, but she had already vanished in the thicket.

The Colonel came up panting. "I've looked all over town for you, and be dashed to you, sir. Who was that with you?"

"A lady." (Culpepper never lied, but he was discreet.)

"D—m 'em all! Look yar, Culp, I've spotted the man who gave the order to put me off the floor" ("flo" was what the Colonel said) "the other night!"

"Who was it?" asked Culpepper, listlessly.

"Jack Folinsbee."

"Who?"

"Why, the son of that dashed nigger-worshipping, psalm-singing Puritan Yankee. What's the matter, now? Look yar, Culp, you ain't goin' back on your blood, ar' ye? You ain't goin back on your word? Ye ain't going down at the feet of this trash, like a whipped hound?"

Culpepper was silent. He was very white. Presently he looked up and said quietly, "No."

CULPEPPER STARBOTTLE had challenged Jack Folinsbee, and the challenge was accepted. The cause alleged was the expelling of Culpepper's uncle from the floor of the Assembly Ball by the order of Folinsbee. Thus much Madroño Hollow knew and could swear to; but there were other strange rumors afloat, of which the blacksmith was an able expounder. "You see, gentlemen, he said to the crowd gathered around his anvil, "I ain't got no theory of this affair, I only give a few facts as have come to my knowledge. Culpepper and Jack meets quite accidental like in Bob's saloon. Jack goes up to Culpepper and says, 'A word with you.' Culpepper bows and steps aside in this way, Jack standing about *here.*" (The blacksmith demonstrates the position of the parties with two old horse-shoes on the anvil.) "Jack pulls a bracelet from his pocket and says, 'Do you know that bracelet?' Culpepper says, 'I do not,' quite cool-like and easy. Jack says, 'You gave it to my sister.' Culpepper says, still cool as you please, 'I did not.' Jack says, 'You lie, G—d d—mn you,' and draws his derringer. Culpepper jumps forward about here" (reference is made to the diagram) "and Jack fires. Nobody hit. It's a mighty cur'o's thing, gentlemen," continued the blacksmith, dropping suddenly into the abstract, and leaning meditatively on his anvil,—"it's a mighty cur'o's thing that nobody gets hit so often. You and me empties our revolvers sociably at each other over a little game, and the room full, and nobody gets hit! That's what gets me."

"Never mind, Thompson," chimed in Bill Masters; "there's another and a better world where we shall know all that, and—become better shots. Go on with your story."

"Well, some grabs Culpepper and some grabs Jack, and so separates them. Then Jack tells 'em as how he had seen his sister wear a bracelet which he knew was one that had been given to Dolores by Colonel Starbottle. That Miss Jo wouldn't say where she got it, but owned up to having seen Culpepper that day. Then, the most cur'o's thing of it yet, what does Culpepper do but rise up and takes all back that he said, and allows that he *did* give her the bracelet. Now my opinion, gentlemen, is that he lied, it ain't like that man to give a gal that he respects anything off of that piece, Dolores. But it's all the same now, and there's but one thing to be done."

The way this one thing was done belongs to the record of Madroño Hollow. The morning was bright and clear; the air was slightly chill, but that was from the mist which arose along the banks of the river. As early as six o'clock the designated ground—a little opening in the madroño grove—was occupied by Culpepper Starbottle, Colonel Starbottle, his second, and the surgeon. The Colonel was exalted and excited, albeit in a rather imposing, dignified way, and pointed out to the surgeon the excellence of the ground, which at that hour was wholly shaded from the sun, whose steady stare is more or less discomposing to your duelist. The surgeon threw himself on the grass and smoked his cigar. Culpepper, quiet and thoughtful, leaned against a tree and gazed up the river. There was a strange suggestion of a picnic about the group, which was heightened when the Colonel drew a bottle from his coat-tails, and, taking a preliminary draught, offered it to the others. "Cocktails, sir," he explained with dignified precision. "A gentleman, sir, should never go out without 'em. Keeps off the morning chill. I remember going out in '58 with Hank Boompirater. Good ged, sir, the man had to put on his overcoat, and was shot in it. Fact!"

But the noise of wheels drowned the Colonel's reminiscences, and a rapidly driven buggy, containing Jack Folinsbee, Calhoun Bungstarter, his second, and Bill Masters, drew up on the ground. Jack Folinsbee leaped out gaily. "I had the jolliest work to get away without the governor's hearing," he began, addressing the group before him with the greatest volubility. Calhoun Bungstarter touched his arm, and the young man blushed. It was his first duel.

"If you are ready, gentlemen," said Mr. Bungstarter, "we had better proceed to business. I believe it is understood that no apology will be offered or accepted. We may as well settle preliminaries at once, or I fear we shall be interrupted. There is a rumor in town that the Vigilance Committee are seeking our friends the Starbottles, and I believe, as their fellow countryman, I have the honor to be included in their warrant."

At this probability of interruption, that gravity which had hitherto been wanting fell upon the group. The preliminaries were soon arranged and the principals placed in position. Then there was a silence.

To a spectator from the hill, impressed with the picnic suggestion, what might have been the popping of two champagne corks broke the stillness.

Culpepper had fired in the air. Colonel Starbottle uttered a low curse. Jack Folinsbee sulkily demanded another shot.

Again the parties stood opposed to each other. Again the word was given, and what seemed to be the simultaneous report of both pistols rose upon the air. But after an interval of a few seconds all were surprised to see Culpepper slowly raise his unexploded weapon and fire it harmlessly above his head. Then throwing the pistol upon the ground, he walked to a tree and leaned silently against it.

Jack Folinsbee flew into a paroxysm of fury. Colonel Starbottle raved and swore. Mr. Bungstarter was properly shocked at their conduct. "Really, gentlemen, if Mr. Culpepper Starbottle declines another shot, I do not see how we can proceed."

But the Colonel's blood was up, and Jack Folinsbee was equally implacable. A hurried consultation ensued, which ended by Colonel Starbottle taking his nephew's place as principal, Bill Masters acting as second, *vice* Mr. Bungstarter, who declined all further connection with the affair.

Two distinct reports rang through the Hollow. Jack Folinsbee dropped his smoking pistol, took a step forward, and then dropped heavily upon his face.

In a moment the surgeon was at his side. The confusion was heightened by the trampling of hoofs, and the voice of the blacksmith bidding them flee for their lives before the coming storm. A moment more and the ground was cleared, and the surgeon, looking up, beheld only the white face of Culpepper bending over him.

"Can you save him?"

"I cannot say. Hold up his head a moment, while I run to the buggy."

Culpepper passed his arm tenderly around the neck of the insensible man. Presently the surgeon returned with some stimulants.

"There, that will do, Mr. Starbottle, thank you. Now my advice is to get away from here while you can. I'll look after Folinsbee. Do you hear?"

Culpepper's arm was still round the neck of his late foe but his head had dropped and fallen on the wounded man's shoulder. The surgeon looked down, and, catching sight of his face, stooped and lifted him gently in his arms. He opened his coat and waistcoat. There was blood upon his shirt and a bullet-hole in his breast. He had been shot unto death at the first fire.

WAN LEE, THE PAGAN

As I opened Hop Sing's letter there fluttered to the ground a square strip of yellow paper covered with hieroglyphics, which at first glance I innocently took to be the label from a pack of Chinese fire-crackers. But the same envelope also contained a smaller strip of rice-paper, with two Chinese characters traced in India ink, that I at once knew to be Hop Sing's visiting card. The whole, as afterwards literally translated, ran as follows:—

> To the stranger the gates of my house are not closed; the rice-jar is on the left, and the sweetmeats on the right, as you enter.
> Two sayings of the Master:
> Hospitality is the virtue of the son and the wisdom of the ancestor.
> The superior man is light-hearted after the crop-gathering; he makes a festival.
> When the stranger is in your melon-patch, observe him not too closely; inattention is often the highest form of civility.
> > Happiness, Peace, and Prosperity.
> > > HOP SING.

Admirable, certainly, as was this morality and proverbial wisdom, and although this last axiom was very characteristic of my friend Hop Sing, who was that most sombre of all humorists, a Chinese philosopher, I must confess that, even after a very free translation, I was at a loss to make any immediate application of the message. Luckily I discovered a third enclosure in the shape of a little note in English and Hop Sing's own commercial hand. It ran thus—

The pleasure of your company is requested at No. —, Sacramento Street, on Friday Evening at 8 o'clock. A cup of tea at 9—sharp.

Hop Sing.

This explained all. It meant a visit to Hop Sing's warehouse, the opening and exhibition of some rare Chinese novelties and *curios*, a chat in the back office, a cup of tea of a perfection unknown beyond these sacred precincts, cigars, and a visit to the Chinese Theater or Temple. This was in fact the favorite program of Hop Sing when he exercised his functions of hospitality as the chief factor or Superintendent of the Ning Foo Company.

At eight o'clock on Friday evening I entered the warehouse of Hop Sing. There was that deliciously commingled mysterious foreign odor that I had so often noticed; there was the old array of uncouth-looking objects, the long procession of jars and crockery, the same singular blending of the grotesque and the mathematically neat and exact, the same endless suggestions of frivolity and fragility, the same want of harmony in colors that were each, in themselves, beautiful and rare. Kites in the shape of enormous dragons and gigantic butterflies; kites so ingeniously arranged as to utter at intervals, when facing the wind, the cry of a hawk; kites so large as to be beyond any boy's power of restraint—so large that you understood why kite-flying in China was an amusement for adults; gods of china and bronze so gratuitously ugly as to be beyond any human interest or sympathy from their very impossibility; jars of sweetmeats covered all over with moral sentiments from Confucius; hats that looked like baskets, and baskets that looked like hats; silks so light that I hesitate to record the incredible number of square yards that you might pass through the ring on your little finger—these and a great many other indescribable objects were all familiar to me. I pushed my way through the dimly-lighted warehouse until I reached the back office or parlor, where I found Hop Sing waiting to receive me.

Before I describe him I want the average reader to discharge from his mind any idea of a Chinaman that he may have gathered from the pantomime. He did not wear beautifully scalloped drawers fringed with little bells—I never met a Chinaman who did; he did not habitually carry his forefinger extended before him at right angles with his body, nor did I ever hear him utter the mysterious sentence, "Ching a ring a ring chaw," nor dance under any provocation. He was, on the whole, a rather grave, decorous, handsome gentleman. His complexion, which extended all over his head except where his long pig-tail grew, was like a very nice piece of glazed brown paper-muslin. His eyes were black and bright, and his eyelids set at an angle of 15°; his nose straight and delicately formed, his mouth small, and his teeth white and clean. He wore a dark blue silk blouse, and in the streets on cold days a short jacket of Astrakhan fur. He wore also a pair of drawers of blue brocade gathered tightly over his calves and ankles, offering a general sort of suggestion that he had forgotten his trousers that morning, but that, so gentlemanly were his manners, his friends had forborne to mention the fact to him. His manner was urbane, although quite serious. He spoke French and English fluently. In brief, I doubt if you could have found the equal of this Pagan shopkeeper among the Christian traders of San Francisco.

There were a few others present: a Judge of the Federal Court, an editor, a high government official, and a prominent merchant. After we had drunk our tea, and tasted a few sweetmeats from a mysterious jar, that looked as if it might contain a preserved mouse among its other nondescript treasures, Hop Sing arose, and gravely beckoning us to follow him, began to descend to the basement. When we got there, we were amazed at finding it brilliantly lighted, and that a number of chairs were arranged in a half-circle on the asphalt pavement. When he had courteously seated us, he said—

"I have invited you to witness a performance which I can at least promise you no other foreigners but yourselves have ever seen. Wang, the court juggler, arrived here yesterday morning. He has never given a performance outside of the palace before. I have asked him to entertain my friends this evening. He requires no theatre, stage, accessories, or any confederate—nothing more than you see here. Will you be pleased to examine the ground yourselves, gentlemen?"

Of course we examined the premises. It was the ordinary basement or cellar of the San Francisco storehouse, cemented to keep out the damp. We poked our sticks into the pavement and rapped on the walls to satisfy our polite host, but for no other purpose. We were quite content to be the victims of any clever deception. For myself, I knew I was ready to be deluded to any extent, and if I had been offered an explanation of what followed, I should have probably declined it.

Although I am satisfied that Wang's general performance was the first of that kind ever given on American soil, it has probably since become so familiar to many of my readers that I shall not bore them with it here. He began by setting to flight, with the aid of his fan the usual number of butterflies made before our eyes of little bits of tissue paper, and kept them in the air during the remainder of the performance. I have a vivid recollection of the judge trying to catch one that had lit on his knee, and of its evading him with the pertinacity of a living insect. And even at this time Wang, still plying his fan, was taking chickens out of hats, making oranges disappear, pulling endless yards of silk from his sleeve, apparently filling the whole area of the basement with goods that appeared mysteriously from the ground, from his own sleeves, from nowhere! He swallowed knives to the ruin of his digestion for years to come; he dislocated every limb of his body; he reclined in the air, apparently upon nothing. But his crowning performance, which I have never yet seen repeated, was the most weird, mysterious, and astounding. It is my apology for this long introduction, my sole excuse for writing this article, the genesis of this veracious history.

He cleared the ground of its encumbering articles for a space of about fifteen feet square, and then invited us all to walk forward and again examine it. We did so gravely; there was nothing but the cemented pavement below to be seen or felt. He then asked for the loan of a handkerchief, and, as I chanced to be nearest him, I offered mine. He took it and spread it open upon the floor. Over this he spread a large square of silk, and over this again a large shawl nearly covering the space he had cleared. He then took a position at one of the points of this rectangle, and began a monotonous chant, rocking his body to and fro in time with the somewhat lugubrious air.

We sat still and waited. Above the chant we could hear the striking of the city clocks, and the occasional rattle of a cart in the street overhead. The absolute watchfulness and expectation, the dim, mysterious half-light of the cellar, falling in a gruesome way upon the misshapen bulk of a Chinese deity in the background, a faint smell of opium smoke mingling with spice, and the dreadful uncertainty of what we were really waiting for, sent an uncomfortable thrill down our backs, and made us look at each other with a forced and unnatural smile. This feeling was heightened when Hop Sing slowly rose, and, without a word, pointed with his finger to the center of the shawl.

There was something beneath the shawl! Surely—and something that was not there before. At first a mere suggestion in relief, a faint outline, but growing more and more distinct and visible every moment. The chant still continued, the perspiration began to roll from the singer's face, gradually the hidden object took upon itself a shape and bulk that raised the shawl in its center some five or six inches. It was now unmistakably the outline of a small but perfect human figure, with extended arms and legs. One or two of us turned pale, there was a feeling of general uneasiness, until the editor broke the silence by a gibe that, poor as it was, was received with spontaneous enthusiasm. Then the chant suddenly ceased, Wang arose, and, with a quick, dexterous movement, stripped both shawl and silk away, and discovered, sleeping peacefully upon my handkerchief, a tiny Chinese baby!

The applause and uproar which followed this revelation ought to have satisfied Wang, even if his audience was a small one; it was loud enough to awaken the baby—a pretty little boy about a year old, looking like a Cupid cut out of sandalwood. He was whisked away almost as mysteriously as he appeared. When Hop Sing returned my handkerchief to me with a bow, I asked if the juggler was the father of the baby. "No sabe!" said the imperturbable Hop Sing, taking refuge in that Spanish form of non-committalism so common in California.

"But does he have a new baby for every performance?" I asked.

"Perhaps; who knows?"

"But what will become of this one?"

"Whatever you choose, gentlemen," replied Hop Sing, with a courteous inclination; "it was born here—you are its godfathers."

There were two characteristic peculiarities of any Californian assemblage in 1856: it was quick to take a hint, and generous to the point of prodigality in its response to any charitable appeal. No matter how sordid or avaricious the individual, he could not resist the infection of sympathy. I doubled the points of my handkerchief into a bag, dropped a coin into it, and, without a word, passed it to the judge. He quietly added a twenty-dollar gold piece, and passed it to the next, when it was returned to me it contained over a hundred dollars. I knotted the money in the handkerchief, and gave it to Hop Sing.

"For the baby, from its godfathers."

"But what name?" said the judge. There was a running fire of "Erebus," "Nox," "Plutus," "Terra Cotta," "Antæus," etc., etc. Finally the question was referred to our host.

"Why not keep his own name," he said quietly—"Wan Lee?" And
he did.

And thus was Wan Lee, on the night of Friday the 5th of March
1856, born into this veracious chronicle.

THE LAST FORM of the *Northern Star* for the 19th of July 1865—the
only daily paper published in Klamath County—had just gone to
press, and at three A.M. I was putting aside my proofs and manu-
scripts, preparatory to going home, when I discovered a letter lying
under some sheets of paper which I must have overlooked. The envelope was considerably soiled, it had no post-mark, but I had no
difficulty in recognizing the hand of my friend Hop Sing. I opened it
hurriedly and read as follows:—

MY DEAR SIR,—I do not know whether the bearer will suit you, but unless the office of "devil" in your newspaper is a purely technical one, I think
he has all the qualities required. He is very quick, active, and intelligent;
understands English better than he speaks it, and makes up for any defect
by his habits of observation and imitation. You have only to show him how
to do a thing once, and he will repeat it, whether it is an offence or a virtue.
But you certainly know him already; you are one of his godfathers, for is he
not Wan Lee, the reputed son of Wang the conjurer, to whose performances
I had the honor to introduce you? But, perhaps, you have forgotten it.

I shall send him with a gang of coolies to Stockton, thence by express to
your town. If you can use him there, you will do me a favor, and probably
save his life, which is at present in great peril from the hands of the younger
members of your Christian and highly-civilized race who attend the en-
lightened schools in San Francisco.

He has acquired some singular habits and customs from his experience of
Wang's profession, which he followed for some years, until he became too
large to go in a hat, or be produced from his father's sleeve. The money you
left with me has been expended on his education; he has gone through the
Tri-literal Classics, but, I think, without much benefit. He knows but little of
Confucius, and absolutely nothing of Mencius. Owing to the negligence of
his father, he associated, perhaps, too much with American children.

I should have answered your letter before, by post, but I thought that
Wan Lee himself would be a better messenger for this.
—Yours respectfully,   HOP SING.

And this was the long-delayed answer to my letter to Hop Sing. But
where was "the bearer"? How was the letter delivered? I summoned
hastily the foreman, printers, and office-boy, but without eliciting

anything; no one had seen the letter delivered, nor knew anything of the bearer. A few days later I had a visit from my laundry-man, Ah Ri.

"You wantee debbil? All lightee; me catchee him."

He returned in a few moments with a bright-looking Chinese boy, about ten years old, with whose appearance and general intelligence I was so greatly impressed that I engaged him on the spot. When the business was concluded, I asked his name.

"Wan Lee," said the boy.

"What! Are you the boy sent out by Hop Sing? What the devil do you mean by not coming here before, and how did you deliver that letter?"

Wan Lee looked at me and laughed. "Me pitchee in top side window."

I did not understand. He looked for a moment perplexed, and then, snatching the letter out of my hand, ran down the stairs. After a moment's pause, to my great astonishment, the letter came flying in at the window, circled twice around the room, and then dropped gently like a bird upon my table. Before I had got over my surprise Wan Lee reappeared, smiled, looked at the letter and then at me, said, "So, John," and then remained gravely silent. I said nothing further, but it was understood that this was his first official act.

His next performance, I grieve to say, was not attended with equal success. One of our regular paper-carriers fell sick, and, at a pinch, Wan Lee was ordered to fill his place. To prevent mistakes he was shown over the route the previous evening, and supplied at about daylight with the usual number of subscribers' copies. He returned after an hour, in good spirits and without the papers. He had delivered them all, he said.

Unfortunately for Wan Lee, at about eight o'clock indignant subscribers began to arrive at the office. They had received their copies; but how? In the form of hard-pressed cannon balls, delivered by a single shot and a mere *tour de force* through the glass of bedroom windows. They had received them full in the face, like a base ball, if they happened to be up and stirring; they had received them in quarter sheets, tucked in at separate windows; they had found them in the chimney, pinned against the door, shot through attic windows, delivered in long slips through convenient keyholes, stuffed into ventilators, and occupying the same can with the morning's milk. One subscriber, who waited for some time at the office door, to have a personal interview with Wan Lee (then comfortably locked in my bedroom), told me, with tears of rage in his eyes, that he had been awakened at five o'clock by a most hideous yelling below his windows; that on rising, in great agitation, he was startled by the sudden appearance of the *Northern Star*, rolled hard and bent into the form of a boomerang or East Indian club, that sailed into the window, described a number of fiendish circles in the room, knocked over the light, slapped the baby's face, "took" him (the subscriber) "in the jaw," and then returned out of the window, and dropped helplessly in the area. During the rest of the day wads and strips of soiled paper, purporting to be copies of the *Northern Star* of that morning's issue, were brought indignantly to the office. An admirable editorial on "The Resources of Humboldt County," which I had constructed the evening before, and which, I have reason to believe, might have changed the whole balance of trade during the ensuing year, and left San Francisco bankrupt at her wharves, was in this way lost to the public.

It was deemed advisable for the next three weeks to keep Wan Lee closely confined to the printing-office and the purely mechanical part of the business. Here he developed a surprising quickness and adaptability, winning even the favor and goodwill of the printers and foreman, who at first looked upon his introduction into the secrets of their trade as fraught with the gravest political significance. He learned to set type readily and neatly, his wonderful skill in manipulation aiding him in the mere mechanical act, and his ignorance of the language confining him simply to the mechanical effort—confirming the printer's axiom that the printer who considers or follows the ideas of his copy makes a poor compositor. He would set up deliberately long diatribes against himself, composed by his fellow-printers, and hung on his hook as copy, and even such short sentences as "Wan Lee is the devil's own imp," "Wan Lee is a Mongolian rascal," and bring the proof to me with happiness beaming from every tooth and satisfaction shining in his huckleberry eyes.

It was not long, however, before he learned to retaliate on his mischievous persecutors. I remember one instance in which his reprisal came very near involving me in a serious misunderstanding. Our foreman's name was Webster, and Wan Lee presently learned to know and recognize the individual and combined letters of his name. It was during a political campaign, and the eloquent and fiery Colonel Starbottle, of Siskiyou, had delivered an effective speech, which was reported especially for the *Northern Star*. In a very sublime per-oration Colonel Starbottle had said, "In the language of the godlike Webster, I repeat,"—and here followed the quotation, which I have forgotten. Now, it chanced that Wan Lee, looking over the galley after it had been revised, saw the name of his chief persecutor, and, of course, imagined the quotation his. After the form was locked up, Wan Lee took advantage of Webster's absence to remove the quota-tion, and substitute a thin piece of lead, of the same size as the type, engraved with Chinese characters, making a sentence which, I had reason to believe, was an utter and abject confession of the incapac-ity and offensiveness of the Webster family generally, and exceed-ingly eulogistic of Wan Lee himself personally.

The next morning's paper contained Colonel Starbottle's speech in full, in which it appeared that the "godlike" Webster had on one occasion uttered his thoughts in excellent but perfectly enigmatical Chinese. The rage of Colonel Starbottle knew no bounds. I have a vivid recollection of that admirable man walking into my office and demanding a retraction of the statement.

"But, my dear sir," I asked, "are you willing to deny, over your own signature, that Webster ever uttered such a sentence? Dare you deny that, with Mr. Webster's well-known attainments, a knowledge of Chinese might not have been among the number? Are you willing to submit a translation suitable to the capacity of our readers, and deny, upon your honor as a gentleman, that the late Mr. Webster ever uttered such a sentiment? If you are, sir, I am willing to publish your denial."

The Colonel was not, and left, highly indignant.

Webster, the foreman, took it more coolly. Happily he was un-aware that for two days after, Chinamen from the laundries, from the gulches, from the kitchens, looked in the front office door with faces beaming with sardonic delight; that three hundred extra cop-ies of the *Star* were ordered for the wash-houses on the river. He only knew that during the day Wan Lee occasionally went off into convulsive spasms, and that he was obliged to kick him into con-sciousness again. A week after the occurrence I called Wan Lee into my office.

"Wan," I said gravely, "I should like you to give me, for my own personal satisfaction, a translation of that Chinese sentence which my gifted countryman, the late godlike Webster, uttered upon a public occasion." Wan Lee looked at me intently, and then the slightest possible twinkle crept into his black eyes. Then he replied, with equal gravity—

"Mishtel Webstel,—he say: 'China boy makee me belly much foolee. China boy makee me heap sick." Which I have reason to think was true.

But I fear I am giving but one side, and not the best, of Wan Lee's character. As he imparted it to me, his had been a hard life. He had known scarcely any childhood—he had no recollection of a father or mother. The conjurer Wang had brought him up. He had spent the first seven years of his life in appearing from baskets, in dropping out of hats, in climbing ladders, in putting his little limbs out of joint in posturing. He had lived in an atmosphere of trickery and deception; he had learned to look upon mankind as dupes of their senses; in fine, if he had thought at all, he would have been a sceptic, if he had been a little older, he would have been a cynic, if he had been older still, he would have been a philosopher. As it was, he was a little imp! A good-natured imp it was, too—an imp whose moral nature had never been wakened, an imp up for a holiday, and willing to try virtue as a diversion. I don't know that he had any spiritual nature; he was very superstitious: he carried about with him a hideous little porcelain god, which he was in the habit of alternately reviling and propitiating. He was too intelligent for the commoner Chinese vices of stealing or gratuitous lying. Whatever discipline he practiced was taught by his intellect.

I am inclined to think that his feelings were not altogether unimpressible—although it was almost impossible to extract an expression from him—and I conscientiously believe he became attached to those that were good to him. What he might have become under more favorable conditions than the bondsman of an over-worked, under-paid literary man, I don't know; I only know that the scant, irregular, impulsive kindnesses that I showed him were gratefully received. He was very loyal and patient—two qualities rare in the average American servant. He was like Malvolio, "sad and civil" with me; only once, and then under great provocation, do I remember of his exhibiting any impatience. It was my habit, after leaving the office at night, to take him with me to my rooms, as the bearer of any supplemental or happy after-thought in the editorial way, that might occur to me before the paper went to press. One night I had been scribbling away past the usual hour of dismissing Wan Lee, and had become quite oblivious of his presence in a chair near my door, when suddenly I became aware of a voice saying, in plaintive accents, something that sounded like "Chy Lee."

I faced around sternly.

"What did you say?"

"Me say, 'Chy Lee.'"

"Well?" I said impatiently.

"You sabe, 'How do, John?'"

"Yes."

"You sabe, 'So long, John?'"

"Yes."

"Well, 'Chy Lee' allee same!"

I understood him quite plainly. It appeared that "Chy Lee" was a form of "good night," and that Wan Lee was anxious to go home. But an instinct of mischief which I fear I possessed in common with him, impelled me to act as if oblivious of the hint. I muttered something about not understanding him, and again bent over my work. In a few minutes I heard his wooden shoes pattering pathetically over the floor. I looked up. He was standing near the door.

"You no sabe, 'Chy Lee'?"

"No," I said sternly.

"You sabe muchee big foolee!—allee same!"

And with this audacity upon his lips he fled. The next morning, however, he was as meek and patient as before, and I did not recall his offence. As a probable peace-offering, he blacked all my boots—a duty never required of him—including a pair of buff deer-skin slippers and an immense pair of horseman's jack-boots, on which he indulged his remorse for two hours.

I have spoken of his honesty as being a quality of his intellect rather than his principle, but I recall about this time two exceptions to the rule. I was anxious to get some fresh eggs, as a change to the heavy diet of a mining town, and knowing that Wan Lee's countrymen were great poultry raisers, I applied to him. He furnished me with them regularly every morning, but refused to take any pay, saying that the man did not sell them—a remarkable instance of self-abnegation, as eggs were then worth half a dollar apiece. One morning, my neighbor, Foster, dropped in upon me at breakfast, and took occasion to bewail his own ill fortune, as his hens had lately stopped laying, or wandered off in the bush. Wan Lee, who was present during our colloquy, preserved his characteristic sad taciturnity. When my neighbor had gone, he turned to me with a slight chuckle— "Flostel's hens—Wan Lee's hens—allee same!" His other offence was more serious and ambitious. It was a season of great irregularities in the mails, and Wan Lee had heard me deplore the delay in the delivery of my letters and newspapers. On arriving at my office one day, I was amazed to find my table covered with letters, evidently just from the post office, but unfortunately not one addressed to me. I turned to Wan Lee, who was surveying them with a calm satisfaction, and demanded an explanation. To my horror he pointed to an empty mail-bag in the corner, and said—"Postman he say 'No lettee, John— no lettee, John.' Postman plentee lie! Postman no good. Me catchee lettee last night—allee same!" Luckily it was still early, the mails had not been distributed; I had a hurried interview with the Postmaster, and Wan Lee's bold attempt at robbing the U.S. Mail was finally condoned, by the purchase of a new mail-bag, and the whole affair thus kept a secret.

If my liking for my little pagan page had not been sufficient, my duty to Hop Sing was enough to cause me to take Wan Lee with me when I returned to San Francisco, after my two years' experience with the *Northern Star*. I do not think he contemplated the change with pleasure. I attributed his feelings to a nervous dread of crowded public streets—when he had to go across town for me on an errand, he always made a long circuit of the outskirts—to his dislike for the discipline of the Chinese and English school to which I proposed to send him, to his fondness for the free, vagrant life of the mines, to sheer wilfulness! That it might have been a superstitious premonition did not occur to me until long after.

Nevertheless it really seemed as if the opportunity I had long looked for and confidently expected had come—the opportunity of placing Wan Lee under gently restraining influences, of subjecting him to a life and experience that would draw out of him what good my superficial care and ill-regulated kindness could not reach. Wan Lee was placed at the school of a Chinese missionary—an intelligent and kind-hearted clergyman, who had shown great interest in the boy, and who, better than all, had a wonderful faith in him. A home was found for him in the family of a widow, who had a bright and interesting daughter about two years younger than Wan Lee. It was this bright, cheery, innocent, and artless child that touched and reached a depth in the boy's nature that hitherto had been unsuspected— that awakened a moral susceptibility which had lain for years insensible alike to the teachings of society or the ethics of the theologian.

These few brief months, bright with a promise that we never saw fulfilled, must have been happy ones to Wan Lee. He worshipped his little friend with something of the same superstition, but without any of the caprice, that he bestowed upon his porcelain pagan god. It was his delight to walk behind her to school, carrying her books—a service always fraught with danger to him from the little hands of his Caucasian Christian brothers. He made her the most marvelous toys, he would cut out of carrots and turnips the most astonishing roses and tulips, he made life-like chickens out of melon-seeds, he constructed fans and kites, and was singularly proficient in the making of dolls' paper dresses. On the other hand she played and sang to him, taught him a thousand little prettinesses and refinements only known to girls, gave him a yellow ribbon for his pig-tail, as best suiting his complexion, read to him, showed him wherein he was original and valuable, took him to Sunday School with her, against the precedents of the school, and, small-womanlike, triumphed. I wish I could add here, that she effected his conversion, and made him give up his porcelain idol, but I am telling a true story, and this little girl was quite content to fill him with her own Christian goodness without letting him know that he was changed. So they got along very well together—thus little Christian girl with her shining cross hanging around her plump, white little neck, and this dark little pagan, with his hideous porcelain god hidden away in his blouse.

There were two days of that eventful year which will long be remembered in San Francisco—two days when a mob of her citizens set upon and killed unarmed, defenceless foreigners, because they were foreigners and of another race, religion, and color, and worked for what wages they could get. There were some public men so timid, that, seeing this, they thought that the end of the world had come; there were some eminent statesmen whose names I am ashamed to write here, who began to think that the passage in the Constitution which guarantees civil and religious liberty to every citizen or foreigner was a mistake. But there were also some men who were not so easily frightened, and in twenty-four hours we had things so arranged that the timid men could wring their hands in safety, and the eminent statesmen utter their doubts without hurting anybody or anything. And in the midst of this I got a note from Hop Sing, asking me to come to him immediately.

I found his warehouse closed and strongly guarded by the police against any possible attack of the rioters. Hop Sing admitted me through a barred grating with his usual imperturbable calm, but, as it seemed to me, with more than his usual seriousness. Without a word he took my hand and led me to the rear of the room, and thence downstairs into the basement. It was dimly lighted, but there was something lying on the floor covered by a shawl. As I approached he drew the shawl away with a sudden gesture, and revealed Wan Lee, the Pagan, lying dead!

Dead, my reverend friends, dead! Stoned to death in the streets of San Francisco, in the year of grace, eighteen hundred and sixty-nine, by a mob of half-grown boys and Christian school-children!

As I put my hand reverently upon his breast, I felt something crumbling beneath his blouse. I looked inquiringly at Hop Sing. He put his hand between the folds of silk and drew out something with the first bitter smile I had ever seen on the face of that pagan gentleman.

It was Wan Lee's porcelain god, crushed by a stone from the hands of those Christian iconoclasts!

HOW SANTA CLAUS
CAME TO SIMPSON'S BAR

I t had been raining in the valley of the Sacramento. The North
Fork had overflowed its banks, and Rattlesnake Creek was impassable. The few boulders that had marked the summer ford at
Simpson's Crossing were obliterated by a vast sheet of water stretch-
ing to the foothills. The up-stage was stopped at Granger's; the last
mail had been abandoned in the tules, the rider swimming for his
life. "An area," remarked the *Sierra Avalanche*, with pensive local pride,
"as large as the State of Massachusetts is now under water."

Nor was the weather any better in the foothills. The mud lay deep
on the mountain road; wagons that neither physical force nor moral
objurgation could move from the evil ways into which they had fallen
encumbered the track, and the way to Simpson's Bar was indicated
by broken-down teams and hard swearing. And further on, cut off
and inaccessible, rained upon and bedraggled, smitten by high winds
and threatened by high water, Simpson's Bar, on the eve of Christmas Day, 1862, clung like a swallow's nest to the rocky entablature
and splintered capitals of Table Mountain, and shook in the blast.

As night shut down on the settlement, a few lights gleamed through
the mist from the windows of cabins on either side of the highway,
now crossed and gullied by lawless streams and swept by marauding
winds. Happily most of the population were gathered at Thompson's
store, clustered around a red-hot stove, at which they silently spat in
some accepted sense of social communion that perhaps rendered conversation unnecessary. Indeed, most methods of diversion had long
since been exhausted on Simpson's Bar; high water had suspended

the regular occupations on gulch and on river, and a consequent lack of money and whiskey had taken the zest from most illegitimate recreation.

Even Mr. Hamlin was fain to leave the Bar with fifty dollars in his pocket—the only amount actually realized of the large sums won by him in the successful exercise of his arduous profession. "Ef I was asked," he remarked somewhat later—"ef I was asked to pint out a purty little village where a retired sport as didn't care for money could exercise hisself, frequent and lively, I'd say Simpson's Bar; but for a young man with a large family depending on his exertions, it don't pay." As Mr. Hamlin's family consisted mainly of female adults, this remark is quoted rather to show the breadth of his humor than the exact extent of his responsibilities.

Howbeit, the unconscious objects of this satire sat that evening in the listless apathy begotten of idleness and lack of excitement. Even the sudden splashing of hoofs before the door did not arouse them. Dick Bullen alone paused in the act of scraping out his pipe, and lifted his head, but no other one of the group indicated any interest in, or recognition of, the man who entered.

It was a figure familiar enough to the company, and known in Simpson's Bar as "The Old Man." A man of perhaps fifty years; grizzled and scant of hair, but still fresh and youthful of complexion. A face full of ready but not very powerful sympathy, with a chameleon-like aptitude for taking on the shade and color of contiguous moods and feelings. He had evidently just left some hilarious companions, and did not at first notice the gravity of the group, but clapped the shoulder of the nearest man jocularly, and threw himself into a vacant chair.

"Jest heard the best thing out, boys! Ye know Smiley, over yar—Jim Smiley—funniest man in the Bar? Well, Jim was jest telling the richest yarn about——"

"Smiley's a——fool," interrupted a gloomy voice.

"A particular——skunk," added another in sepulchral accents.

A silence followed these positive statements. The Old Man glanced quickly around the group. Then his face slowly changed. "That's so," he said reflectively, after a pause, "certainly a sort of a skunk and suthin' of a fool. In course." He was silent for a moment, as in painful contemplation of the unsavoriness and folly of the unpopular Smiley. "Dismal weather, ain't it?" he added, now fully embarked on the current of prevailing sentiment. "Mighty rough papers on the boys, and no show for money this season. And tomorrow's Christmas."

There was a movement among the men at this announcement, but whether of satisfaction or disgust was not plain. "Yes," continued the Old Man in the lugubrious tone he had, within the last few moments, unconsciously adopted,—"yes, Christmas, and tonight's Christmas Eve. Ye see, boys, I kinder thought—that is, I sorter had an idee, jest passin' like, you know—that maybe ye'd all like to come over to my house tonight and have a sort of tear round. But I suppose, now, you wouldn't? Don't feel like it, maybe?" he added with anxious sympathy, peering into the faces of his companions.

"Well, I don't know," responded Tom Flynn with some cheerfulness. "P'r'aps we may. But how about your wife, Old Man? What does *she* say to it?"

The Old Man hesitated. His conjugal experience had not been a happy one, and the fact was known to Simpson's Bar. His first wife, a delicate, pretty little woman, had suffered keenly and secretly from the jealous suspicions of her husband, until one day he invited the whole Bar to his house to expose her infidelity. On arriving, the party found the shy, petite creature quietly engaged in her household duties, and retired abashed and discomfited. But the sensitive woman did not easily recover from the shock of this extraordinary outrage. It was with difficulty she regained her equanimity sufficiently to release her lover from the closet in which he was concealed, and escape with him. She left a boy of three years to comfort her bereaved husband. The Old Man's present wife had been his cook. She was large, loyal, and aggressive.

Before he could reply, Joe Dimmick suggested with great directness that it was the "Old Man's house," and that, invoking the Divine Power, if the case were his own, he would invite whom he pleased, even if in so doing he imperiled his salvation. The Powers of Evil, he further remarked, should contend against him vainly. All this delivered with a terseness and vigor lost in this necessary translation.

"In course. Certainly. Thet's it," said the Old Man with a sympathetic frown. "Thar's no trouble about thet. It's my own house, built every stick on it myself. Don't you be afeard o' her, boys. She may cut up a trifle rough—ez wimmin do—but she'll come round." Secretly the Old Man trusted to the exaltation of liquor and the power of courageous example to sustain him in such an emergency.

As yet, Dick Bullen, the oracle and leader of Simpson's Bar, had not spoken. He now took his pipe from his lips. "Old Man, how's that yer Johnny gettin' on? Seems to me he didn't look so peart last time I seed him on the bluff heavin' rocks at Chinamen. Didn't seem to take much interest in it. Thar was a gang of 'em by yer yesterday—drownded out up the river—and I kinder thought o' Johnny, and how he'd miss 'em! Maybe now, we'd be in the way ef he wus sick?"

The father, evidently touched not only by this pathetic picture of Johnny's deprivation, but by the considerate delicacy of the speaker, hastened to assure him that Johnny was better, and that a "little fun might 'liven him up." Whereupon Dick arose, shook himself, and saying, "I'm ready. Lead the way, Old Man: here goes," himself led the way with a leap, a characteristic howl, and darted out into the night. As he passed through the outer room he caught up a blazing brand from the hearth. The action was repeated by the rest of the party, closely following and elbowing each other, and before the astonished proprietor of Thompson's grocery was aware of the intention of his guests, the room was deserted.

The night was pitchy dark. In the first gust of wind their temporary torches were extinguished, and only the red brands dancing and flitting in the gloom like drunken will-o'-the-wisps indicated their whereabouts. Their way led up Pine-Tree Cañon, at the head of which a broad, low, bark-thatched cabin burrowed in the mountain-side. It was the home of the Old Man, and the entrance to the tunnel in which he worked when he worked at all. Here the crowd paused for a moment, out of delicate deference to their host, who came up panting in the rear.

"P'r'aps ye'd better hold on a second out yer, whilst I go in and see that things is all right," said the Old Man, with an indifference he was far from feeling. The suggestion was graciously accepted, the door opened and closed on the host, and the crowd, leaning their backs against the wall and cowering under the eaves, waited and listened.

For a few moments there was no sound but the dripping of water from the eaves, and the stir and rustle of wrestling boughs above them. Then the men became uneasy, and whispered suggestion and suspicion passed from the one to the other. "Reckon she's caved in his head the first lick!" "Decoyed him inter the tunnel and barred him up, likely." "Got him down and sittin' on him." "Prob'ly biling suthin' to heave on us: stand clear the door, boys!" For just then the latch clicked, the door slowly opened, and a voice said, "Come in out o' the wet."

The voice was neither that of the Old Man nor of his wife. It was the voice of a small boy, its weak treble broken by that preternatural hoarseness which only vagabondage and the habit of premature self-assertion can give.

It was the face of a small boy that looked up at theirs—a face that might have been pretty, and even refined, but that it was darkened by evil knowledge from within, and dirt and hard experience from without. He had a blanket around his shoulders, and had evidently just risen from his bed.

"Come in," he repeated, "and don't make no noise. The Old Man's in there talking to mar," he continued, pointing to an adjacent room which seemed to be a kitchen, from which the Old Man's voice came in deprecating accents. "Let me be," he added querulously, to Dick Bullen, who had caught him up, blanket and all, and was affecting to toss him into the fire, "let go o' me, you d——d old fool, d' ye hear ?"

Thus adjured, Dick Bullen lowered Johnny to the ground with a smothered laugh, while the men, entering quietly, ranged themselves around a long table of rough boards which occupied the center of the room. Johnny then gravely proceeded to a cupboard and brought out several articles, which he deposited on the table. "Thar's whiskey. And crackers. And red herons. And cheese." He took a bite of the latter on his way to the table. "And sugar." He scooped up a mouthful *en route* with a small and very dirty hand. "And terbacker. Thar's dried appils too on the shelf, but I don't admire 'em. Appils is swellin'. Thar," he concluded, "now wade in, and don't be afeard. I don't mind the old woman. She don't b'long to me. S'long."

He had stepped to the threshold of a small room, scarcely larger than a closet, partitioned off from the main apartment, and holding in its dim recess a small bed. He stood there a moment looking at the company, his bare feet peeping from the blanket, and nodded.

"Hello, Johnny! You ain't goin' to turn in agin, are ye?" said Dick.

"Yes, I are," responded Johnny decidedly.

"Why, wot's up, old fellow?"

"I'm sick."

"How sick?"

"I've got a fevier. And childblains. And roomatiz," returned Johnny, and vanished within. After a moment's pause, he added in the dark, apparently from under the bedclothes—"And biles!"

There was an embarrassing silence. The men looked at each other and at the fire. Even with the appetizing banquet before them, it seemed as if they might again fall into the despondency of Thompson's grocery, when the voice of the Old Man, incautiously lifted, came deprecatingly from the kitchen.

"Certainly! Thet's so. In course they is. A gang o' lazy, drunken loafers, and that ar Dick Bullen's the ornariest of all. Didn't hev no more *sabe* than to come round yar with sickness in the house and no provision. Thet's what I said: 'Bullen,' sez I, 'it's crazy drunk you are, or a fool,' sez I; to think o' such a thing.' 'Staples,' I sez, ' be you a man, Staples, and 'spect to raise h—ll under my roof and invalids lyin' round?' But they would come—they would. Thet's wot you must 'spect o' such trash as lays round the Bar."

A burst of laughter from the men followed this unfortunate exposure. Whether it was overheard in the kitchen, or whether the Old Man's irate companion had just then exhausted all other modes of expressing her contemptuous indignation, I cannot say, but a back door was suddenly slammed with great violence. A moment later and the Old Man reappeared, haply unconscious of the cause of the late hilarious outburst, and smiled blandly.

"The old woman thought she'd jest run over to Mrs. MacFadden's for a sociable call," he explained with jaunty indifference, as he took a seat at the board.

Oddly enough it needed this untoward incident to relieve the embarrassment that was beginning to be felt by the party, and their natural audacity returned with their host. I do not propose to record the convivialities of that evening. The inquisitive reader will accept the statement that the conversation was characterized by the same intellectual exaltation, the same cautious reverence, the same fastidious delicacy, the same rhetorical precision, and the same logical and coherent discourse somewhat later in the evening, which distinguish similar gatherings of the masculine sex in more civilized localities and under more favorable auspices. No glasses were broken in the absence of any; no liquor was uselessly spilt on the floor or table in the scarcity of that article.

It was nearly midnight when the festivities were interrupted.

"Hush," said Dick Bullen, holding up his hand. It was the querulous voice of Johnny from his adjacent closet: "O dad!"

The Old Man arose hurriedly and disappeared in the closet. Presently he reappeared. "His rheumatiz is coming on agin bad," he explained, "and he wants rubbin'." He lifted the demijohn of whiskey from the table and shook it. It was empty. Dick Bullen put down his tin cup with an embarrassed laugh. So did the others. The Old Man examined their contents and said hopefully, "I reckon that's enough; he don't need much. You hold on all o' you for a spell, and I'll be back'; and vanished in the closet with an old flannel shirt and the whiskey. The door closed but imperfectly, and the following dialogue was distinctly audible:

"Now, sonny, whar does she ache worst?"

"Sometimes over yar and sometimes under yer; but it's most powerful from yer to yer. Rub yer, dad."

A silence seemed to indicate a brisk rubbing. Then Johnny:

"Hevin' a good time out yer, dad?"

"Yes, sonny."

"To-morrer's Chrismuss—ain't it?"

"Yes, sonny. How does she feel now?"

"Better. Rub a little furder down. Wot's Chrismuss, anyway? Wot's it all about?"

"Oh, it's a day."

This exhaustive definition was apparently satisfactory, for there was a silent interval of rubbing. Presently Johnny again:

"Mar sez that everywhere else but yer everybody gives things to everybody Chrismuss, and then she jist waded inter you. She sez thar's a man they call Sandy Claws, not a white man, you know, but a kind o' Chinemin, comes down the chimbley night afore Chrismuss and gives things to chillern—boys like me. Puts 'em in their butes! Thet's what she tried to play upon me. Easy now, pop, whar are you rubbin' to—thet's a mile from the place. She jest made that up, didn't she, jest to aggrewate me and you? Don't rub thar. . . . Why, dad!"

In the great quiet that seemed to have fallen upon the house the sigh of the near pines and the drip of leaves without was very distinct. Johnny's voice, too, was lowered as he went on, "Don't you take on now, for I'm gettin' all right fast. Wot's the boys doin' out thar?"

The Old Man partly opened the door and peered through. His

guests were sitting there sociably enough, and there were a few silver coins and a lean buckskin purse on the table. "Bettin' on suthin'—
some little game or 'nother. They're all right," he replied to Johnny,
and recommended his rubbing.

"I'd like to take a hand and win some money," said Johnny reflectively after a pause.

The Old Man glibly repeated what was evidently a familiar formula, that if Johnny would wait until he struck it rich in the tunnel
he'd have lots of money, etc., etc.

"Yes," said Johnny, "but you don't. And whether you strike it or I
win it, it's about the same. It's all luck. But it's mighty cur'o's about
Chrismuss—ain't it? Why do they call it Chrismuss?"

Perhaps from some instinctive deference to the overhearing of his
guests, or from some vague sense of incongruity, the Old Man's reply
was so low as to be inaudible beyond the room.

"Yes," said Johnny, with some slight abatement of interest, "I've
heerd o' him before. Thar, that'll do, dad. I don't ache near so bad as
I did. Now wrap me tight in this yer blanket. So. Now," he added in
a muffled whisper, "sit down yer by me till I go asleep." To assure
himself of obedience, he disengaged one hand from the blanket, and,
grasping his father's sleeve, again composed himself to rest.

For some moments the Old Man waited patiently. Then the un-
wonted stillness of the house excited his curiosity, and without moving from the bed he cautiously opened the door with his disengaged
hand, and looked into the main room. To his infinite surprise it was
dark and deserted. But even then a smouldering log on the hearth
broke, and by the upspringing blaze he saw the figure of Dick Bullen
sitting by the dying embers.

"Hello!"

Dick started, rose, and came somewhat unsteadily toward him.

"Whar's the boys?" said the Old Man.

"Gone up the cañon on a little *pasear.* They're coming back for
me in a minit. I'm waitin' round for 'em. What are you starin' at,
Old Man?" he added, with a forced laugh; "do you think I'm drunk?"

The Old Man might have been pardoned the supposition, for
Dick's eyes were humid and his face flushed. He loitered and lounged
back to the chimney, yawned, shook himself, buttoned up his coat
and laughed. "Liquor ain't so plenty as that, Old Man. Now don't
you git up," he continued, as the Old Man made a movement to

release his sleeve from Johnny's hand. "Don't you mind manners. Sit jest whar you be; I'm goin' in a jiffy. Thar, that's them now."

There was a low tap at the door. Dick Bullen opened it quickly, nodded "Good-night" to his host, and disappeared. The Old Man would have followed him but for the hand that still unconsciously grasped his sleeve. He could have easily disengaged it: it was small, weak, and emaciated. But perhaps because it was small, weak, and emaciated he changed his mind, and, drawing his chair closer to the bed, rested his head upon it. In this defenseless attitude the potency of his earlier potations surprised him. The room flickered and faded before his eyes, reappeared, faded again, went out, and left him—asleep.

Meantime Dick Bullen, closing the door, confronted his companions. "Are you ready?" said Staples.

"Ready," said Dick; "What's the time?"

"Past twelve," was the reply; "can you make it?—it's nigh on fifty miles, the round trip hither and yon."

"I reckon," returned Dick shortly. "Whar's the mare?"

"Bill and Jack's holdin' her at the crossin'."

"Let 'em hold on a minit longer," said Dick.

He turned and re-entered the house softly. By the light of the guttering candle and dying fire he saw that the door of the little room was open. He stepped toward it on tiptoe and looked in. The Old Man had fallen back in his chair, snoring, his helpless feet thrust out in a line with his collapsed shoulders, and his hat pulled over his eyes. Beside him, on a narrow wooden bedstead, lay Johnny, muffled tightly in a blanket that hid all save a strip of forehead and a few curls damp with perspiration.

Dick Bullen made a step forward, hesitated, and glanced over his shoulder into the deserted room. Everything was quiet. With a sudden resolution he parted his huge mustaches with both hands and stooped over the sleeping boy. But even as he did so a mischievous blast, lying in wait, swooped down the chimney, rekindled the hearth, and lit up the room with a shameless glow from which Dick fled in bashful terror.

His companions were already waiting for him at the crossing. Two of them were struggling in the darkness with some strange misshapen bulk, which as Dick came nearer took the semblance of a great yellow horse.

It was the mare. She was not a pretty picture. From her Roman nose to her rising haunches, from her arched spine hidden by the stiff *machillas* of a Mexican saddle, to her thick, straight bony legs, there was not a line of equine grace. In her half-blind but wholly vicious white eyes, in her protruding under-lip, in her monstrous color, there was nothing but ugliness and vice.

"Now then," said Staples, "stand cl'ar of her heels, boys, and up with you. Don't miss your first holt of her mane, and mind ye get your off stirrup quick. Ready!"

There was a leap, a scrambling struggle, a bound, a wild retreat of the crowd, a circle of flying hoofs, two springless leaps that jarred the earth, a rapid play and jingle of spurs, a plunge, and then the voice of Dick somewhere in the darkness. "All right!"

"Don't take the lower road back onless you're hard pushed for time! Don't hold her in down hill. We'll be at the ford at five. G'lang! Hoopa! Mula! GO!"

A splash, a spark struck from the ledge in the road, a clatter in the rocky cut beyond, and Dick was gone.

• • •

SING, O MUSE, the ride of Richard Bullen! Sing, O Muse, of chivalrous men! the sacred quest, the doughty deeds, the battery of low churls, the fearsome ride and gruesome perils of the Flower of Simpson's Bar! Alack! she is dainty, this Muse! She will have none of this bucking brute and swaggering, ragged rider, and I must fain follow him in prose, afoot!

It was one o'clock, and yet he had only gained Rattlesnake Hill. For in that time Jovita had rehearsed to him all her imperfections and practiced all her vices. Thrice had she stumbled. Twice had she thrown up her Roman nose in a straight line with the reins, and, resisting bit and spur, struck out madly across country. Twice had she reared, and, rearing, fallen backward; and twice had the agile Dick, unharmed, regained his seat before she found her vicious legs again. And a mile beyond them, at the foot of a long hill, was Rattlesnake Creek.

Dick knew that here was the crucial test of his ability to perform his enterprise, set his teeth grimly, put his knees well into her flanks, and changed his defensive tactics to brisk aggression. Bullied and maddened, Jovita began the descent of the hill. Here the artful Richard pretended to hold her in with ostentatious objurgation and well-feigned cries of alarm. It is unnecessary to add that Jovita instantly ran away. Nor need I state the time made in the descent; it is written in the chronicles of Simpson's Bar. Enough that in another moment, as it seemed to Dick, she was splashing on the overflowed banks of Rattlesnake Creek.

As Dick expected, the momentum she had acquired carried her beyond the point of balking, and, holding her well together for a mighty leap, they dashed into the middle of the swiftly flowing current. A few moments of kicking, wading, and swimming, and Dick drew a long breath on the opposite bank.

The road from Rattlesnake Creek to Red Mountain was tolerably level. Either the plunge in Rattlesnake Creek had dampened her baleful fire, or the art which led to it had shown her the superior wickedness of her rider, for Jovita no longer wasted her surplus energy in wanton conceits. Once she bucked, but it was from force of habit; once she shied, but it was from a new, freshly painted meeting-house at the crossing of the county road. Hollows, ditches, gravelly deposits, patches of freshly springing grasses, flew from beneath her rattling hoofs. She began to smell unpleasantly, once or twice she coughed slightly, but there was no abatement of her strength or speed.

By two o'clock he had passed Red Mountain and begun the descent to the plain. Ten minutes later the driver of the fast Pioneer coach was overtaken and passed by a "man on a Pinto hoss"—an event sufficiently notable for remark. At half past two Dick rose in his stirrups with a great shout. Stars were glittering through the rifted clouds, and beyond him, out of the plain, rose two spires, a flagstaff, and a straggling line of black objects. Dick jingled his spurs and swung his *riata*, Jovita bounded forward, and in another moment they swept into Tuttleville, and drew up before the wooden piazza of "The Hotel of All Nations."

What transpired that night at Tuttleville is not strictly a part of this record. Briefly I may state, however, that after Jovita had been handed over to a sleepy ostler, whom she at once kicked into unpleasant consciousness, Dick sallied out with the barkeeper for a tour of the sleeping town.

Lights still gleamed from a few saloons and gambling houses; but, avoiding these, they stopped before several closed shops, and by persistent tapping and judicious outcry roused the proprietors from their beds, and made them unbar the doors of their magazines and expose their wares. Sometimes they were met by curses, but oftener by interest and some concern in their needs, and the interview was invariably concluded by a drink.

It was three o'clock before this pleasantry was given over, and with a small waterproof bag of India-rubber strapped on his shoulders, Dick returned to the hotel. But here he was waylaid by Beauty—Beauty opulent in charms, affluent in dress, persuasive in speech, and Spanish in accent! In vain she repeated the invitation in "Excelsior," happily scorned by all Alpine-climbing youth, and rejected by this child of the Sierras—a rejection softened in this instance by a laugh and his last gold coin.

And then he sprang to the saddle and dashed down the lonely street and out into the lonelier plain, where presently the lights, the black line of houses, the spires, and the flagstaff sank into the earth behind him again and were lost in the distance.

The storm had cleared away, the air was brisk and cold, the outlines of adjacent landmarks were distinct, but it was half past four before Dick reached the meeting-house and the crossing of the county road. To avoid the rising grade he had taken a longer and more circuitous road, in whose viscid mud Jovita sank fetlock deep at every bound. It was a poor preparation for a steady ascent of five miles more; but Jovita, gathering her legs under her, took it with her usual blind, unreasoning fury, and a half-hour later reached the long level that led to Rattlesnake Creek. Another half-hour would bring him to the creek. He threw the reins lightly upon the neck of the mare, chirruped to her, and began to sing.

Suddenly Jovita shied with a bound that would have unseated a less practiced rider. Hanging to her rein was a figure that had leaped from the bank, and at the same time from the road before her arose a shadowy horse and rider.

"Throw up your hands," commanded the second apparition, with an oath.

Dick felt the mare tremble, quiver, and apparently sink under him. He knew what it meant and was prepared.

"Stand aside, Jack Simpson. I know you, you d——d thief! Let me pass, or——"

He did not finish the sentence. Jovita rose straight in the air with a terrific bound, throwing the figure from her bit with a single shake

{105}

of her vicious head, and charged with deadly malevolence down on the impediment before her. An oath, a pistol-shot, horse and highwayman rolled over in the road, and the next moment Jovita was a hundred yards away. But the good right arm of her rider, shattered by a bullet, dropped helplessly at his side.

Without slacking his speed he shifted the reins to his left hand. But a few moments later he was obliged to halt and tighten the saddle-girths that had slipped in the onset. This in his crippled condition took some time. He had no fear of pursuit, but looking up he saw that the eastern stars were already paling, and that the distant peaks had lost their ghostly whiteness, and now stood out blackly against a lighter sky. Day was upon him. Then completely absorbed in a single idea, he forgot the pain of his wound, and mounting again dashed on toward Rattlesnake Creek. But now Jovita's breath came broken by gasps, Dick reeled in his saddle, and brighter and brighter grew the sky.

Ride, Richard; run, Jovita; linger, O day!

For the last few rods there was a roaring in his ears. Was it exhaustion from loss of blood, or what? He was dazed and giddy as he swept down the hill, and did not recognize his surroundings. Had he taken the wrong road, or was this Rattlesnake Creek?

It was. But the brawling creek he had swam a few hours before had risen, more than doubled its volume, and now rolled a swift and resistless river between him and Rattlesnake Hill. For the first time that night Richard's heart sank within him. The river, the mountain, the quickening east, swam before his eyes. He shut them to recover his self-control. In that brief interval, by some fantastic mental process, the little room at Simpson's Bar and the figures of the sleeping father and son rose upon him.

He opened his eyes wildly, cast off his coat, pistol, boots, and saddle, bound his precious pack tightly to his shoulders, grasped the bare flanks of Jovita with his bared knees, and with a shout dashed into the yellow water. A cry rose from the opposite bank as the head of a man and horse struggled for a few moments against the battling current, and then were swept away amidst uprooted trees and whirling driftwood.

• • •

THE OLD MAN STARTED and woke. The fire on the hearth was dead, the candle in the outer room flickering in its socket, and somebody was rapping at the door. He opened it, but fell back with a cry before the dripping, half-naked figure that reeled against the doorpost.

"Dick?"

"Hush! Is he awake yet?"

"No; but, Dick——"

"Dry up, you old fool! Get me some whiskey, *quick!*" The Old Man flew and returned with—an empty bottle! Dick would have sworn, but his strength was not equal to the occasion. He staggered, caught at the handle of the door, and motioned to the Old Man.

"Thar's suthin' in my pack yer for Johnny. Take it off. I can't."

The Old Man unstrapped the pack, and laid it before the exhausted man.

"Open it, quick."

He did so with trembling fingers. It contained only a few poor toys—cheap and barbaric enough, goodness knows, but bright with paint and tinsel. One of them was broken; another, I fear, was irretrievably ruined by water, and on the third—ah me! there was a cruel spot.

"It don't look like much, that's a fact," said Dick ruefully. . . . "But it's the best we could do. . . . Take 'em, Old Man, and put 'em in his stocking, and tell him—tell him, you know—hold me, Old Man——" The Old Man caught at his sinking figure. "Tell him," said Dick, with a weak little laugh—"tell him Sandy Claus has come."

And even so, bedraggled, ragged, unshaven and unshorn, with one arm hanging helplessly at his side, Santa Claus came to Simpson's Bar and fell fainting on the first threshold. The Christmas dawn came slowly after, touching the remoter peaks with the rosy warmth of ineffable love. And it looked so tenderly on Simpson's Bar that the whole mountain, as if caught in a generous action, blushed to the skies.

BULGER'S REPUTATION

We all remembered very distinctly Bulger's advent in Rattle-snake Camp. It was during the rainy season—a season singularly inducive to settled reflective impressions as we sat and smoked around the stove in Mosby's grocery. Like older and more civilized communities, we had our periodic waves of sentiment and opinion, with the exception that they were more evanescent with us, and, as we had just passed through a fortnight of dissipation and extravagance, owing to a visit from some gamblers and speculators, we were now undergoing a severe moral revulsion, partly induced by reduced finances and partly by the arrival of two families with grown-up daughters on the hill. It was raining, with occasional warm breaths, through the open window, of the southwest trades, redolent of the saturated spices of the woods and springing grasses, which perhaps were slightly inconsistent with the hot stove around which we had congregated. But the stove was only an excuse for our listless, gregarious gathering; warmth and idleness went well together, and it was currently accepted that we had caught from the particular reptile which gave its name to our camp much of its pathetic, life-long search for warmth, and its habit of indolently basking in it.

A few of us still went through the affectation of attempting to dry our damp clothes by the stove, and sizzling our wet boots against it; but as the same individuals calmly permitted the rain to drive in upon them through the open window without moving, and seemed to take infinite delight in the amount of steam they generated, even that pretense dropped. Crotalus himself, with his tail in a muddy ditch, and the sun striking cold fire from his slit eyes as he basked his head on a warm stone beside it, could not have typified us better.

Percy Briggs took his pipe from his mouth at last and said, with reflective severity:—

"Well, gentlemen, if we can't get the wagon road over here, and if we're going to be left out by the stage-coach company, we can at least straighten up the camp, and not have it look like a cross between a tenement alley and a broken-down circus. I declare, I was just sick when these two Baker girls started to make a short cut through the camp. Darned if they didn't turn round and take to the woods and the rattlers again afore they got half-way. And that benighted idiot, Tom Rollins, standin' there in the ditch, spattered all over with slumgullion 'til he looked like a spotted tarrypin, wavin' his fins and sashaying backwards and forrards and sayin', 'This way, ladies; this way!'"

"*I* didn't," returned Tom Rollins, quite casually, without looking up from his steaming boots; "*I* didn't start in night afore last to dance 'The Green Corn Dance' outer 'Hiawatha,' with feathers in my hair and a red blanket on my shoulders, round that family's new potato patch, in order that it might 'increase and multiply.' I didn't sing 'Sabbath Morning Bells' with an anvil accompaniment until twelve o'clock at night over at the Crossing, so that they might dream of their Happy Childhood's Home. It seems to me that it wasn't *me* did it. I might be mistaken—it was late—but I have the impression that it wasn't *me.*"

From the silence that followed, this would seem to have been clearly a recent performance of the previous speaker, who, however, responded quite cheerfully:—

"An evenin' o' simple, childish gayety don't count. We've got to start in again *fair.* What we want here is to clear up and encourage decent immigration, and get rid o' gamblers and blatherskites that are makin' this yer camp their happy hunting-ground. We don't want any more permiskus shootin'. We don't want any more paintin' the town red. We don't want any more swaggerin' galoots ridin' up to this grocery and emptyin' their six-shooters in the air afore they 'light. We want to put a stop to it peacefully and without a row—and we kin. We ain't got no bullies of our own to fight back, and they know it, so they know they won't get no credit bullyin' us; they'll leave, if we're only firm. It's all along of our cussed fool good-nature; they see it amuses us, and they'll keep it up as long as the whiskey's free. What we want to do is, when the next man comes waltzin' along"—

A distant clatter from the rocky hillside here mingled with the puff of damp air through the window.

"Looks as ef we might hev a show even now," said Tom Rollins, removing his feet from the stove as we all instinctively faced towards the window.

"I reckon you're in with us in this, Mosby?" said Briggs, turning towards the proprietor of the grocery, who had been leaning listlessly against the wall behind his bar.

"Arter the man's had a fair show," said Mosby, cautiously. He deprecated the prevailing condition of things, but it was still an open question whether the families would prove as valuable customers as his present clients. "Everything in moderation, gentlemen."

The sound of galloping hoofs came nearer, now swishing in the soft mud of the highway, until the unseen rider pulled up before the door. There was no shouting, however, nor did he announce himself with the usual salvo of fire-arms. But when, after singularly heavy tread and the jingle of spurs on the platform, the door flew open to the new-comer, he seemed a realization of our worst expectations. Tall, broad, and muscular, he carried in one hand a shot-gun, while from his hip dangled a heavy navy revolver. His long hair, unkempt but oiled, swept a greasy circle around his shoulders; his enormous mustache, dripping with wet, completely concealed his mouth. His costume of fringed buckskin was wild and *outré* even for our frontier camp. But what was more confirmative of our suspicions was that he was evidently in the habit of making an impression, and after a distinct pause at the doorway, with only a side glance at us, he strode towards the bar.

"As there don't seem to be no hotel hereabouts, I reckon I kin put up my mustang here and have a shakedown somewhere behind that counter," he said. His voice seemed to have added to its natural depth the hoarseness of frequent over-straining.

"Ye ain't got no bunk to spare, you boys, hev ye?" asked Mosby, evasively, glancing at Percy Briggs, without looking at the stranger. We all looked at Briggs also; it was *his* affair after all—he had originated this opposition. To our surprise he said nothing.

The stranger leaned heavily on the counter.

"I was speaking to *you*," he said, with his eyes of Mosby and slightly accenting the pronoun with a tap of his revolver-butt on the bar. "Ye don't seem to catch on."

Mosby smiled feebly, and again cast an imploring glance at Briggs. To our greater astonishment, Briggs said, quietly: "Why don't you answer the stranger, Mosby?"

"Yes, yes," said Mosby, suavely, to the newcomer, while an angry flush crossed his cheek as he recognized the position in which Briggs had placed him. "Of course, you're welcome to what doings *I* hev here, but I reckoned these gentlemen over there," with a vicious glance at Briggs, "might fix ye up suthin' better; they're so pow'ful kind to your sort."

The stranger threw down a gold piece on the counter and said: "Fork out your whiskey, then," waited until his glass was filled, took it in his hand, and then, drawing an empty chair to the stove, sat down beside Briggs. "Seein' as you're that kind," he said, placing his heavy hand on Briggs's knee, "mebbe ye kin tell me ef thar's a shanty or a cabin at Rattlesnake that I kin get for a couple o' weeks. I saw an empty one at the head o' the hill. You see, gennelmen," he added confidentially as he swept the drops of whiskey from his long mustache with his fingers and glanced around our group, "I've got some business over at Bigwood," our nearest town, "but ez a place to *stay at* it ain't my style."

"What's the matter with Bigwood?" said Briggs abruptly.

"It's too howlin', too festive, too rough; thar's too much yellin' and shootin' goin' day and night. Thar's too many card sharps and gay gamboliers cavortin' about the town to please me. Too much permiskus soakin' at the bar and free jim-jams. What I want is a quiet place what a man kin give his mind and elbow a rest from betwixt grippin' his shootin'-irons and crookin' in his whiskey. A sort o' slow, quiet, easy place *like this.*"

We all stared at him, Percy Briggs as fixedly as any. But there was not the slightest trace of irony, sarcasm, or peculiar significance in his manner. He went on slowly:—

"When I struck this yer camp a minit ago; when I seed that thar ditch meanderin' peaceful like through the street, without a hotel or free saloon or express office on either side; with the smoke just a curlin' over the chimbley of that log shanty, and the bresh just set fire to and a smoulderin' in that potato patch with a kind o' old-time stingin' in your eyes and nose, and a few women's duds just a flutterin' on a line by the fence, I says to myself: 'Bulger—this is peace! This is wot you're lookin' for, Bulger—this is wot you're wantin'—this is wot *you'll hev!*'"

"You say you've business over at Bigwood. What business?" said Briggs.

"It's a peculiar business, young fellow," returned the stranger, gravely. "Thar's different men ez had different opinions about it. Some allows it's an easy business, some allows it's a rough business; some says it's a sad business, others say it's gay and festive. Some wonders ez how I've got into it, and others wonder how I'll ever get out of it. It's a payin' business—it's a peaceful sort o' business when left to itself. It's a peculiar business—a business that sort o' b'longs to me, though I ain't got no patent from Washington for it. It's *my own* business." He paused, rose, and saying, "Let's meander over and take a look at that empty cabin, and ef she suits me, why, I'll plank down a slug for her on the spot, and move in to-morrow," walked towards the door. "I'll pick up suthin' in the way o' boxes and blankets from the grocery," he added, looking at Mosby, "and ef thar's a corner whar I kin stand my gun and a nail to hang up my revolver—why, I'm all thar!"

By this time we were no longer astonished when Briggs rose also, and not only accompanied the sinister-looking stranger to the empty cabin, but assisted him in negotiating with its owner for a fortnight's occupancy. Nevertheless, we eagerly assailed Briggs on his return for some explanation of this singular change in his attitude towards the stranger. He coolly reminded us, however, that while his intention of excluding ruffianly adventurers from the camp remained the same, he had no right to go back on the stranger's sentiments, which were evidently in accord with our own, and although Mr. Bulger's appearance was inconsistent with them, that was only an additional reason why we should substitute a mild firmness for that violence which we all deprecated, but which might attend his abrupt dismissal. We were all satisfied except Mosby, who had not yet recovered from Briggs's change of front, which he was pleased to call "craw-fishing." "Seemed to me his account of his business was extraordinary satisfactory! Sorter filled the bill all round—no mistake thar,"—he suggested, with a malicious irony. "I like a man that's outspoken."

"I understood him very well," said Briggs, quietly.

"In course you did. Only when you've settled in *your* mind whether he was describing horse-stealing or tract-distributing, mebbe you'll let *me* know."

It would seem, however, that Briggs did not interrogate the stranger again regarding it, nor did we, who were quite content to leave matters in Briggs's hands. Enough that Mr. Bulger moved into the empty cabin that next day, and, with the aid of a few old boxes from the grocery, which he quickly extemporized into tables and chairs, and the purchase of some necessary cooking-utensils, soon made himself at home. The rest of the camp, now thoroughly aroused, made a point of leaving their work in the ditches, whenever they could, to stroll carelessly around Bulger's tenement in the vague hope of satis- fying a curiosity that had become tormenting. But they could not find that he was doing anything of a suspicious character—except, perhaps, from the fact that it was not *outwardly* suspicious, which I grieve to say did not lull them to security. He seemed to be either fixing up his cabin or smoking in his doorway. On the second day he checked this itinerant curiosity by taking the initiative himself, and quietly walking from claim to claim and from cabin to cabin with a pacific but by no means a satisfying interest. The shadow of his tall figure carrying his inseparable gun, which had not yet apparently "stood in the corner," falling upon an excavated bank beside the delv- ing miners, gave them a sense of uneasiness they could not explain; a few characteristic yells of boisterous hilarity from their noontide gathering under a cottonwood somehow ceased when Mr. Bulger was seen gravely approaching, and his casual stopping before a poker party in the gulch actually caused one of the most reckless gamblers to weakly recede from "a bluff" and allow his adversary to sweep the board. After this it was felt that matters were becoming serious. There was no subsequent patrolling of the camp before the stranger's cabin. Their curiosity was singularly abated. A general feeling of repulsion, kept within bounds partly by the absence of any overt act from Bulger, and partly by an inconsistent over-consciousness of his shot-gun, took its place. But an unexpected occurrence revived it.

One evening, as the usual social circle were drawn around Mosby's stove, the lazy silence was broken by the familiar sounds of pistol- shots and a series of more familiar shrieks and yells from the rocky hill road. The circle quickly recognized the voices of their old friends the roysterers and gamblers from Sawyer's Dam; they as quickly rec- ognized the returning shouts here and there from a few companions who were welcoming them. I grieve to say that in spite of their pre- vious attitude of reformation a smile of gratified expectancy lit up the faces of the younger members, and even the older ones glanced dubiously at Briggs. Mosby made no attempt to conceal a sigh of relief as he carefully laid out an extra supply of glasses in his bar.

Suddenly the oncoming yells ceased, the wild gallop of hoofs slackened into a trot, and finally halted, and even the responsive shouts of the camp stopped also. We all looked vacantly at each other; Mosby leaped over his counter and went to the door: Briggs followed with the rest of us. The night was dark, and it was a few minutes before we could distinguish a straggling, vague, but silent procession moving through the moist, heavy air on the hill. But, to our surprise, it was moving *away* from us—absolutely *leaving* the camp! We were still staring in expectancy when out of the darkness slowly emerged a figure which we recognized at once as Captain Jim, one of the most reckless members of our camp. Pushing us back into the grocery he entered without a word, closed the door behind him, and threw himself vacantly into a chair. We at once pressed around him. He looked up at us dazedly, drew a long breath, and said slowly:—

"It's no use, gentlemen! Suthin's *got* to be done with that Bulger; and mighty quick."

"What's the matter?" we asked eagerly.

"Matter!" he repeated, passing his hand across his forehead. "Matter! Look yere! Ye all of you heard them boys from Sawyer's Dam coming over the hill? Ye heard their music—mebbe ye heard *us* join in the chorus? Well, they came waltzing down the hill, like old times, and we waitin' for 'em. Then, jest as they passed the old cabin, who do you think they ran right into—shooting-iron, long hair and mustache, and all that—standing there plump in the road?—why, Bulger!"

"Well?"

"Well!—Whatever it was—don't ask *me*—but, dern my skin, ef after a word or two from *him*—them boys just stopped yellin', turned round like lambs, and rode away, peaceful-like, along with him. We ran after them a spell, still yellin', when that thar Bulger faced around, said to us that he'd 'come down here for quiet,' and ef he couldn't hev it he'd have to leave with those gentlemen *who wanted it* too! And I'm gosh darned ef those *gentlemen*—you know 'em all—Patsey Carpenter, Snap-shot Harry, and the others—ever said a darned word, but kinder nodded 'So long' and went away!"

Our astonishment and mystification were complete; and I regret to say, the indignation of Captain Jim and Mosby equally so. "If we're going to be bossed by the first new-comer," said the former, gloomily, "I reckon we might as well take our chances with the Sawyer's Dam boys, whom we know."

{114}

"Ef we are going to hev legitimate trade of Rattlesnake interfered with by the cranks of some hidin' horse-thief or retired road agent," said Mosby, "we might as well invite the hull of Joaquin Murietta's gang here at once! But I suppose this is part o' Bulger's particular 'business,'" he added, with a withering glance at Briggs.

"I understand it all," said Briggs, quietly. "You know I told you that bullies couldn't live in the same camp together. That's human nature—and that's how plain men like you and me manage to scud along without getting plugged. You see, Bulger wasn't going to hev any of his own kind jumpin' his claim here. And I reckon he was pow'ful enough to back down Sawyer's Dam. Anyhow, the bluff told—and here we are in peace and quietness."

"Until he lets us know what *is* his little game," sneered Mosby.

Nevertheless, such is the force of mysterious power that, although it was exercised against what we firmly believed was the independence of the camp, it extorted a certain respect from us. A few thought it was not a bad thing to have a professional bully, and even took care to relate the discomfiture of the wicked youth of Sawyer's Dam for the benefit of a certain adjacent and powerful camp who had looked down upon us. He, himself, returning the same evening from his self-imposed escort, vouchsafed no other reason than the one he had already given. Preposterous as it seemed, we were obliged to accept it, and the still more preposterous inference that he had sought Rattlesnake Camp solely for the purpose of acquiring and securing its peace and quietness. Certainly he had no other occupation; the little work he did upon the tailings of the abandoned claim which went with his little cabin was scarcely a pretense. He rode over on certain days to Bigwood on account of his business, but no one had ever seen him there, nor could the description of his manner and appearance evoke any information from the Bigwoodians. It remained a mystery.

It had also been feared that the advent of Bulger would intensify that fear and dislike of riotous Rattlesnake which the two families had shown, and which was the origin of Briggs's futile attempt at reformation. But it was discovered that since his arrival the young girls had shown less timidity in entering the camp, and had even exchanged some polite conversation and good-humored badinage with its younger and more impressible members. Perhaps this tended to make these youths more observant, for a few days later, when the vexed question of Bulger's business was again under discussion, one of them remarked, gloomily:—

"I reckon there ain't no doubt *what* he's here for!"

The youthful prophet was instantly sat upon after the fashion of all elderly critics since Job's. Nevertheless, after a pause he was permitted to explain.

"Only this morning, when Lance Forester and me were chirping with them gals out on the hill, who should we see hanging around in the bush but that cussed Bulger! We allowed at first that it might be only a new style of his interferin', so we took no notice, except to pass a few remarks about listeners and that sort o' thing, and perhaps to bedevil the girls a little more than we'd hev done if we'd been alone. Well, they laughed, and we laughed— and that was the end of it. But this afternoon, as Lance and me were meandering down by their cabin, we sorter turned into the woods to wait till they'd come out. Then all of a sudden Lance stopped as rigid as a pointer that's flushed somethin', and says, 'B'gosh!' And thar, under a big redwood, sat that slimy hypocrite Bulger, twisting his long mustaches and smiling like clockwork alongside o' little Meely Baker—you know her, the pootiest of the two sisters—and she smilin' back on him. Think of it!— that unknown, unwashed, long-haired tramp and bully, who must be forty if a day, and that innocent gal of sixteen. It was simply disgustin'!"

I need not say that the older cynics and critics already alluded to at once improved the occasion. What more could be expected? Women, the world over, were noted for this sort of thing! This long-haired, swaggering bully, with his air of mystery, had captivated them, as he always had done since the days of Homer. Simple merit, which sat lowly in bar-rooms, had conceived projects for the public good around the humble, unostentatious stove, was nowhere! Youth could not too soon learn this bitter lesson. And in this case youth too, perhaps, was right in its conjectures, for this *was*, no doubt, the little game of the perfidious Bulger.

We recalled the fact that his unhallowed appearance in camp was almost coincident with the arrival of the two families. We glanced at Briggs; to our amazement, for the first time he looked seriously concerned. But Mosby in the mean time leaned his elbows lazily over the counter and, in a slow voice, added fuel to the flame.

"I wouldn't hev spoken of it before," he said, with a sidelong glance at Briggs, "for it might be all in the line o' Bulger's 'business,' but suthin' happened the other night that, for a minit, got me! I was passin' the Bakers' shanty, and I heard one of them gals a-singing a camp-meeting hymn. I don't calkilate to run agin you young fellers in any sparkin' or canoodlin' that's goin' on, but her voice sounded so pow'ful soothin' and pretty thet I jest stood there and listened. Then the old woman—old Mother Baker—*she* joined in, and I listened too. And then—dern my skin!—but a man's voice joined in—jest belching outer that cabin!—and I sorter lifted myself up and kem away.

"That voice, gentlemen," said Mosby, lingering artistically as he took up a glass and professionally eyed it before wiping it with his towel, "that voice, cumf'bly fixed thar in thet cabin among them wimen folks, was Bulger's!"

Briggs got up, with his eyes looking the darker for his flushed face. "Gentlemen," he said huskily, "thar's only one thing to be done. A lot of us have got to ride over to Sawyer's Dam tomorrow morning and pick up as many square men as we can muster; there's a big camp-meeting goin' on there, and there won't be no difficulty in that. When we've got a big enough crowd to show we mean business, we must march back here and ride Bulger out of this camp! I don't hanker arter Vigilance Committees, as a rule—it's a rough remedy—it's like drinkin' a quart o' whisky agin rattlesnake poison—but it's got to be done! We don't mind being *sold* ourselves—but when it comes to our standin' by and seein' the only innocent people in Rattlesnake given away—we kick! Bulger's got to be fired outer this camp! And he will be!"

But he was not.

For when, the next morning, a determined and thoughtful procession of the best and most characteristic citizens of Rattlesnake Camp filed into Sawyer's Dam, they found that their mysterious friends had disappeared, although they met with a fraternal but subdued welcome from the general camp. But any approach to the subject of their visit, however, was received with a chilling disapproval. Did they not know that lawlessness of any kind, even under the rude mantle of frontier justice, was to be deprecated and scouted when a "means of salvation, a power of regeneration," such as was now sweeping over Sawyer's Dam, was at hand? Could they not induce this man who was to be violently deported to accompany them willingly to Sawyer's Dam and subject himself to the powerful influence of the "revival" then in full swing?

The Rattlesnake boys laughed bitterly, and described a man of whom they talked so lightly; but in vain. "It's no use, gentlemen," said a more worldly bystander, in a lower voice, "the camp-meetin's got a strong grip here, and betwixt you and me there ain't no wonder. For the man that runs it—the big preacher—has got new ways and methods that fetches the boys every time. He don't preach no cut-and-dried gospel; he don't carry around no slop-shop robes and clap 'em on you whether they fit or not; but he samples and measures the camp afore he wades into it. He scouts and examines; he ain't no mere Sunday preacher with a comfortable house and once-a-week church, but he gives up his days and nights to it, and makes his family work with him, and even sends 'em forward to explore the field. And he ain't no white-choker shadbelly either, but fits himself, like his gospel, to the men he works among. Ye ought to hear him afore you go. His tent is just out your way. I'll go with you."

Too dejected to offer any opposition, and perhaps a little curious to see this man who had unwittingly frustrated their design of lynching Bulger, they halted at the outer fringe of worshipers who packed the huge inclosure. They had not time to indulge their cynicisms over this swaying mass of emotional, half-thinking, and almost irresponsible beings, not to detect any similarity between *their* extreme methods and the scheme of redemption they themselves were seeking, for in a few moments, apparently lifted to his feet on a wave of religious exultation, the famous preacher arose. The men of Rattlesnake gasped for breath.

It was Bulger!

But Briggs quickly recovered himself. "By what name," said he, turning passionately towards his guide, "does this man—this imposter—call himself here?"

"Baker."

"Baker?" echoed the Rattlesnake contingent.

"Baker?" repeated Lance Forester, with a ghastly smile.

"Yes," returned their guide. "You oughter know it too! For he sent his wife and daughters over, after his usual style, to sample your camp, a week ago! Come, now, what are you givin' us?"

A YELLOW DOG

I never knew why in the Western States of America a yellow dog should be proverbially considered the acme of canine degradation and incompetency, nor why the possession of one should seriously affect the social standing of its possessor. But the fact being established, I think we accepted it at Rattlers Ridge without question. The matter of ownership was more difficult to settle; and although the dog I have in my mind at the present writing attached himself impartially and equally to every one in camp, no one ventured to exclusively claim him; while, after the perpetration of any canine atrocity, everybody repudiated him with indecent haste.

"Well, I can swear he hasn't been near our shanty for weeks," or the retort, "He was last seen comin' out of *your* cabin," expressed the eagerness with which Rattlers Ridge washed its hands of any responsibility. Yet he was by no means a common dog, nor even an unhandsome dog; and it was a singular fact that his severest critics vied with each other in narrating instances of his sagacity, insight, and agility which they themselves had witnessed.

He had been seen crossing the "flume" that spanned Grizzly Cañon, at a height of nine hundred feet, on a plank six inches wide. He had tumbled down the "shoot" to the South Fork, a thousand feet below, and was found sitting on the river bank "without a scratch, 'cept that he was lazily givin' himself with his off hind paw." He had been forgotten in a snowdrift on a Sierran shelf, and had come home in the early spring with the conceited complacency of an Alpine traveler and a plumpness alleged to have been the result of an exclusive diet of buried mail bags and their contents. He was generally believed to read the advance election posters, and disappear a day or two before the candidates and the brass band—which he hated—

came to the Ridge. He was suspected of having overlooked Colonel Johnson's hand at poker, and of having conveyed to the Colonel's adversary, by a succession of barks, the danger of betting against four kings.

While these statements were supplied by wholly unsupported witnesses, it was a very human weakness of Rattlers Ridge that the responsibility of corroboration was passed to *the dog* himself, and *he* was looked upon as a consummate liar.

"Snoopin' round yere, and *callin'* yourself a poker sharp, are ye! Scoot, you yaller pizin!" was a common adjuration whenever the unfortunate animal intruded upon a card party. "Ef thar was a spark, an *atom* of truth in *that dog*, I'd believe my own eyes that I saw him sittin' up and trying to magnetize a jay bird off a tree. But wot are ye goin' to do with a yaller equivocator like that?"

I have said that he was yellow—or, to use the ordinary expression, "yaller." Indeed, I am inclined to believe that much of the ignominy attached to the epithet lay in this favorite pronunciation. Men who habitually spoke of a *"yellow* bird," a *"yellow* hammer," a *"yellow* leaf," always alluded to him as a *"yaller* dog."

He certainly *was* yellow. After a bath—usually compulsory—he presented a decided gamboge streak down his back, from the top of his forehead to the stump of his tail, fading in his sides and flank to a delicate straw color. His breast, legs, and feet—when not reddened by "slumgullion," in which he was fond of wading—were white. A few attempts at ornamental decoration from the India-ink pot of the storekeeper failed, partly through the yellow dog's excessive agility, which would never give the paint time to dry on him, and partly through his success in transferring his markings to the trousers and blankets of the camp.

The size and shape of his tail—which had been cut off before his introduction to Rattlers Ridge—were favorite sources of speculation to the miners, both as determining his breed and his moral responsibility in coming into camp in that defective condition. There was a general opinion that he couldn't have looked worse with a tail, and its removal was therefore a gratuitous effrontery.

His best feature was his eyes, which were a lustrous Vandyke brown, and sparkling with intelligence; but here again he suffered from evolution through environment, and their original trustful openness was marred by the experience of watching for flying stones, sods, and passing kicks from the rear, so that the pupils were continually reverting to the outer angle of the eyelid.

Nevertheless, none of these characteristics decided the vexed question of his *breed*. His speed and scent pointed to a "hound," and it is related that on one occasion he was laid on the trail of a wildcat with such success that he followed it apparently out of the State, returning at the end of two weeks, footsore, but blandly contented.

Attaching himself to a prospecting party, he was sent under the same belief "into the brush" to drive off a bear, who was supposed to be haunting the camp-fire. He returned in a few minutes *with* the bear, *driving it into* the unarmed circle and scattering the whole party. After this the theory of his being a hunting dog was abandoned. Yet it was said—on the usual uncorroborated evidence—that he had "put up" a quail; and his qualities as a retriever were for a long time accepted, until, during a shooting expedition for wild ducks, it was discovered that the one he had brought back had never been *shot*, and the party were obliged to compound damages with an adjacent settler.

His fondness for paddling in the ditches and "slumgullion" at one time suggested a water spaniel. He could swim, and would occasionally bring out of the river sticks and pieces of bark that had been thrown in; but as *he* always had to be thrown in with them, and was a good-sized dog, his aquatic reputation faded also. He remained simply "a yaller dog." What more could be said? His actual name was "Bones"—given to him, no doubt, through the provincial custom of confounding the occupation of the individual with his quality, for which it was pointed out precedent could be found in some old English family names.

But if Bones generally exhibited no preference for any particular individual in camp, he always made an exception in favor of drunkards. Even an ordinary roistering bacchanalian party brought him out from under a tree or a shed in the keenest satisfaction. He would accompany them through the long straggling street of the settlement, barking his delight at every step or mis-step of the revelers, and exhibiting none of that mistrust of eye which marked his attendance upon the sane and the respectable. He accepted even their uncouth play without a snarl or a yelp, hypocritically pretending even to like it; and I conscientiously believe would have allowed a tin can to be attached to his tail if the hand that tied it on were only unsteady, and the voice that bade him "lie still" were hushy with liquor. He would "see" the party cheerfully into a saloon, wait outside the door—his tongue fairly lolling from his mouth in enjoyment—until they reappeared, permit them even to tumble over him with pleasure, and then gambol away before them, heedless of awkwardly projected stones and epithets. He would afterwards accompany them separately home, or lie with them at crossroads until they were assisted to their cabins. Then he would trot rakishly to his own haunt by the saloon stove, with the slightly conscious air of having been a bad dog, yet of having had a good time.

We never could satisfy ourselves whether his enjoyment arose from some merely selfish conviction that he was more *secure* with the physically and mentally incompetent, from some active sympathy with active wickedness, or from a grim sense of his own mental superiority at such moments. But the general belief leant towards his kindred sympathy as a "yaller dog" with all that was disreputable. And this was supported by another very singular canine manifestation—the "sincere flattery" of simulation or imitation.

"Uncle Billy" Riley for a short time enjoyed the position of being the camp drunkard, and at once became an object of Bones' greatest solicitude. He not only accompanied him everywhere, curled at his feet or head according to Uncle Billy's attitude at the moment, but, it was noticed, began presently to undergo a singular alteration in his own habits and appearance. From being an active, tireless scout and forager, a bold and unovertakable marauder, he became lazy and apathetic; allowed gophers to burrow under him without endeavoring to undermine the settlement in his frantic endeavors to dig them out, permitted squirrels to flash their tails at him a hundred yards away, forgot his usual *caches*, and let his favorite bones unburied and bleaching in the sun. His eyes grew dull, his coat lustreless, in proportion as his companion became blear-eyed and ragged; in running, his usual arrow-like directness began to deviate, and it was not unusual to meet the pair together, zig-zagging up the hill. Indeed, Uncle Billy's condition could be predetermined by Bones' appearance at times when his temporary master was invisible. "The old man must have an awful jag on to-day," was casually remarked when an extra fluffiness and imbecility was noticeable in the passing Bones. At first it was believed that he drank also, but when careful investigation proved this hypothesis untenable, he was freely called a "derned time-servin', yaller hypocrite." Not a few advanced the opinion that if Bones did not actually lead Uncle Billy astray, he at least "slavered him over and coddled him until the old man got conceited in his wickedness." This undoubtedly led to a compulsory divorce between them, and Uncle Billy was happily despatched to a neighboring town and a doctor.

Bones seemed to miss him greatly, ran away for two days, and was supposed to have visited him, to have been shocked at his convalescence, and to have been "cut" by Uncle Billy in his reformed character; and he returned to his old active life again, and buried his past with his forgotten bones. It was said that he was afterwards detected in trying to lead an intoxicated tramp into camp after the methods employed by a blind man's dog, but was discovered in time by the— of course—uncorroborated narrator.

I should be tempted to leave him thus in his original and picturesque sin, but the same veracity which compelled me to transcribe his faults and iniquities obliges me to describe his ultimate and somewhat monotonous reformation, which came from no fault of his own.

It was a joyous day at Rattlers Ridge that was equally the advent of his change of heart and the first stagecoach that had been induced to diverge from the highroad and stop regularly at our settlement. Flags were flying from the post office and Polka saloon—and Bones was flying before the brass band that he detested, when the sweetest girl in the county—Pinkey Preston—daughter of the county judge and hopelessly beloved by all Rattlers Ridge, stepped from the coach which she had glorified by occupying as an invited guest.

"What makes him run away?" she asked quickly, opening her lovely eyes in a possible innocent wonder that anything could be found to run away from her.

"He don't like the brass band," we explained eagerly.

"How funny," murmured the girl; "is it as out of tune as all that?"

This irresistible witticism alone would have been enough to satisfy us—we did nothing but repeat it to each other all the next day—but we were positively transported when we saw her suddenly gather her dainty skirts in one hand and trip off through the red dust towards Bones, who, with his eyes over his yellow shoulder, had halted in the road, and half turned in mingled disgust and rage at the spectacle of the descending trombone. We held our breath as she approached him. Would Bones evade her as he did us at such moments, or would he save our reputation, and consent, for the moment, to accept her as a new kind of inebriate? She came nearer; he saw her; he began to slowly quiver with excitement—his stump of a tail vibrating with such rapidity that the loss of the missing portion was scarcely noticeable. Suddenly she stopped before him, took his yellow head between her little hands, lifted it, and looked down in his handsome brown eyes with her two lovely blue ones. What passed between them in that magnetic glance no one ever knew. She returned with him; said to him casually: "We're not afraid of brass bands, are we?" to which he apparently acquiesced, at least stifling his disgust of them, while he was near her—which was nearly all the time.

During the speech-making her gloved hand and his yellow head were always near together, and at the crowning ceremony—her public checking of Yuba Bill's "waybill," on behalf of the township, with a gold pencil, presented to her by the Stage Company—Bones' joy, far from knowing no bounds, seemed to know nothing but them, and he witnessed it apparently in the air. No one dared to interfere. For the first time a local pride in Bones sprang up in our hearts—and we lied to each other in his praises openly and shamelessly.

Then the time came for parting. We were standing by the door of the coach, hats in hand, as Miss Pinkey was about to step into it; Bones was waiting by her side, confidently looking into the interior, and apparently selecting his own seat on the lap of Judge Preston in the corner, when Miss Pinkey held up the sweetest of admonitory fingers. Then, taking his head between her two hands, she again looked into his brimming eyes, and said, simply, *"Good* dog," with the gentlest of emphasis on the adjective, and popped into the coach.

The six bay horses started as one, the gorgeous green and gold vehicle bounded forward, the red dust rose behind, and the yellow dog danced in and out of it to the very outskirts of the settlement. And then he soberly returned.

A day or two later he was missed—but the fact was afterwards known that he was at Spring Valley, the county town where Miss Preston lived—and he was forgiven. A week afterwards he was missed again, but this time for a longer period, and then a pathetic letter arrived from Sacramento for the storekeeper's wife.

"Would you mind," wrote Miss Pinkey Preston, "asking some of your boys to come over here to Sacramento and bring back Bones? I don't mind having the dear dog walk out with me at Spring Valley,

where every one knows me; but here he *does* make one so noticeable, on account of *his color.* I've got scarcely a frock that he
agrees with. He don't go with my pink muslin, and that lovely
buff tint he makes three shades lighter. You know yellow is *so*
trying."

A consultation was quickly held by the whole settlement,
and a deputation sent to Sacramento to relieve the unfortunate girl. We were all quite indignant with Bones—but, oddly
enough, I think it was greatly tempered with our new pride in
him. While he was with us alone, his peculiarities had been
scarcely appreciated, but the recurrent phrase, "that yellow dog
that they keep at the Rattlers," gave us a mysterious importance along the country side, as if we had secured a "mascot" in
some zoölogical curiosity.

This was further indicated by a singular occurrence. A new
church had been built at the crossroads, and an eminent divine
had come from San Francisco to preach the opening sermon.
After a careful examination of the camp's wardrobe, and some
felicitous exchange of apparel, a few of us were deputed to
represent "Rattlers" at the Sunday service. In our white ducks,
straw hats, and flannel blouses, we were sufficiently picturesque
and distinctive as "honest miners" to be shown off in one of the
front pews.

Seated near the prettiest girls, who offered us their hymn-
books—in the cleanly odor of fresh pine shavings, and ironed
muslin, and blown over by the spices of our own woods through
the open windows, a deep sense of the abiding peace of Christian
communion settled upon us. At this supreme moment some one
murmured in an awe-stricken whisper:—

"Will you look at Bones?"

We looked. Bones had entered the church and gone up in
the gallery through a pardonable ignorance and modesty; but,
perceiving his mistake, was now calmly walking along the gallery rail before the astounded worshipers. Reaching the end,
he paused for a moment, and carelessly looked down. It was
about fifteen feet to the floor below—the simplest jump in the
world for the mountain-bred Bones. Daintily, gingerly, lazily,
and yet with a conceited airiness of manner, as if, humanly speaking, he had one leg in his pocket and were doing it on three, he

cleared the distance, dropping just in front of the chancel, without a sound, turned himself around three times, and then lay comfortably down.

Three deacons were instantly in the aisle coming up before the eminent divine, who, we fancied, wore a restrained smile. We heard the hurried whispers: "Belongs to them." "Quite a local institution here, you know." "Don't like to offend sensibilities"; and the minister's prompt "By no means," as he went on with his service.

A short month ago we would have repudiated Bones; to-day we sat there in slightly supercilious attitudes, as if to indicate that any affront offered to Bones would be an insult to ourselves, and followed by our instantaneous withdrawal in a body.

All went well, however, until the minister, lifting the large Bible from the communion table and holding it in both hands before him, walked towards a reading-stand by the altar rails. Bones uttered a distinct growl. The minister stopped.

We, and we alone, comprehended in a flash the whole situation. The Bible was nearly the size and shape of one of those soft clods of sod which we were in the playful habit of launching at Bones when he lay half asleep in the sun, in order to see him cleverly evade it.

We held our breath. What was to be done? But the opportunity belonged to our leader, Jeff Briggs—a confoundedly good-looking fellow, with the golden mustache of a northern viking and the curls of an Apollo. Secure in his beauty and bland in his self-conceit, he rose from the pew, and stepped before the chancel rails.

"I would wait a moment, if I were you, sir," he said, respectfully, "and you will see that he will go out quietly."

"What is wrong?" whispered the minister in some concern.

"He thinks you are going to heave that book at him, sir, without giving him a fair show, as we do."

The minister looked perplexed, but remained motionless, with the book in his hands. Bones arose, walked half way down the aisle, and vanished like a yellow flash!

With this justification of his reputation, Bones disappeared for a week. At the end of that time we received a polite note from Judge Preston, saying that the dog had become quite domiciled in their house, and begged that the camp, without yielding up their valuable *property* in him, would allow him to remain at Spring Valley for an indefinite time; that both the judge and his daughter—with whom Bones was already an old friend—would be glad if the members of the camp would visit their old favorite whenever they desired, to assure themselves that he was well cared for.

I am afraid that the bait thus ingenuously thrown out had a good deal to do with our ultimate yielding. However, the reports of those who visited Bones were wonderful and marvelous. He was residing there in state, lying on rugs in the drawing-room, coiled up under the judicial desk in the judge's study, sleeping regularly on the mat outside Miss Pinkey's bedroom door, or lazily snapping at flies on the judge's lawn.

"He's as yallar as ever," said one of our informants, "but it don't somehow seem to be the same back that we used to break clods over in the old time, just to see him scoot out of the dust."

And now I must record a fact which I am aware all lovers of dogs will indignantly deny, and which will be furiously bayed at by every faithful hound since the days of Ulysses. Bones not only *forgot*, but absolutely *cut us!* Those who called upon the judge in "store clothes" he would perhaps casually notice, but he would sniff at them as if detecting and resenting them under their superficial exterior. The rest he simply paid no attention to. The more familiar term of "Bonesy"—formerly applied to him, as in our rare moments of endearment—produced no response. This pained, I think, some of the more youthful of us; but, through some strange human weakness, it also increased the camp's respect for him. Nevertheless, we spoke of him familiarly to strangers at the very moment he ignored us. I am afraid that we also took some pains to point out that he was getting fat and unwieldy, and losing his elasticity, implying covertly that his choice was a mistake and his life a failure.

A year after he died, in the odor of sanctity and respectability, being found one morning coiled up and stiff on the mat outside Miss Pinkey's door. When the news was conveyed to us, we asked permission, the camp being in a prosperous condition, to erect a stone over his grave. But when it came to the inscription we could only think of the two words murmured to him by Miss Pinkey, which we always believe effected his conversion:—

"*Good* Dog!"

DICK SPINDLER'S
FAMILY CHRISTMAS

There was surprise and sometimes disappointment in Rough and Ready, when it was known that Dick Spindler intended to give a "family" Christmas party at his own house. That he should take an early opportunity to celebrate his good fortune and show hospitality was only expected from the man who had just made a handsome "strike" on his claim; but that it should assume so conservative, old-fashioned, and respectable a form was quite unlooked-for by Rough and Ready, and was thought by some a trifle pretentious. There were not half-a-dozen families in Rough and Ready; nobody ever knew before that Spindler had any relations, and this "ringing in" of strangers to the settlement seemed to indicate at least a lack of public spirit. "He might," urged one of his critics, "hev given the boys,—that had worked alongside o' him in the ditches by day, and slung lies with him around the camp-fire by night,—he might hev given them a square 'blow out,' and kep' the leavin's for his old Spindler crew, just as other families do. Why, when old man Scudder had his house-raisin' last year, his family lived for a week on what was left over, arter the boys had waltzed through the house that night,— and the Scudders warn't strangers, either." It was also evident that there was an uneasy feeling that Spindler's action indicated an unhallowed leaning towards the minority of respectability and exclusiveness, and a desertion—without the excuse of matrimony—of the convivial and independent bachelor majority of Rough and Ready.

"Ef he was stuck after some gal and was kinder looking ahead, I'd hev understood it," argued another critic.

"Don't ye be too sure he ain't," said Uncle Jim Starbuck gloomily.

"Ye'll find that some blamed woman is at the bottom of this yer 'family' gathering. That and trouble is almost all they're made for!"

There happened to be some truth in this dark prophecy but none of the kind that the misogynist supposed. In fact, Spindler had called a few evenings before at the house of the Rev. Mr. Saltover, and Mrs. Saltover, having one of her "Saleratus headaches," had turned him over to her widow sister, Mrs. Huldy Price, who obediently bestowed upon him that practical and critical attention which she divided with the stocking she was darning. She was a woman of thirty-five, of singular nerve and practical wisdom, who had once smuggled her wounded husband home from a border affray, calmly made coffee for his deceived pursuers while he lay hidden in the loft, walked four miles for that medical assistance which arrived too late to save him, buried him secretly in his own "quarter section," with only one other witness and mourner, and so saved her position and property in that wild community, who believed he had fled. There was very little of this experience to be traced in her round, fresh-colored brunette cheek, her calm black eyes, set in a prickly hedge of stiff lashes, her plump figure, or her frank, courageous laugh. The latter appeared as a smile when she welcomed Mr. Spindler. "She hadn't seen him for a coon's age," but "reckon he was busy fixin' up his new house."

"Well, yes," said Spindler, with a slight hesitation, "ye see, I'm reckonin' to hev a kinder Christmas gatherin' of my"— he was about to say "folks," but dismissed it for "relations," and finally settled upon "relatives" as being more correct in a preacher's house.

Mrs. Price thought it a very good idea. Christmas was the natural season for the family to gather to "see who's here and who's there, who's gettin' on and who isn't, and who's dead and buried. It was lucky for them who were so placed that they could do so and be joyful." Her invincible philosophy probably carried her past any dangerous recollections of the lonely grave in Kansas, and holding up the stocking to the light, she glanced cheerfully along its level to Mr. Spindler's embarrassed face by the fire.

"Well, I can't say much ez to that," responded Spindler, still awkwardly, "for you see I don't know much about it anyway."

"How long since you've seen 'em?" asked Mrs. Price, apparently addressing herself to the stocking.

Spindler gave a weak laugh. "Well, you see, ef it comes to that, I've never seen 'em!"

Mrs. Price put the stocking in her lap and opened her direct eyes on Spindler. "Never seen 'em?" she repeated. "Then, they're not near relations?"

"There are three cousins," said Spindler, checking them off on his fingers, "a half-uncle, a kind of brother-in-law,—that is, the brother of my sister-in-law's second husband,—and a niece. That's six."

"But if you've not seen them, I suppose they've corresponded with you?" said Mrs. Price.

"They've nearly all of 'em written to me for money, seeing my name in the paper ez hevin' made a strike," returned Spindler simply; "and hevin' sent it, I jest know their addresses."

"Oh!" said Mrs. Price, returning to the stocking.

Something in the tone of her ejaculation increased Spindler's embarrassment, but it also made him desperate. "You see, Mrs. Price," he blurted out, "I oughter tell ye that I reckon they are the folks that 'hevn't got on,' don't you see, and so it seemed only the square thing for me, ez had got on, to give them a sort o' Christmas festival. Suthin', don't ye know, like what your brother-in-law was sayin' last Sunday in the pulpit about this yer peace and goodwill 'twixt man and man."

Mrs. Price looked again at the man before her. His sallow, perplexed face exhibited some doubt, yet a certain determination, regarding the prospect the quotation had opened to him. "A very good idea, Mr. Spindler, and one that does you great credit," she said gravely.

"I'm mighty glad to hear you say so, Mrs. Price," he said, with an accent of great relief, "for I reckoned to ask you a great favor! You see," he fell into his former hesitation, "that is—the fact is—that this sort o' thing is rather suddent to me,—a little outer my line, don't you see, and I was goin' to ask ye ef you'd mind takin' the hull thing in hand and runnin' it for me."

"Runnin' it for you," said Mrs. Price, with a quick eyeshot from under the edge of her lashes. "Man alive! What are you thinking of?"

"Bossin' the whole job for me," hurried on Spindler, with nervous desperation. "Gettin' together all the things and makin' ready for 'em,—orderin' in everythin' that's wanted, and fixin' up the rooms,—I kin step out while you're doin' it,—and then helpin' me receivin' 'em, and sittin' at the head o' the table, you know,—like ez ef you was the mistress."

"But," said Mrs. Price, with her frank laugh, "that's the duty of one of your relations,—your niece, for instance,—or cousin, if one of them is a woman."

"But," persisted Spindler, "you see, they're strangers to me; I don't know 'em, and I do you. You'd make it easy for 'em,—and for me,— don't you see? Kinder introduce 'em,— don't you know? A woman of your gin'ral experience would smooth down all them little diffi-culties," continued Spindler, with a vague recollection of the Kansas story, "and put everybody on velvet. Don't say 'No,' Mrs. Price! I'm just calkilatin' on you."

Sincerity and persistency in a man goes a great way with even the best of women. Mrs. Price, who had at first received Spindler's re-quest as an amusing originality, now began to incline secretly to-wards it. And, of course, began to suggest objections.

"I'm afraid it won't do," she said thoughtfully, awakening to the fact that it would do and could be done. "You see, I've promised to spend Christmas at Sacramento with my nieces from Baltimore. And then there's Mr. Saltover and my sister to consult."

But here Spindler's simple face showed such signs of distress that the widow declared she would "think it over,"—a process which the sanguine Spindler seemed to consider so nearly akin to talking it over that Mrs. Price began to believe it herself, as he hopefully de-parted.

She "thought it over" sufficiently to go to Sacramento and excuse herself to her nieces. But here she permitted herself to "talk it over," to the infinite delight of those Baltimore girls, who thought this ex-travaganza of Spindler's "so Californian and eccentric!" So that it was not strange that presently the news came back to Rough and Ready, and his old associates learned for the first time that he had never seen his relatives, and that they would be doubly strangers. This did not increase his popularity; neither, I grieve to say, did the intelligence that his relatives were probably poor, and that the Rev-erend Mr. Saltover had approved of his course, and had likened it to the rich man's feast, to which the halt and blind were invited. In-deed, the allusion was supposed to add hypocrisy and a bid for popu-larity to Spindler's defection, for it was argued that he might have feasted "Wall-eyed Joe" or "Tanglefoot Billy,"—who had once been "chawed" by a bear while prospecting,—if he had been sincere. How-beit, Spindler's faith was oblivious to these criticisms, in his joy at Mr. Saltover's adhesion to his plans and the loan of Mrs. Price as a hostess. In fact, he proposed to her that the invitations should also convey that information in the expression, "by the kind permission of the Rev. Mr. Saltover," as a guarantee of good faith, but the widow would have none of it. The invitations were duly written and dispatched.

"Suppose," suggested Spindler, with a sudden lugubrious apprehension,—"suppose they shouldn't come?"

"Have no fear of that," said Mrs. Price, with a frank laugh.

"Or ef they was dead," continued Spindler.

"They couldn't all be dead," said the widow cheerfully.

"I've written to another cousin by marriage," said Spindler dubiously, "in case of accident; I didn't think of him before, because he was rich."

"And have you ever seen him either, Mr. Spindler?" asked the widow, with a slight mischievousness.

"Lordy! No!" he responded, with unaffected concern.

Only one mistake was made by Mrs. Price in her arrangements for the party. She had noticed what the simple-minded Spindler could never have conceived,—the feeling towards him held by his old associates, and had tactfully suggested that a general invitation should be extended to them in the evening.

"You can have refreshments, you know, too, after the dinner, and games and music."

"But," said the unsophisticated host, "won't the boys think I'm playing it rather low down on them, so to speak, givin' 'em a kind o' second table, as ef it was the tailings after a strike?"

"Nonsense," said Mrs. Price, with decision. "It's quite fashionable in San Francisco, and just the thing to do."

To this decision Spindler, in his blind faith in the widow's management, weakly yielded. An announcement in the "Weekly Banner" that, "On Christmas evening Richard Spindler, Esq., proposed to entertain his friends and fellow citizens at an 'at home,' in his own residence," not only widened the breach between him and the "boys," but awakened an active resentment that only waited for an outlet. It was understood that they were all coming; but that they should have "some fun out of it" which might not coincide with Spindler's nor his relatives' sense of humor seemed a foregone conclusion.

Unfortunately, too, subsequent events lent themselves to this irony of the situation. A few mornings after the invitations were dispatched,

Spindler, at one of his daily conferences with Mrs. Price, took a newspaper from his pocket. "It seems," he said, looking at her with an embarrassed gravity, "that we will have to take one o' them names off that list,—the name o' Sam Spindler,—and calkilate upon only six relations coming."

"Ah," said Mrs. Price interestedly, "then you have had an answer, and he has declined?"

"Not that exactly," said Spindler slowly, "but from remarks in this yer paper, he was hung last week by the Vigilance Committee of Yolo."

Mrs. Price opened her eyes on Spindler's face as she took the paper from his hand. "But," she said quickly, "this may be all a mistake, some other Spindler! You know, you say you've never seen them!"

"I reckon it's no mistake," said Spindler, with patient gravity, "for the Committee sent me back my invitation, with the kinder disparagin' remark that they've 'sent him where it ain't bin the habit to keep Christmas!'"

Mrs. Price gasped, but a glance at Spindler's patient, wistful, inquiring eyes brought back her old courage. "Well," she said cheerfully, "perhaps it's just as well he didn't come."

"Are ye sure o' that, Mrs. Price?" said Spindler, with a slightly troubled expression. "Seems to me, now, that he was the sort as might hev bin gathered in at the feast, and kinder snatched like a brand from the burnin', accordin' to Scripter. But ye know best."

"Mr. Spindler," said Mrs. Price suddenly, with a slight snap in her black eyes; "are your—are the others like this? Or"—here her eyes softened again, and her laugh returned, albeit slightly hysterical—"is this kind of thing likely to happen again?"

"I think we're pretty sartin o' hevin' six to dinner," returned Spindler simply. Then, as if noticing some other significance in her speech, he added wistfully, "But you won't go back on me, Mrs. Price, ef things ain't pannin' out exackly as I reckoned? You see, I never really knew these yer relations."

He was so obviously sincere in his intent, and, above all, seemed to place such a pathetic reliance on her judgment, that she hesitated to let him know the shock his revelation had given her. And what might his other relations prove to be? Good Lord! Yet, oddly enough, she was so prepossessed by him, and so fascinated by his very Quixotism, that it was perhaps for these complex reasons that she said a little stiffly:—

"One of these cousins, I see, is a lady, and then there is your niece. Do you know anything about them, Mr. Spindler?"

His face grew serious. "No more than I know of the others," he said apologetically. After a moment's hesitation he went on: "Now you speak of it, it seems to me I've heard that my niece was di-vorced. But," he added, brightening up, "I've heard that she was popular."

Mrs. Price gave a short laugh, and was silent for a few minutes. Then this sublime little woman looked up at him. What he might have seen in her eyes was more than he expected, or, I fear, deserved. "Cheer up, Mr. Spindler," she said manfully. "I'll see you through this thing, don't you mind! But don't you say anything about—about—this Vigilance Committee business to anybody. Nor about your niece —it was your niece, wasn't it?—being divorced. Charley [the late Mr. Price] had a queer sort of sister, who—but that's neither here nor there! And your niece mayn't come, you know; or if she does, you ain't bound to bring her out to the general company."

At parting, Spindler, in sheer gratefulness, pressed her hand, and lingered so long over it that a little color sprang into the widow's brown cheek. Perhaps a fresh courage sprang into her heart, too, for she went to Sacramento the next day, previously enjoining Spindler on no account to show any answers he might receive. At Sacramento her nieces flew to her with confidences.

"We so wanted to see you, Aunt Huldy, for we've heard something so delightful about your funny Christmas Party!" Mrs. Price's heart sank, but her eyes snapped. "Only think of it! One of Mr. Spindler's long-lost relatives—a Mr. Wragg—lives in this hotel, and papa knows him. He's a sort of half-uncle, I believe, and he's just furious that Spindler should have invited him. He showed papa the letter; said it was the greatest piece of insolence in the world; that Spindler was an ostentatious fool, who had made a little money and wanted to use him to get into society; and the fun of the whole thing was that this half-uncle and whole brute is himself a parvenu,—a vulgar, ostentatious creature, who was only a"—

"Never mind what he was, Kate," interrupted Mrs. Price hastily. "I call his conduct a shame."

"So do we," said both girls eagerly. After a pause Kate clasped her knees with her locked fingers, and rocking backwards and forwards said, "Milly and I have got an idea, and don't you say 'No' to it. We've had it ever since that brute talked in that way. Now, through him we know more about this Mr. Spindler's family connections than you do; and we know all the trouble you and he'll have in getting up this party. You understand? Now, we first want to know what Spindler's like. Is he a savage, bearded creature, like the miners we saw on the boat?"

Mrs. Price said that, on the contrary, he was very gentle, soft-spoken, and rather good-looking.

"Young or old?"

"Young,—in fact, a mere boy, as you may judge from his actions," returned Mrs. Price, with a suggestive matronly air.

Kate here put up a long-handled eyeglass to her fine gray eyes, fitted it ostentatiously over her aquiline nose, and then said, in a voice of simulated horror, "Aunt Huldy,—this revelation is shocking!"

Mrs. Price laughed her usual frank laugh, albeit her brown cheek took upon it a faint tint of Indian red. "If that's the wonderful idea you girls have got, I don't see how it's going to help matters," she said dryly.

"No, that's not it! We really have an idea. Now look here."

Mrs. Price "looked here." This process seemed to the superficial observer to be merely submitting her waist and shoulders to the arms of her nieces, and her ears to their confidential and coaxing voices.

Twice she said "it couldn't be thought of," and "it was impossible"; once addressed Kate as "You limb!" and finally said that she "wouldn't promise, but might write!"

IT WAS TWO DAYS before Christmas. There was nothing in the air, sky, or landscape of that Sierran slope to suggest the season to the Eastern stranger. A soft rain had been dropping for a week on laurel, pine, and buckeye, and the blades of springing grasses and shyly opening flowers. Sedate and silent hillsides that had grown dumb and parched towards the end of the dry season became gently articulate again; there were murmurs in hushed and forgotten cañons, the leap and laugh of water among the dry bones of dusty creeks, and the full song of the larger forks and rivers. Southwest winds brought the warm odor of the pine sap swelling in the forest, or the faint, far-off spice of wild mustard springing in the lower valleys. But, as if by some irony of Nature, this gentle invasion of spring in the wild wood brought only disturbance and discomfort to the haunts and works of man. The ditches were overflowed, the fords of the Fork impassable, the sluicing adrift, and the trails and wagon roads to Rough and Ready knee-deep in mud. The stagecoach from Sacramento, entering the settlement by the mountain highway, its wheels and panels clogged and crusted with an unctuous pigment like mud and blood, passed out of it through the overflowed and dangerous ford, and emerged in spotless purity, leaving its stains behind with Rough and Ready. A week of enforced idleness on the river "Bar" had driven the miners to the more comfortable recreation of the saloon bar, its mirrors, its florid paintings, its armchairs, and its stove. The steam of their wet boots and the smoke of their pipes hung over the latter like the sacrificial incense from an altar. But the attitude of the men was more critical and censorious than contented, and showed little of the gentleness of the weather or season.

"Did you hear if the stage brought down any more relations of Spindler's?"

The bar-keeper, to whom this question was addressed, shifted his lounging position against the bar and said, "I reckon not, ez far ez I know."

"And that old bloat of a second cousin—that crimson beak—what kem down yesterday,—he ain't bin hangin' round here to-day for his reg'lar pizon?"

"No," said the bar-keeper thoughtfully, "I reckon Spindler's got him locked up, and is settin' on him to keep him sober till after Christmas, and prevent you boys gettin' at him."

"He'll have the jimjams before that," returned the first speaker; "and how about that dead beat of a half-nephew who borrowed twenty dollars of Yuba Bill on the way down, and then wanted to get off at Shootersville, but Bill wouldn't let him, and scooted him down to Spindler's and collected the money from Spindler himself afore he'd give him up?"

"He's up thar with the rest of the menagerie," said the bar-keeper, "but I reckon that Mrs. Price hez bin feedin' him up. And ye know the old woman—that fifty-fifty cousin by marriage—whom Joe Chandler swears he remember ez an old cook for a Chinese restaurant in Stockton,—darn my skin ef that Mrs. Price hasn't rigged her out in some fancy duds of her own, and made her look quite decent."

A deep groan here broke from Uncle Jim Starbuck.

"Didn't I tell ye?" he said, turning appealingly to the others. "It's that darned widow that's at the bottom of it all! She first put Spindler up to givin' the party, and now, darn my skin, ef she ain't goin' to fix up these ragamuffins and drill 'em so we can't get any fun outer 'em after all! And it's bein' a woman that's bossin' the job, and not Spindler, we've got to draw things mighty fine and not cut up too rough, or some of the boys will kick."

"You bet," said a surly but decided voice in the crowd.

"And," said another voice, "Mrs. Price didn't live in 'Bleeding Kansas' for nothing."

"Wot's the program you've settled on, Uncle Jim?" said the bar-keeper lightly, to check what seemed to promise a dangerous discussion.

"Well," said Starbuck, "we calkilate to gather early Christmas night in Hooper's Hollow and rig ourselves up Injun fashion, and then start for Spindler's with pitch-pine torches, and have a 'torchlight dance' around the house; them who does the dancin' and yellin' outside takin' their turn at goin' in and hevin' refreshment. Jake Cooledge, of Boston, sez if anybody objects to it, we've only got to say we're 'Mummers of the Olden Times,' sabe? Then, later, we'll have 'Them Sabbath Evening Bells' performed on prospectin' pans by the band. Then, at the finish, Jake Cooledge is goin' to give one of his surkastic speeches,— kinder welcomin' Spindler's family to the Free Openin' o' Spindler's Almshouse and Reformatory." He paused, possibly for that approbation which, however, did not seem to come spontaneously. "It ain't much," he added apologetically, "for we're hampered by women; but we'll add to the program ez we see how things pan out. Ye see, from what we can hear, all of Spindler's relations ain't on hand yet! We've got to wait, like in elekshun times, for 'returns from the back counties.' Hello! What's that?"

It was the swish and splutter of hoofs on the road before the door. The Sacramento coach! In an instant every man was expectant, and Starbuck darted outside on the platform. Then there was the usual greeting and bustle, the hurried ingress of thirsty passengers into the saloon, and a pause. Uncle Jim returned, excitedly and pantingly. "Look yer, boys! Ef this ain't the richest thing out! They say there's two more relations o' Spindler's on the coach, come down as express freight, consigned,—d' ye hear?—consigned to Spindler!"

"Stiffs, in coffins?" suggested an eager voice.

"I didn't get to hear more. But here they are."

There was the sudden irruption of a laughing, curious crowd into the bar-room, led by Yuba Bill, the driver. Then the crowd parted, and out of their midst stepped two children, a boy and a girl, the oldest apparently of not more than six years, holding each other's hands. They were coarsely yet cleanly dressed, and with a certain uniform precision that suggested formal charity. But more remarkable than all, around the neck of each was a little steel chain, from which depended the regular check and label of the powerful Express Company, Wells, Fargo & Co., and the words: "To Richard Spindler." "Fragile." "With great care." "Collect on delivery." Occasionally their little hands went up automatically and touched their labels, as if to show them. They surveyed the crowd, the floor, the gilded bar, and Yuba Bill without fear and without wonder. There was a pathetic suggestion that they were accustomed to this observation.

"Now, Bobby," said Yuba Bill, leaning back against the bar, with an air half paternal, half managerial, "tell these gents how you came here."

"By Wellth, Fargoth Expreth," lisped Bobby.

"Whar from?"

"Wed Hill, Owegon."

"Red Hill, Oregon? Why, it's a thousand miles from here," said a bystander.

"I reckon," said Yuba Bill coolly, "they kem by stage to Portland, by steamer to 'Frisco, steamer again to Stockton, and then by stage over the whole line. Allers by Wells, Fargo & Co.'s Express, from agent to agent, and from messenger to messenger. Fact! They ain't bin tetched or handled by any one but the Kempany's agents; they ain't had a line or direction except them checks around their necks! And they've wanted for nothin' else. Why, I've carried heaps o' treasure before, gentlemen, and once a hundred thousand dollars in greenbacks, but I never carried anythin' that was watched and guarded as them kids! Why, the division inspector at Stockton wanted to go with 'em over the line; but Jim Bracy, the messenger, said he'd call it a reflection on himself and resign, ef they didn't give 'em to him with the other packages! Ye had a pretty good time, Bobby, didn't ye? Plenty to eat and drink, eh?"

The two children laughed a little weak laugh, turned each other bashfully around, and then looked up shyly at Yuba Bill and said, "Yeth."

"Do you know where you are goin'?" asked Starbuck, in a constrained voice.

It was the little girl who answered quickly and eagerly:—

"Yes, to Krissmass and Sandy Claus."

"To what?" asked Starbuck.

Here the boy interposed with a superior air:—

"Thee meanth Couthin Dick. He'th got Krithmath."

"Where's your mother?"

"Dead."

"And your father?"

"In orthpittal."

There was a laugh somewhere on the outskirts of the crowd. Every one faced angrily in that direction, but the laughter had disappeared. Yuba Bill, however, sent his voice after him. "Yes, in hospital! Funny, ain't it?—amoosin' place! Try it. Step over here, and in five minutes, by the living Hoky, I'll qualify you for admission, and not charge you a cent!" He stopped, gave a sweeping glance of dissatisfaction around him, and then, leaning back against the bar, beckoned to some one near the door, and said in a disgusted tone, "You tell these galoots how it happened, Bracy. They make me sick!"

Thus appealed to, Bracy, the express messenger, stepped forward in Yuba Bill's place.

"It's nothing particular, gentlemen," he said, with a laugh, "only it seems that some man called Spindler, who lives about here, sent an invitation to the father of these children to bring his family to a Christmas party. It wasn't a bad sort of thing for Spindler to do, considering that they were his poor relations, though they didn't know him from Adam,—was it?" He paused; several of the bystanders cleared their throats, but said nothing. "At least," resumed Bracy, "that's what the boys up at Red Hill, Oregon, thought, when they heard of it. Well, as the father was in hospital with a broken leg, and the mother only a few weeks dead, the boys thought it mighty rough on these poor kids if they were done out of their fun because they had no one to bring them. The boys couldn't afford to go themselves, but they got a little money together, and then got the idea of sendin' 'em by express. Our agent at Red Hill tumbled to the idea at once; but he wouldn't take any money in advance, and said he would send 'em 'C. O. D.' like any other package. And he did, and here they are! That's all! And now, gentlemen, as I've got to deliver them personally to this Spindler, and get his receipt and take off their checks, I reckon we must toddle. Come, Bill, help take 'em up!"

"Hold on! " said a dozen voices. A dozen hands were thrust into a dozen pockets; I grieve to say some were regretfully withdrawn empty, for it was a hard season in Rough and Ready. But the expressman stepped before them, with warning, uplifted hand.

"Not a cent, boys,—not a cent! Wells, Fargo's Express Company don't undertake to carry bullion with those kids, at least on the same contract!" He laughed, and then, looking around him, said confidentially in a lower voice, which, however, was quite audible to the children, "There's as much as three bags of silver in quarter and half dollars in my treasure box in the coach that has been poured, yes, just showered upon them, ever since they started, and has been passed over from agent to agent and messenger to messenger,—enough to pay their passage from here to China! It's time to say quits now. But bet your life, they are not going to that Christmas party poor!"

He caught up the boy, as Yuba Bill lifted the little girl to his shoulder, and both passed out. Then one by one the loungers in the barroom silently and awkwardly followed, and when the bar-keeper turned back from putting away his decanters and glasses, to his astonishment the room was empty.

Spindler's house, or "Spindler's Splurge," as Rough and Ready chose to call it, stood above the settlement, on a deforested hillside, which, however, revenged itself by producing not enough vegetation to cover even the few stumps that were ineradicable. A large wooden structure in the pseudoclassic style affected by Westerners, with an incongruous cupola, it was oddly enough relieved by a still more incongruous veranda extending around its four sides, upheld by wooden Doric columns, which were already picturesquely covered with flowering vines and sun-loving roses. Mr. Spindler had trusted the furnishing of its interior to the same contractor who had upholstered the gilded bar-room of the Eureka Saloon, and who had apparently bestowed the same design and material, impartially, on each. There were gilded mirrors all over the house and chilly marble-topped tables, gilt plaster Cupids in the corners, and stuccoed lions "in the way" everywhere. The tactful hands of Mrs. Price had screened some of these with seasonable laurels, fir boughs, and berries, and had imparted a slight Christmas flavor to the house. But the greater part of her time had been employed in trying to subdue the eccentricities of Spindler's amazing relations; in tranquilizing Mrs. "Aunt" Martha Spindler,—the elderly cook before alluded to,—who was inclined to regard the gilded splendors of the house as indicative of dangerous immorality; in restraining "Cousin" Morley Hewlett from consider-ing the dining-room buffet as a bar for "intermittent refreshment"; and in keeping the weak-minded nephew, Phinney Spindler, from shooting at bottles from the veranda, wearing his uncle's clothes, or running up an account in his uncle's name for various articles at the general stores. Yet the unlooked-for arrival of the two children had been the one great compensation and diversion for her. She wrote at once to her nieces a brief account of her miraculous deliverance. "I think these poor children dropped from the skies here to make our Christmas party possible, to say nothing of the sympathy they have created in Rough and Ready for Spindler. He is going to keep them as long as he can, and is writing to the father. Think of the poor little tots traveling a thousand miles to 'Krissmass,' as they call it!—though they were so well cared for by the messengers that their little bodies were positively stuffed like quails. So you see, dear, we will be able to get along without airing your famous idea. I'm sorry, for I know you're just dying to see it all."

Whatever Kate's "idea" might have been, there certainly seemed now no need of any extraneous aid to Mrs. Price's management. Christmas came at last, and the dinner passed off without serious disaster. But the ordeal of the reception of Rough and Ready was still to come. For Mrs. Price well knew that although "the boys" were more subdued, and, indeed, inclined to sympathize with their host's uncouth endeavor, there was still much in the aspect of Spindler's relations to excite their sense of the ludicrous.

But here Fortune again favored the house of Spindler with a dra-matic surprise, even greater than the advent of the children had been. In the change that had come over Rough and Ready, "the boys" had decided, out of deference to the women and children, to omit the first part of their program, and had approached and entered the house as soberly and quietly as ordinary guests. But before they had shaken hands with the host and hostess, and seen the relations, the clatter of wheels was heard before the open door, and its lights flashed upon a carriage and pair,—an actual private carriage,—the like of which had not been seen since the governor of the State had come down to open the new ditch! Then there was a pause, the flash of the carriage lamps upon white silk, the light tread of a satin foot on the veranda and in the hall, and the entrance of a vision of loveliness! Middle-aged men and old dwellers of cities remembered their youth; younger men bethought themselves of Cinderella and the Prince! There was a thrill and a hush as this last guest—a beautiful girl, radiant with youth and adornment—put a dainty glass to her sparkling eye and advanced familiarly with outstretched hand, to Dick Spindler. Mrs. Price gave a single gasp, and drew back speechless.

"Uncle Dick," said a laughing contralto voice, which, indeed, somewhat recalled Mrs. Price's own, in its courageous frankness, "I am so delighted to come, even if a little late, and so sorry that Mr. M'Kenna could not come on account of business."

Everybody listened eagerly, but none more eagerly and surprisingly than the host himself. M'Kenna! The rich cousin who had never answered the invitation! And Uncle Dick! This, then, was his divorced niece! Yet even in his astonishment he remembered that of course no one but himself and Mrs. Price knew it,—and that lady had glanced discreetly away.

"Yes," continued the half-niece brightly. "I came from Sacramento with some friends to Shootersville, and from thence I drove here; and though I must return tonight, I could not forego the pleasure of coming, if it was only for an hour or two, to answer the invitation of the uncle I have not seen for years." She paused, and, raising her glasses, turned a politely questioning eye towards Mrs. Price. "One of our relations?" she said smilingly to Spindler.

"No," said Spindler, with some embarrassment, "a—a friend!"

The half-niece extended her hand. Mrs. Price took it.

But the fair stranger,—what she did and said were the only things remembered in Rough and Ready on that festive occasion; no one thought of the other relations; no one recalled them nor their eccentricities; Spindler himself was forgotten. People only recollected how Spindler's lovely niece lavished her smiles and courtesies on every one, and brought to her feet particularly the misogynist Starbuck and the sarcastic Cooledge, oblivious of his previous speech; how she sat at the piano and sang like an angel, hushing the most hilarious and excited into sentimental and even maudlin silence; how, graceful as a nymph, she led with "Uncle Dick" a Virginia reel until the whole assembly joined, eager for a passing touch of her dainty hand in its changes; how, when two hours had passed,—all too swiftly for the guests,—they stood with bared heads and glistening eyes on the veranda to see the fairy coach whirl the fairy princess away! How—but this incident was never known to Rough and Ready.

It happened in the sacred dressing-room, where Mrs. Price was cloaking with her own hands the departing half-niece of Mr. Spindler. Taking that opportunity to seize the lovely relative by the shoulders and shake her violently, she said: "Oh, yes, and it's all very well for you, Kate, you limb! For you're going away, and will never see Rough and Ready and poor Spindler again. But what am I to do, miss? How am I to face it out? For you know I've got to tell him at least that you're no half-niece of his!"

"Have you?" said the young lady.

"Have I?" repeated the widow impatiently. "Have I? Of course I have! What are you thinking of?"

"I was thinking, aunty," said the girl audaciously, "that from what I've seen and heard to-night, if I'm not his half-niece now, it's only a question of time! So you'd better wait. Good-night, dear."

And, really,—it turned out that she was right!

IN THE TULES

He had never seen a steamboat in his life. Born and reared in one of the Western Territories, far from a navigable river, he had only known the "dug-out" or canoe as a means of conveyance across the scant streams whose fordable waters made even those scarcely a necessity. The long, narrow, hooded wagon, drawn by swaying oxen, known familiarly as a "prairie schooner," in which he journeyed across the plains to California in '53, did not help his conception by that nautical figure. And when at last he dropped upon the land of promise through one of the Southern mountain passes he halted all unconsciously upon the low banks of a great yellow river amidst a tangled brake of strange, reed-like grasses that were unknown to him. The river, broadening as it debouched through many channels into a lordly bay, seemed to him the *ultima thule* of his journeyings. Unyoking his oxen on the edge of the luxuriant meadows which blended with scarcely any line of demarcation into the great stream itself, he found the prospect "good" according to his lights and prairial experiences, and, converting his halted wagon into a temporary cabin, he resolved to rest here and "settle."

There was little difficulty in so doing. The cultivated clearings he had passed were few and far between; the land would be his by discovery and occupation; his habits of loneliness and self-reliance made him independent of neighbors. He took his first meal in his new solitude under a spreading willow, but so near his natural boundary that the waters gurgled and oozed in the reeds but a few feet from him. The sun sank, deepening the gold of the river until it might have been the stream of Paetolus itself. But Martin Morse had no imagination; he was not even a gold-seeker; he had simply obeyed the roving instinct of the frontiersman in coming hither. The land was virgin and unoccupied; it was his; he was alone. These questions settled, he smoked his pipe with less concern over his three thousand miles' transference of habitation than the man of cities who had moved into a next street. When the sun sank, he rolled himself in his blankets in the wagon bed and went quietly to sleep.

But he was presently awakened by something which at first he could not determine to be a noise or an intangible sensation. It was a deep throbbing through the silence of the night—a pulsation that seemed even to be communicated to the rude bed whereon he lay. As it came nearer it separated itself into a labored, monotonous panting, continuous, but distinct from an equally monotonous but fainter beating of the waters, as if the whole track of the river were being coursed and trodden by a multitude of swiftly-trampling feet. A strange feeling took possession of him—half of fear, half of curious expectation. It was coming nearer. He rose, leaped hurriedly from the wagon, and ran to the bank. The night was dark; at first he saw nothing before him but the steel-black sky pierced with far-spaced, irregularly scattered stars. Then there seemed to be approaching him, from the left, another and more symmetrical constellation—a few red and blue stars high above the river, with three compact lines of larger planetary lights flashing towards him and apparently on his own level. It was almost upon him; he involuntarily drew back as the strange phenomenon swept abreast of where he stood, and resolved itself into a dark yet airy bulk, whose vagueness, topped by enormous towers, was yet illuminated by those open squares of light that he had taken for stars, but which he saw now were brilliantly-lit windows.

Their vivid rays shot through the reeds and sent broad bands across the meadow, the stationary wagon, and the slumbering oxen. But all this was nothing to the inner life they disclosed through lifted curtains and open blinds, which was the crowning revelation of this strange and wonderful spectacle. Elegantly dressed men and women moved through brilliantly lit and elaborately gilt saloons; in one a banquet seemed to be spread, served by white-jacketed servants; in another were men playing cards around marble-topped tables; in another the light flashed back again from the mirrors and glistening glasses and decanters of a gorgeous refreshment saloon; in smaller openings there was the shy disclosure of dainty white curtains and velvet lounges of more intimate apartments.

Martin Morse stood enthralled and mystified. It was as if some invisible Asmodeus had revealed to this simple frontiersman a world of which he had never dreamed. It was *the* world—a world of which he knew nothing in his simple, rustic habits and profound Western isolation—sweeping by him with the rush of an unknown planet. In another moment it was gone: a shower of sparks shot up from one of the towers and fell all around him, and then vanished, even as he remembered the set piece of "Fourth of July" fireworks had vanished in his own rural town when he was a boy. The darkness fell with it too. But such was his utter absorption and breathless preoccupation that only a cold chill recalled him to himself, and he found he was standing mid-leg deep in the surge cast over the low banks by this passage of the first steamboat he had ever seen!

He waited for it the next night, when it appeared a little later from the opposite direction on its return trip. He watched it the next night and the next. Hereafter he never missed it, coming or going—whatever the hard and weary preoccupations of his new and lonely life. He felt he could not have slept without seeing it go by. Oddly enough, his interest and desire did not go further. Even had he the time and money to spend in a passage on the boat, and thus actively realize the great world of which he had only these rare glimpses, a certain proud, rustic shyness kept him from it. It was not *his* world; he could not affront the snubs that his ignorance and in-experience would have provoked, and he was dimly conscious, as so many of us are in our ignorance, that in mingling with it he would simply lose the privileges of alien criticism. For there was much that he did not understand, and some things that grated upon his lonely independence.

One night, a lighter one than those previous, he lingered a little longer in the moonlight to watch the phosphorescent wake of the retreating boat. Suddenly it struck him that there was a certain ir-regular splashing in the water, quite different from the regular, di-agonally crossing surges that the boat swept upon the bank. Looking at it more intently, he saw a black object turning in the water like a porpoise, and then the unmistakable uplifting of a black arm in an unskillful swimmer's overhand stroke. It was a struggling man. But it was quickly evident that the current was too strong and the turbu-lence of the shallow water too great for his efforts. Without a moment's hesitation, clad as he was in only his shirt and trousers,

Morse strode into the reeds, and the next moment, with a call of warning, was swimming towards the now wildly struggling figure. But, from some unknown reason, as Morse approached him nearer the man uttered some incoherent protest and desperately turned away, throwing off Morse's extended arm.

Attributing this only the vague convulsions of a drowning man, Morse, a skilled swimmer, managed to clutch his shoulder, and propelled him at arm's length, still struggling, apparently with as much reluctance as incapacity, towards the bank. As their feet touched the reeds and slimy bottom the man's resistance ceased, and he lapsed quite listlessly in Morse's arms. Half lifting, half dragging his burden, he succeeded at last in gaining the strip of meadow, and deposited the unconscious man beneath the willow tree. Then he ran to his wagon for whiskey.

But, to his surprise, on his return the man was already sitting up and wringing the water from his clothes. He then saw for the first time, by the clear moonlight, that the stranger was elegantly dressed and of striking appearance, and was clearly a part of that bright and fascinating world which Morse had been contemplating in his solitude. He eagerly took the proffered tin cup and drank the whiskey. Then he rose to his feet, staggered a few steps forward, and glanced curiously around him at the still motionless wagon, the few felled trees and evidence of "clearing," and even at the rude cabin of logs and canvas just beginning to rise from the ground a few paces distant, and said, impatiently:—

"Where the devil am I?"

Morse hesitated. He was unable to name the locality of his dwelling-place. He answered briefly:—

"On the right bank of the Sacramento."

The stranger turned upon him a look of suspicion not unmingled with resentment. "Oh!" he said, with ironical gravity, "and I suppose that this water you picked me out of was the Sacramento River. Thank you!"

Morse, with slow Western patience, explained that he had only settled there three weeks ago, and the place had no name.

"What's your nearest town, then?"

"Thar ain't any. Thar's a blacksmith's shop and grocery at the crossroads, twenty miles further on, but it's got no name as I've heard on."

The stranger's look of suspicion passed. "Well," he said, in an imperative fashion, which, however, seemed as much the result of habit as the occasion, "I want a horse, and mighty quick, too."

"H'aint got any."

"No horse? How did you get to this place?"

Morse pointed to the slumbering oxen.

The stranger again stared curiously at him. After a pause he said, with a half-pitying, half-humorous smile: "Pike—aren't you?"

Whether Morse did or did not know that this current California slang for a denizen of the bucolic West implied a certain contempt, he replied simply:—

"I'm from Pike County, Mizzouri."

"Well," said the stranger, resuming his impatient manner, "You must beg or steal a horse from your neighbors."

"Thar ain't any neighbor nearer than fifteen miles."

"Then send fifteen miles! Stop." He opened his still clinging shirt and drew out a belt pouch, which he threw to Morse. "There! there's two hundred and fifty dollars in that. Now, I want a horse. *Sabe?*"

"Thar ain't any one to send," said Morse, quietly.

"Do you mean to say you are all alone here?"

"Yes."

"And you fished me out—all by yourself?"

"Yes."

The stranger again examined him curiously. Then he suddenly stretched out his hand and grasped his companion's.

"All right; if you can't send, I reckon I can manage to walk over there to-morrow."

"I was goin' on to say," said Morse, simply, "that if you'll lie by to-night, I'll start over sun up, after puttin' out the cattle, and fetch you back a horse afore noon."

"That's enough." He, however, remained looking curiously at Morse. "Did you never hear," he said, with a singular smile, "that it was about the meanest kind of luck that could happen to you to save a drowning man?"

"No," said Morse, simply. "I reckon it orter be the meanest if you *didn't.*"

"That depends upon the man you save," said the stranger, with the same ambiguous smile, "and whether the *saving* him is only putting things off. Look here," he added, with an abrupt return to his imperative style, "can't you give me some dry clothes?"

Morse brought him a pair of overalls and a "hickory shirt," well worn, but smelling strongly of a recent wash with coarse soap. The stranger put them on while his companion busied himself in collecting a pile of sticks and dry leaves.

"What's that for?" said the stranger, suddenly.

"A fire to dry your clothes."

The stranger calmly kicked the pile aside.

"Not any fire to-night if I know it," he said, brusquely. Before Morse could resent his quickly changing moods he continued, in another tone, dropping to an easy reclining position beneath the tree, "Now, tell me all about yourself, and what you are doing here."

Thus commanded, Morse patiently repeated his story from the time he had left his backwoods cabin to his selection of the river bank for a "location." He pointed out the rich quality of this alluvial bottom and its adaptability for the raising of stock, which he hoped soon to acquire. The stranger smiled grimly, raised himself to a sitting position, and, taking a penknife from his damp clothes, began to clean his nails in the bright moonlight—an occupation which made the simple Morse wander vaguely in his narration.

"And you don't know that this hole will give you chills and fever till you'll shake yourself out of your boots?"

Morse had lived before in aguish districts, and had no fear.

"And you never heard that some night the whole river will rise up and walk over you and your cabin and your stock?"

"No. For I reckon to move my shanty farther back."

The man shut up his penknife with a click and rose.

"If you've got to get up at sunrise, we'd better be turning in. I suppose you can give me a pair of blankets?"

Morse pointed to the wagon. "Thar's a shakedown in the wagon bed; you kin lie there." Nevertheless he hesitated, and, with the inconsequence and abruptness of a shy man, continued the previous conversation.

"I shouldn't like to move far away, for them steamboats is pow'ful kempany o' nights. I never seed one afore I kem here," and then, with the inconsistency of a reserved man, and without a word of further preliminary, he launched into a confidential disclosure of his late experiences. The stranger listened with a singular interest and a quietly searching eye.

"Then you were watching the boat very closely just now when

you saw me. What else did you see? Anything before that—before you saw me in the water?"

"No—the boat had got well off before I saw you at all."

"Ah," said the stranger. "Well, I'm going to turn in." He walked to the wagon, mounted it, and by the time that Morse had reached it with his wet clothes he was already wrapped in the blankets. A moment later he seemed to be in a profound slumber.

It was only then, when his guest was lying helplessly at his mercy, that he began to realize his strange experiences. The domination of this man had been so complete that Morse, although by nature independent and self-reliant, had not permitted himself to question his right or to resent his rudeness. He had accepted his guest's careless or premeditated silence regarding the particulars of his accident as a matter of course, and had never dreamed of questioning him. That it was a natural accident of that great world so apart from his own experiences he did not doubt, and thought no more about it. The advent of the man himself was greater to him than the causes which brought him there. He was as yet quite unconscious of the complete fascination this mysterious stranger held over him, but he found himself shyly pleased with even the slight interest he had displayed in his affairs, and his hand felt yet warm and tingling from his sudden soft but expressive grasp, as if it had been a woman's. There is a simple intuition of friendship in some lonely, self-abstracted natures that is nearly akin to love at first sight. Even the audacities and insolence of this stranger affected Morse as he might have been touched and captivated by the coquetries or imperiousness of some bucolic virgin. And this reserved and shy frontiersman found himself that night sleepless, and hovering with an abashed timidity and consciousness around the wagon that sheltered his guest, as if he had been a very Corydon watching the moonlit couch of some slumbering Amaryllis.

He was off by daylight—after having placed a rude breakfast by the side of the still sleeping guest—and before mid-day he had returned with a horse. When he handed the stranger his pouch, less the amount he had paid for the horse, the man said curtly—

"What's that for?"

"Your change. I paid only fifty dollars for the horse."

The stranger regarded him with his peculiar smile. Then, replacing the pouch in his belt, he shook Morse's hand again and mounted the horse.

"So your name's Martin Morse! Well—good-by, Morsey!"

Morse hesitated. A blush rose to his dark cheek. "You didn't tell me *your* name," he said. "In case"—

"In case I'm *wanted?* Well, you can call me Captain Jack." He smiled, and, nodding his head, put spurs to his mustang and cantered away.

Morse did not do much work that day, falling into abstracted moods and living over his experiences of the previous night, until he fancied he could almost see his strange guest again. The narrow strip of meadow was haunted by him. There was the tree under which he had first placed him, and that was where he had seen him sitting up in his dripping but well-fitting clothes. In the rough garments he had worn and returned lingered a new scent of some delicate soap, overpowering the strong alkali flavor of his own. He was early by the river side, having a vague hope, he knew not why, that he should again see him and recognize him among the passengers. He was wading out among the reeds, in the faint light of the rising moon, recalling the exact spot where he had first seen the stranger, when he was suddenly startled by the rolling over in the water of some black object that had caught against the bank, but had been dislodged by his movements. To his horror it bore a faint resemblance to his first vision of the preceding night. But a second glance at the helplessly floating hair and bloated outline showed him that it was a *dead* man, and of a type and build far different from his former companion. There was a bruise upon his matted forehead and an enormous wound in his throat already washed bloodless, white, and waxen. An inexplicable fear came upon him, not at the sight of the corpse, for he had been in Indian massacres and had rescued bodies mutilated beyond recognition; but from some moral dread that, strangely enough, quickened and deepened with the far-off pant of the advancing steamboat. Scarcely knowing why, he dragged the body hurriedly ashore, concealing it in the reeds, as if he were disposing of the evidence of his own crime. Then, to his preposterous terror, he noticed that the panting of the steamboat and the beat of its paddles were "slowing" as the vague bulk came in sight, until a huge wave from the suddenly arrested wheels sent a surge like an enormous heartbeat pulsating through the sedge that half submerged him. The flashing of three or four lanterns on deck and the motionless line of lights abreast of him dazzled his eyes, but he knew that the low fringe of willows hid his house and wagon completely from view. A vague murmur of voices from the deck was suddenly over-ridden by a sharp order, and to his relief the slowly revolving wheels again sent a pulsation through the water, and the great fabric moved solemnly away. A sense of relief came over him, he knew not why, and he was conscious that for the first time he had not cared to look at the boat.

When the moon arose he again examined the body, and took from its clothing a few articles of identification and some papers of formality and precision, which he vaguely conjectured to be some law papers from their resemblance to the phrasing of sheriffs' and electors' notices which he had seen in the papers. He then buried the corpse in a shallow trench, which he dug by the light of the moon. He had no question of responsibility; his pioneer training had not included coroners' inquests in its experience; in giving the body a speedy and secure burial from predatory animals he did what one frontiersman would do for another—what he hoped might be done for *him*. If his previous unaccountable feelings returned occasionally, it was not from that; but rather from some uneasiness in regard to his late guest's possible feelings, and a regret that he had not been here at the finding of the body. That it would in some way have explained his own accident he did not doubt.

The boat did not "slow up" the next night, but passed as usual; yet three or four days elapsed before he could look forward to its coming with his old extravagant and half-exalted curiosity—which was his nearest approach to imagination. He was then able to examine it more closely, for the appearance of the stranger whom he now began to call "his friend" in his verbal communings with himself—but whom he did not seem destined to again discover; until one day, to his astonishment, a couple of fine horses were brought to his clearing by a stock-drover. They had been "ordered" to be left there. In vain Morse expostulated and questioned.

"Your name's Martin Morse, ain't it?" said the drover, with business brusqueness; "and I reckon there ain't no other man o' that name around here?"

"No," said Morse.

"Well, then, they're *yours*."

"But who sent them?" insisted Morse. "What was his name, and where does he live?"

"I didn't know ez I was called upon to give the pedigree o' buyers," said the drover drily; "but the horses is 'Morgan,' you can bet your life." He grinned as he rode away.

That Captain Jack sent them, and that it was a natural prelude to his again visiting him, Morse did not doubt, and for a few days he lived in that dream. But Captain Jack did not come. The animals were of great service to him in "rounding up" the stock he now easily took in for pasturage, and saved him the necessity of having a partner or a hired man. The idea that this superior gentleman in fine clothes might ever appear to him in the former capacity had even flitted through his brain, but he had rejected it with a sigh. But the thought that, with luck and industry, he himself might, in course of time, approximate to Captain Jack's evident station, *did* occur to him, and was an incentive to energy. Yet it was quite distinct from the ordinary working man's ambition of wealth and state. It was only that it might make him more worthy of his friend. The great world was still as it had appeared to him in the passing boat—a thing to wonder at—to be above—and to criticize.

For all that, he prospered in his occupation. But one day he woke with listless limbs and feet that scarcely carried him through his daily labors. At night his listlessness changed to active pain and a feverishness that seemed to impel him towards the fateful river, as if his one aim in life was to drink up its waters and bathe in its yellow stream. But whenever he seemed to attempt it, strange dreams assailed him of dead bodies arising with swollen and distorted lips to touch his own as he strove to drink, or of his mysterious guest battling with him in its current, and driving him ashore. Again, when he assayed to bathe his parched and crackling limbs in its flood, he would be confronted with the dazzling lights of the motionless steamboat and the glare of stony eyes—until he fled in aimless terror. How long this lasted he knew not, until one morning he awoke in his new cabin with a strange man sitting by his bed and a negress in the doorway.

"You've had a sharp attack of 'tule fever,'" said the stranger, dropping Morse's listless wrist and answering his questioning eyes, "but you're all right now, and will pull through."

"Who are you?" stammered Morse feebly.

"Dr. Duchesne, of Sacramento."

"How did you come here?"

"I was ordered to come to you and bring a nurse, as you were alone. There she is." He pointed to the smiling negress.

"*Who* ordered you?"

The doctor smiled with professional tolerance. "One of your friends, of course."

"But what was his name?"

"Really, I don't remember. But don't distress yourself. He has settled for everything right royally. You have only to get strong now. My duty is ended, and I can safely leave you with the nurse. Only when you are strong again, I say—and *he* says—keep back farther from the river."

And that was all he knew. For even the nurse who attended him through the first days of his brief convalescence would tell him nothing more. He quickly got rid of her and resumed his work, for a new and strange phase of his simple, childish affection for his benefactor, partly superinduced by his illness, was affecting him. He was beginning to feel the pain of an unequal friendship; he was dimly conscious that his mysterious guest was only coldly returning his hospitality and benefits, while holding aloof from any association with him—and indicating the immeasurable distance that separated their future intercourse. He had withheld any kind message or sympathetic greeting; he had kept back even his *name*. The shy, proud, ignorant heart of the frontiersman swelled beneath the fancied slight, which left him helpless alike of reproach or resentment. He could not return the horses, although in a fit of childish indignation he had resolved not to use them; he could not reimburse him for the doctor's bill, although he had sent away the nurse.

He took a foolish satisfaction in not moving back from the river, with a faint hope that his ignoring Captain Jack's advice might mysteriously be conveyed to him. He even thought of selling out his location and abandoning it, that he might escape the cold surveillance of his heartless friend. All this was undoubtedly childish—but there is an irrepressible simplicity of youth in all deep feeling, and the worldly inexperience of the frontiersman left him as innocent as a child. In this phase of his unrequited affection he even went so far so to seek some news of Captain Jack at Sacramento, and, following out his foolish quest, to even take the steamboat from thence to Stockton.

What happened to him then was perhaps the common experience of such natures. Once upon the boat the illusion of the great world it contained for him utterly vanished. He found it noisy, formal, insincere, and—had he ever understood or used the word in his limited vocabulary—*vulgar.* Rather, perhaps, it seemed to him that the prevailing sentiment and action of those who frequented it—and for whom it was built—were of a lower grade than his own. And, strangely enough, this gave him none of his former sense of critical superiority, but only of his own utter and complete isolation. He wandered in his rough frontiersman's clothes from deck to cabin, from airy galleries to long saloons, alone, unchallenged, unrecognized, as if he were again haunting it only in spirit, as he had so often done in his dreams.

His presence on the fringe of some voluble crowd caused no interruption; to him their speech was almost foreign in its allusions to things he did not understand, or, worse, seemed inconsistent with their eagerness and excitement. How different from all this were his old recollections of slowly oncoming teams, uplifted above the level horizon of the plains in his former wanderings; the few sauntering figures that met him as man to man, and exchanged the chronicle of the road; the record of Indian tracks; the finding of a spring; the discovery of pasturage, with the lazy, restful hospitality of the night! And how fierce here this continual struggle for dominance and existence, even in this lull of passage. For above all and through all he was conscious of the feverish haste of speed and exertion.

The boat trembled, vibrated, and shook with every stroke of the ponderous piston. The laughter of the crowd, the exchange of gossip and news, the banquet at the long table, the newspapers and books in the reading-room, even the luxurious couches in the state-rooms, were all dominated, thrilled, and pulsating with the perpetual throb of the demon of hurry and unrest. And when at last a horrible fascination dragged him into the engine-room, and he saw the cruel relentless machinery at work, he seemed to recognize and understand some intelligent but pitiless Moloch, who was dragging this feverish world at its heels.

Later he was seated in a corner of the hurricane deck, whence he could view the monotonous banks of the river; yet, perhaps by certain signs unobservable to others, he knew he was approaching his own locality. He knew that his cabin and clearing would be indiscernible behind the fringe of willows on the bank, but he already distinguished the points where a few cottonwoods struggled into a promontory of lighter foliage beyond them. Here voices fell upon his ear, and he was suddenly aware that two men had lazily crossed over from the other side of the boat, and were standing before him looking upon the bank.

"It was about here, I reckon," said one, listlessly, as if continuing a previous lagging conversation, "that it must have happened. For it was after we were making for the bend we've just passed that the deputy, goin' to the state-room below us, found the door locked and the window open. But both men—Jack Despard and Seth Hall, the sheriff—weren't to be found. Not a trace of 'em. The boat was searched, but all for nothing. The idea is that the sheriff, arter getting his prisoner comf'ble in the state room, took off Jack's handcuffs and locked the door; that Jack, who was mighty desp'rate, bolted through the window into the river, and the sheriff, who was no slouch, arter him. Others allow—for the chairs and things all tossed about in the state-room—that the two men clinched *thar*, and Jack choked Hall and chucked him out, and then slipped cl'ar into the water himself, for the state-room window was just ahead of the paddle-box, and the cap'n allows that no man or men could fall afore the paddles and live. Anyhow, that was all they ever knew of it."

"And there wasn't no trace of them found?" said the second man, after a long pause.

"No. Cap'n says them paddles would hev' just snatched 'em and slung 'em round and round and buried 'em 'way down in the ooze of the river bed, with all the silt of the current atop of 'em, and they mightn't come up for ages; or else the wheels might have waltzed 'em 'way up to Sacramento until there wasn't enough left of 'em to float, and dropped 'em when the boat stopped."

"It was a mighty fool risk for a man like Despard to take," resumed the second speaker as he turned away with a slight yawn.

"Bet your life! but he was desp'rate, and the sheriff had got him sure! And they *do* say that he was superstitious, like all them gamblers, and allowed that a man who was fixed to die by a rope or a pistol wasn't to be washed out of life by water."

The two figures drifted lazily away, but Morse sat rigid and motionless. Yet, strange to say, only one idea came to him clearly out of this awful revelation—the thought that his friend was still true to him—and that his strange absence and mysterious silence were fully accounted for and explained. And with it came the more thrilling fancy that this man was alive now to *him* alone.

He was the sole custodian of his secret. The morality of the question, while it profoundly disturbed him, was rather in reference to its effect upon the chances of Captain Jack and the power it gave his enemies than his own conscience. He would rather that his friend should have proven the proscribed outlaw who retained an unselfish interest in him than the superior gentleman who was coldly wiping out his gratitude. He thought he understood now the reason of his visitor's strange and varying moods—even his bitter superstitious warning in regard to the probable curse entailed upon one who should save a drowning man. Of this he recked little; enough that he fancied that Captain Jack's concern in his illness was heightened by that fear, and this assurance of his protecting friendship thrilled him with pleasure.

There was no reason now why he should not at once go back to his farm, where, at least, Captain Jack would always find him; and he did so, returning on the same boat. He was now fully recovered from his illness, and calmer in mind; he redoubled his labors to put himself in a position to help the mysterious fugitive when the time should come. The remote farm should always be a haven of refuge for him, and in this hope he forbore to take any outside help, remaining solitary and alone, that Captain Jack's retreat should be inviolate. And so the long dry season passed, the hay was gathered, the pasturing herds sent home, and the first rains, dimpling like shot the broadening surface of the river, were all that broke his unending solitude. In this enforced attitude of waiting and expectancy he was exalted and strengthened by a new idea. He was not a religious man, but, dimly remembering the exhortations of some camp-meeting of his boyhood, he conceived the idea that he might have been selected to work out the regeneration of Captain Jack. What might not come of this meeting and communing together in this lonely spot? That anything was due to the memory of the murdered sheriff, whose bones were rotting in the trench that he daily but unconcernedly passed, did not occur to him. Perhaps his mind was not large enough for the double consideration. Friendship and love—and, for the matter of that, religion—are eminently one-ideaed.

But one night he awakened with a start. His hand, which was hanging out of his bunk, was dabbling idly in water. He had barely time to spring to his middle in what seemed to be a slowly filling tank before the door fell out as from that inward pressure, and his whole shanty collapsed like a pack of cards. But it fell outwards, the roof sliding from over his head like a withdrawn canopy; and he was swept from his feet against it, and thence out into what might have been another world! For the rain had ceased, and the full moon revealed only one vast, illimitable expanse of water! It was not an overflow, but the whole rushing river magnified and repeated a thousand times, which, even as he gasped for breath and clung to the roof, was bearing him away he knew not whither. But it was bearing him away upon its center, for as he cast one swift glance towards his meadows he saw they were covered by the same sweeping torrent, dotted with his sailing hay-ricks and reaching to the wooded foothills. It was the great flood of '54. In its awe-inspiring completeness it might have seemed to him the primeval Deluge.

As his frail raft swept under a cottonwood he caught at one of the overhanging limbs, and, working his way desperately along the bough, at last reached a secure position in the fork of the tree. Here he was for the moment safe. But the devastation viewed from this height was only the more appalling. Every sign of his clearing, all evidence of his past year's industry, had disappeared. He was now conscious for the first time of the lowing of the few cattle he had kept, as, huddled together on a slight eminence, they one by one slipped over struggling into the flood. The shining bodies of his dead horses rolled by him as he gazed. The lower-lying limbs of the sycamore near him were bending with the burden of the lighter articles from his overturned wagon and cabin which they had caught and retained, and a rake was securely lodged in a bough. The habitual solitude of his locality was now strangely invaded by drifting sheds, agricultural implements, and fence rails from unknown and remote neighbors, and he could faintly hear the far-off calling of some unhappy farmer adrift upon a spar of his wrecked and shattered house. When day broke he was cold and hungry.

Hours passed in hopeless monotony, with no slackening or diminution of the waters. Even the drifts became less, and a vacant sea at last spread before him on which nothing moved. An awful silence impressed him. In the afternoon rain again began to fall on this gray, nebulous expanse, until the whole world seemed made of aqueous vapor. He had but one idea now—the coming of the evening boat, and he would reserve his strength to swim to it. He did not know until later that it could no longer follow the old channel of the river, and passed far beyond his sight and hearing. With his disappointment and exposure that night came a return of his old fever. His limbs were alternately racked with pain or benumbed and lifeless. He could scarcely retain his position—at times he scarcely cared to—and speculated upon ending his sufferings by a quick plunge downwards. In other moments of lucid misery he was conscious of having wandered in his mind; of having seen the dead face of the murdered sheriff, washed out of his shallow grave by the flood, staring at him from the water; to this was added the hallucination of noises. He heard voices, his own name called by a voice he knew—Captain Jack's!

Suddenly he started, but in that fatal movement lost his balance and plunged downwards. But before the water closed above his head he had had a cruel glimpse of help near him: of a flashing light—of the black hull of a tug not many yards away—of moving figures—the sensation of a sudden plunge following his own, the grip of a strong hand upon his collar, and—unconsciousness!

When he came to he was being lifted in a boat from the tug and rowed through the deserted streets of a large city, until he was taken in through the second-story window of a half-submerged hotel and cared for. But all his questions yielded only the information that the tug—a privately procured one, not belonging to the Public Relief Association—had been dispatched for him with special directions, by a man who acted as one of the crew, and who was the one who had plunged in for him at the last moment. The man had left the boat at Stockton. There was nothing more? Yes!—he had left a letter. Morse seized it feverishly. It contained only a few lines:—

"We are quits now. You are all right. I have saved *you* from drowning, and shifted the curse to my own shoulders. Good-by.

'CAPTAIN JACK.'"

The astounded man attempted to rise—to utter an exclamation—but fell back, unconscious.

Weeks passed before he was able to leave his bed—and then only as an impoverished and physically shattered man. He had no means to re-stock the farm left bare by the subsiding water. A kindly train-packer offered him a situation as muleteer in a pack-train going to the mountains—for he knew tracks and passes and could ride. The mountains gave him back a little of the vigor he had lost in the river valley, but none of its dreams and ambitions. One day, while tracking a lost mule, he stopped to slake his thirst in a water-hole—all that the summer had left of a lonely mountain torrent. Enlarging the hole to give drink to his beast also, he was obliged to dislodge and throw out with the red soil some bits of honeycomb rock, which were so queer-looking and so heavy as to attract his attention. Two of the largest he took back to camp with him. They were gold! From the locality he took out a fortune. Nobody wondered. To the Californian's superstition it was perfectly natural. It was "nigger luck"—the luck of the stupid, the ignorant, the inexperienced, the non-seeker—the irony of the gods!

But the simple, bucolic nature that had sustained itself against temptation with patient industry and lonely self-concentration succumbed to rapidly acquired wealth. So it chanced that one day, with a crowd of excitement-loving spendthrifts and companions, he found himself on the outskirts of a lawless mountain town. An eager, frantic crowd had already assembled there—a desperado was to be lynched! Pushing his way through the crowd for a nearer view of the exciting spectacle, the changed and reckless Morse was stopped by armed men only at the foot of a cart, which upheld a quiet, determined man, who, with a rope around his neck, was scornfully surveying the mob, that held the other end of the rope drawn across the limb of a tree above him. The eyes of the doomed man caught those of Morse—his expression changed—a kindly smile lit his face—he bowed his proud head for the first time, with an easy gesture of farewell.

And then, with a cry, Morse threw himself upon the nearest armed guard, and a fierce struggle began. He had overpowered one adversary and seized another in his hopeless fight towards the cart when the half-astonished crowd felt that something must be done. It was done with a sharp report, the upward curl of smoke and the falling back of the guard as Morse staggered forward *free*—with a bullet in his heart. Yet even then he did not fall until he reached the cart, when he lapsed forward, dead, with his arms outstretched and his head at the doomed man's feet.

There was something so supreme and all-powerful in this hopeless act of devotion that the heart of the multitude thrilled and then recoiled aghast at its work, and a single word or a gesture from the doomed man himself would have set him free. But they say—and it is credibly recorded—that as Captain Jack Despard looked down upon the hopeless sacrifice at his feet his eyes blazed, and he flung upon the crowd a curse so awful and sweeping that, hardened as they were, their blood ran cold, and then leaped furiously to their cheeks.

"And now," he said, coolly tightening the rope around his neck with a jerk of his head—"Go on, and be d——d to you! I'm ready."

They did not hesitate this time. And Martin Morse and Captain Jack Despard were buried in the same grave.

LANTY FOSTER'S MISTAKE

L anty Foster was crouching on a low stool before the dying
kitchen fire, the better to get its fading radiance on the book
she was reading. Beyond, through the open window and door,
the fire was also slowly fading from the sky and the mountain ridge
whence the sun had dropped half an hour before. The view was up-
hill, and the sky-line of the hill was marked by two or three gibbet-
like poles from which, on a now invisible line between them, depended
certain objects—mere black silhouettes against the sky—which bore
weird likeness to human figures. Absorbed as she was in her book,
she nevertheless occasionally cast an impatient glance in that direction, as the sunlight faded more quickly than her fire. For the fluttering objects were the "week's wash" which had to be brought in before
night fell and the mountain wind arose. It was strong at that altitude,
and before this had ravished the clothes from the line, and scattered
them along the highroad leading over the ridge, once even lashing
the shy schoolmaster with a pair of Lanty's own stockings, and blinding the parson with a really tempestuous petticoat.

A whiff of wind down the big-throated chimney stirred the long
embers on the hearth, and the girl jumped to her feet, closing the
book with an impatient snap. She knew her mother's voice would
follow. It was hard to leave her heroine at the crucial moment of
receiving an explanation from a presumed faithless lover, just to climb
a hill and take in a lot of soulless washing, but such are the infelici-
ties of stolen romance reading. She threw the clothes-basket over
her head like a hood, the handle resting across her bosom and shoulders, and with both her hands free started out of the cabin. But the
darkness had come up from the valley in one stride after its mountain

{164}

fashion, had outstripped her, and she was instantly plunged in it. Still the outline of the ridge above her was visible, with the white, steadfast stars that were not there a moment ago, and by that sign she knew she was late. She had to battle against the rushing wind now, which sung through the inverted basket over her head and held her back, but with bent shoulders she at last reached the top of the ridge and the level. Yet here, owing to the shifting of the lighter background above her, she now found herself again encompassed with the darkness. The outlines of the poles had disappeared, the white fluttering garments were distinct apparitions waving in the wind, like dancing ghosts. But there certainly was a queer misshapen bulk moving beyond, which she did not recognize, and as she at last reached one of the poles, a shock was communicated to it, through the clothes-line and the bulk beyond. Then she heard a voice say impatiently,—

"What in h——ll am I running into now?"

It was a man's voice, and, from its elevation, the voice of a man on horseback. She answered without fear and with slow deliberation,—

"Inter our clothes-line, I reckon."

"Oh!" said the man in a half-apologetic tone. Then in brisker accents, "The very thing I want! I say, can you give me a bit of it? The ring of my saddle girth has fetched loose. I can fasten it with that."

"I reckon," replied Lanty, with the same unconcern, moving nearer the bulk, which now separated into two parts as the man dismounted. "How much do you want?"

"A foot or two will do."

They were now in front of each other, although their faces were not distinguishable to either. Lanty, who had been following the lines with her hand, here came upon the end knotted around the last pole. This she began to untie.

"What a place to hang clothes," he said curiously.

"Mighty dryin', though," returned Lanty laconically.

"And your house? Is it near by?" he continued.

"Just down the ridge—ye kin see from the edge. Got a knife?" She had untied the knot.

"No—yes—wait." He had hesitated a moment and then produced something from his breast pocket, which he however kept in his hand. As he did not offer it to her she simply held out a section of the rope between her hands, which he divided with a single cut. She saw only that the instrument was long and keen. Then she lifted the flap of the saddle for him as he attempted to fasten the loose ring with the rope, but the darkness made it impossible. With an ejaculation, he fumbled in his pockets. "My last match!" he said, striking it, as he crouched over it to protect it from the wind. Lanty leaned over also, with her apron raised between it and the blast. The flame for an instant lit up the ring, the man's dark face, mustache, and white teeth set together as he tugged at the girth, and Lanty's brown, velvet eyes and soft, round cheek framed in the basket. Then it went out, but the ring was secured.

"Thank you," said the man, with a short laugh, "but I thought you were a hump-backed witch in the dark there."

"And I couldn't make out whether you was a cow or a b'ar," returned the young girl simply.

Here, however, he quickly mounted his horse, but in the action something slipped from his clothes, struck a stone, and bounded away into the darkness.

"My knife," he said hurriedly. "Please hand it to me." But although the girl dropped on her knees and searched the ground diligently, it could not be found. The man with a restrained ejaculation again dismounted, and joined in the search.

"Haven't you got another match?" suggested Lanty.

"No—it was my last!" he said impatiently

"Just you hol' on here," she said suddenly, "and I'll run down to the kitchen and fetch you a light. I won't be long."

"No! no!" said the man quickly; "don't! I couldn't wait. I've been here too long now. Look here. You come in daylight and find it, and— just keep it for me, will you?" He laughed. "I'll come for it. And now, if you'll only help to set me on that road again, for it's so infernal black I can't see the mare's ears ahead of me, I won't bother you any more. Thank you."

Lanty had quietly moved to his horse's head and taken the bridle in her hand, and at once seemed to be lost in the gloom. But in a few moments he felt the muffled thud of his horse's hoof on the thick dust of the highway, and its still hot, impalpable powder rising to his nostrils.

"Thank you," he said again, "I'm all right now," and in the pause that followed it seemed to Lanty that he had extended a parting hand to her in the darkness. She put up her own to meet it, but missed his, which had blundered onto her shoulder. Before she could grasp it, she felt him stooping over her, the light brush of his soft mustache on her cheek, and then the starting forward of his horse. But the retaliating box on the ear she had promptly aimed at him spent itself in the black space which seemed suddenly to have swallowed up the man, and even his light laugh.

For an instant she stood still, and then, swinging the basket indignantly from her shoulder, took up her suspended task. It was no light one in the increasing wind, and the unfastened clothes-line had precipitated a part of its burden to the ground through the loosening of the rope. But on picking up the trailing garments her hand struck an unfamiliar object. The stranger's lost knife! She thrust it hastily into the bottom of the basket and completed her work. As she began to descend with her burden she saw that the light of the kitchen fire, seen through the windows, was augmented by a candle. Her mother was evidently awaiting her.

"Pretty time to be fetchin' in the wash," said Mrs. Foster querulously. "But what can you expect when folks stand gossipin' and philanderin' on the ridge instead o' tendin' to their work?"

Now Lanty knew that she had *not* been "gossipin'" nor "philanderin'," yet as the parting salute might have been open to that imputation, and as she surmised that her mother might have overheard their voices, she briefly said, to prevent further questioning, that she had shown a stranger the road. But for her mother's unjust accusation she would have been more communicative. As Mrs. Foster went back grumblingly into the sitting-room Lanty resolved to keep the knife at present a secret from her mother, and to that purpose removed it from the basket. But in the light of the candle she saw it for the first time plainly—and started.

For it was really a dagger! jeweled-handled and richly wrought— such as Lanty had never looked upon before. The hilt was studded with gems, and the blade, which had a cutting edge, was damascened in blue and gold. Her soft eyes reflected the brilliant setting, her lips parted breathlessly; then, as her mother's voice arose in the other room, she thrust it back into its velvet sheath and clapped it into her pocket. Its rare beauty had confirmed her resolution of absolute secrecy. To have shown it now would have made "no end of talk." And she was not sure but that her parents would have demanded its custody! And it was given to her by *him* to keep. This settled the question of moral ethics. She took the first opportunity to run up to her bedroom and hide it under the mattress.

Yet the thought of it filled the rest of her evening. When her household duties were done she took up her novel again, partly from force of habit and partly as an attitude in which she could think of *It* undisturbed. For what was fiction to her now? True, it possessed a certain reminiscent value. A "dagger" had appeared in several romances she had devoured, but she never had a clear idea of one before. "The Count sprang back, and, drawing from his belt a richly jeweled dagger, hissed between his teeth," or, more to the purpose. "'Take this,' said Orlando, handing her the ruby-hilted poniard which had gleamed upon his thigh, 'and should the caitiff attempt thy unguarded innocence—'"

"Did ye hear what your father was sayin'?" Lanty started. It was her mother's voice in the doorway, and she had been vaguely conscious of another voice pitched in the same querulous key, which, indeed, was the dominant expression of the small ranchers of that fertile neighborhood. Possibly a too complaisant and unaggressive Nature had spoiled them.

"Yes!—no!" said Lanty abstractedly, "what did he say?"

"If you wasn't taken up with that fool book," said Mrs. Foster, glancing at her daughter's slightly conscious color, "ye'd know! He allowed ye'd better not leave yer filly in the far pasture nights. That gang o' Mexican horse-thieves is out again, and raided McKinnon's stock last night."

This touched Lanty closely. The filly was her own property, and she was breaking it for her own riding. But her distrust of her parents' interference was greater than any fear of horse-stealers. "She's mighty uneasy in the barn; and," she added, with a proud consciousness of that beautiful yet carnal weapon upstairs, "I reckon I ken protect her and myself agin any Mexican horse-thieves."

"My! but we're gettin' high and mighty," responded Mrs. Foster, with deep irony. "Did you git all that outer your fool book?"

"Mebbe," said Lanty curtly.

Nevertheless, her thoughts that night were not entirely based on written romance. She wondered if the stranger knew that she had really tried to box his ears in the darkness, also if he had been able to see her face. *His* she remembered, at least the flash of his white teeth against his dark face and darker mustache, which was quite as soft as her own hair. But if he thought "for a minnit" that she was "goin' to allow an entire stranger to kiss her—he was mighty mistaken." She should let him know it "pretty quick"! She should hand him back the dagger "quite careless like," and never let on that she'd thought anything of it. Perhaps that was the reason why, before she went to bed, she took a good look at it, and after taking off her straight, beltless, calico gown she even tried the effect of it, thrust in the stiff waistband of her petticoat, with the jeweled hilt displayed, and thought it looked charming—as indeed it did. And then, having said her prayers like a good girl, and supplicated that she should be less "tetchy" with her parents, she went to sleep and dreamed that she had gone out to take in the wash again, but that the clothes had all changed to the queerest lot of folks, who were all fighting and struggling with each other until she, Lanty, drawing her dagger, rushed up single-handed among them, crying, "Disperse, ye craven curs,—disperse, I say!" And they dispersed.

Yet even Lanty was obliged to admit the next morning that all this was somewhat incongruous with the baking of "corn dodgers," the frying of fish, the making of beds, and her other household duties, and dismissed the stranger from her mind until he should "happen along." In her freer and more acceptable outdoor duties she even tolerated the advances of neighboring swains who made a point of passing by "Foster's Ranch," and who were quite aware that Atalanta Foster, *alias* "Lanty," was one of the prettiest girls in the country. But Lanty's toleration consisted in that singular performance known to herself as "giving them as good as they sent," being a lazy traversing, qualified with scorn, of all that they advanced. How long they would have put up with this from a plain girl I do not know, but Lanty's short upper lip seemed framed for indolent and fascinating scorn, and her dreamy eyes usually looked beyond the questioner, or blunted his bolder glances in their velvety surfaces. The libretto of these scenes was not exhaustive, *e.g.*:—

The Swain (with bold, bad gayety). "Saw that shy schoolmaster hangin' round your ridge yesterday! Orter know by this time that shyness with a gal don't pay."

Lanty (decisively). "Mebbe he allows it don't get left as often as impudence."

The Swain (ignoring the reply and his previous attitude and becoming more direct). "I was calkilatin' to say that with these yer hoss-thieves about, yer filly ain't safe in the pasture. I took a turn round there two or three times last evening to see if she was all right."

Lanty (with a flattering show of interest). "No! *did* ye now? I was jest wonderin'—"

The Swain (eagerly). "I did—quite late, too! Why, that's nothin', Miss Atalanty to what I'd do for you."

Lanty (musing, with far-off eyes). "Then that's why she was so awful skeerd and frightened! Just jumpin' outer her skin with horror. I reckoned it was a b'ar or panther or a spook! You ought to have waited till she got accustomed to your looks."

Nevertheless, despite this elegant raillery, Lanty was enough concerned in the safety of her horse to visit it the next day with a view of bringing it nearer home. She had just stepped into the alder fringe of a dry "run" when she came suddenly upon the figure of a horseman in the "run," who had been hidden by the alders from the plain beyond and who seemed to be engaged in examining the hoof marks in the dust of the old ford. Something about his figure struck her recollection, and as he looked up quickly she saw it was the owner of the dagger. But he appeared to be lighter of hair and complexion, and was dressed differently, and more like a *vaquero*. Yet there was the same flash of his teeth as he recognized her, and she knew it was the same man.

Alas for her preparation! Without the knife she could not make that haughty return of it which she had contemplated. And more than that, she was conscious she was blushing! Nevertheless she managed to level her pretty brown eyebrows at him, and said sharply that if he followed her to her home she would return his property at once.

"But I'm in no hurry for it," he said with a laugh,—the same light laugh and pleasant voice she remembered,—"and I'd rather not come to the house just now. The knife is in good hands, I know, and I'll call for it when I want it! And until then—if it's all the same to you— keep it to yourself,—keep it dark, as dark as the night I lost it!"

"I don't go about blabbing my affairs," said Lanty indignantly, "and if it hadn't *been* dark that night you'd have your ears boxed—you know why!"

The stranger laughed again, waved his hand to Lanty, and galloped away.

Lanty was a little disappointed. The daylight had taken away some of her illusions. He was certainly very good-looking, but not quite as picturesque, mysterious, and thrilling as in the dark! And it was very queer—he certainly did look darker that night! Who was he? And why was he lingering near her? He was different from her neighbors—her admirers. He might be one of those locaters, from the big towns, who prospect the lands, with a view of settling government warrants on them,—they were always so secret until they had found what they wanted. She did not dare to seek information of her friends, for the same reason that she had concealed his existence from her mother,—it would provoke awkward questions; and it was evident that he was trusting to her secrecy, too. The thought thrilled her with a new pride, and was some compensation for the loss of her more intangible romance. It would be mighty fine, when he did call openly for his beautiful knife and declared himself, to have them all know that *she* knew about it all along.

When she reached home, to guard against another such surprise she determined to keep the weapon with her, and, distrusting her pocket, confided it to the cheap little country-made corset which only for the last year had confined her budding figure, and which now, perhaps, heaved with an additional pride. She was quite abstracted during the rest of the day, and paid but little attention to the gossip of the farm lads, who were full of a daring raid, two nights before, by the Mexican gang on the large stock farm of a neighbor. The Vigilance Committee had been baffled; it was even alleged that some of the smaller ranchmen and herders were in league with the gang. It was also believed to be a widespread conspiracy; to have a political complexion in its combination of an alien race with Southwestern filibusters. The legal authorities had been reinforced by special detectives from San Francisco. Lanty seldom troubled herself with these matters; she knew the exaggeration, she suspected the ignorance of her rural neighbors. She roughly referred it, in her own vocabulary, to "jaw," a peculiarly masculine quality. But later in the evening, when the domestic circle in the sitting-room had been augmented by a neighbor, and Lanty had taken refuge behind her novel as an excuse for silence, Zob Hopper, the enamored swain of the previous evening, burst in with more astounding news. A posse of the sheriff had just passed along the ridge; they had "corraled" part of the gang, and rescued some of the stock. The leader of the gang had escaped, but his capture was inevitable, as the roads were stopped. "All the same, I'm glad to see ye took my advice, Miss Atalanty, and brought in your filly," he concluded, with an insinuating glance at the young girl.

But "Miss Atalanty," curling a quarter of an inch of scarlet lip above the edge of her novel, here "allowed" that if his advice or the filly had to be "took," she didn't know which was worse.

"I wonder ye kin talk to sech peartness, Mr. Hopper," said Mrs. Foster severely; "she ain't got eyes nor senses for anythin' but that book."

"Talkin' o' what's to be 'took,'" put in the diplomatic neighbor, "you bet it ain't that Mexican leader! No, sir! he's been 'stopped' before this—and then got clean away all the same! One o' them detectives got him once and disarmed him—but he managed to give them the slip, after all. Why, he's that full o' shifts and disguises thar ain't no spottin' him. He walked right under the constable's nose oncet, and took a drink with the sheriff that was arter him—and the blamed fool never knew it. He kin change even the color of his hair quick as winkin'."

"Is he a real Mexican,—a regular Greaser?" asked the paternal Foster. "Cos I never heard that they wuz smart."

"No! They say he comes o' old Spanish stock, a bad egg they threw outer the nest, I reckon," put in Hopper eagerly, seeing a strange animated interest dilating Lanty's eyes, and hoping to share in it; "but he's reg'lar high-toned, you bet! Why, I knew a man who seed him in his own camp—prinked out in a velvet jacket and silk sash, with gold chains and buttons down his wide pants and a dagger stuck in his sash, with a handle just blazin' with jew'ls. Yes! Miss Atalanty, they say that one stone at the top—a green stone, what they call an 'em'ral'—was worth the price o' a 'Frisco house-lot. True ez you live! Eh—what's up now?"

Lanty's book had fallen on the floor as she was rising to her feet with a white face, still more strange and distorted in an affected yawn behind her little hand. "Yer makin' me that sick and nervous with yer fool yarns," she said hysterically, "that I'm goin' to get a little fresh air. It's just stifling here with lies and terbacker!" With another high laugh, she brushed past him into the kitchen, opened the door, and then paused, and, turning, ran rapidly up to her bedroom. Here she locked herself in, tore open the bosom of her dress, plucked out the dagger, threw it on the bed, where the green stone gleamed for an instant in the candle-light, and then dropped on her knees beside the bed with her whirling head buried in her cold red hands.

It had all come to her in a flash, like a blaze of lightning,—the black, haunting figure on the ridge, the broken saddle girth, the abandonment of the dagger in the exigencies of flight and concealment; the second meeting, the skulking in the dry, alder-hidden "run," the changed dress, the lighter-colored hair, but always the same voice and laugh,—the leader, the fugitive, the Mexican horse-thief! And she, the God-forsaken fool, the chuckle-headed nigger baby, with not half the sense of her own filly or that sop-headed Hopper—had never seen it! She—*she* who would be the laughing-stock of them all—she had thought him a "locater," a "towny" from 'Frisco! And she had consented to keep his knife until he would call for it,—yes, call for it, with fire and flame perhaps, the trampling of hoofs, pistol shots—and—yet—

Yet!—he had *trusted* her. Yes! trusted her when he knew a word from her lips would have brought the whole district down on him! when the mere exposure of that dagger would have identified and damned him! Trusted her a second time, when she was within cry of her house! When he might have taken her filly without her knowing it! And now she remembered vaguely that the neighbors had said how strange it was that her father's stock had not suffered as theirs had. *He* had protected them—he who was now a fugitive—and their men pursuing him! She rose suddenly with a single stamp of her narrow foot, and as suddenly became cool and sane. And then, quite her old self again, she lazily picked up the dagger and restored it to its place in her bosom. That done, with her color back and her eyes a little brighter, she deliberately went downstairs again, stuck her little brown head into the sitting-room, said cheerfully, "Still yawpin', you folks," and quietly passed out into the darkness.

She ran swiftly up to the ridge, impelled by the blind memory of having met him there at night and the one vague thought to give him warning. But it was dark and empty, with no sound but the rushing wind. And then an idea seized her. If he were haunting the vicinity still, he might see the fluttering of the clothes upon the line and believe she was there. She stooped quickly, and in the merciful and exonerating darkness stripped off her only white petticoat and pinned it on the line. It flapped, fluttered, and streamed in the mountain wind. She lingered and listened. But there came a sound she had not counted on,—the clattering hoofs of not one, but many, horses on the lower road. She ran back to the house to find its inmates already hastening towards the road for news. She took that chance to slip in quietly, go to her room, whose window commanded a view of the ridge, and crouching low behind it, she listened. She could hear the sound of voices, and the dull trampling of heavy boots on the dusty path towards the barnyard on the other side of the house— a pause and then the return of the trampling boots, and the final clattering of hoofs on the road again. Then there was a tap on her door and her mother's querulous voice.

"Oh! yer there, are ye? Well—it's the best place fer a girl—with all these man's doin's goin' on! They've got that Mexican horse-thief and have tied him up in your filly's stall in the barn—till the 'Frisco deputy gets back from rounding up the others. So ye jest stay where ye are till they've come and gone, and we're shut o' all that cattle. Are ye mindin'?"

"All right, maw; 'tain't no call o' mine, anyhow," returned Lanty through the half-open door.

At another time her mother might have been startled at her passive obedience. Still more would she have been startled had she seen her daughter's face now, behind the closed door—with her little mouth set over her clinched teeth. And yet it was her own child, and Lanty was her mother's real daughter; the same pioneer blood filled their veins, the blood that had never nourished cravens or degenerates, but had given itself to sprinkle and fertilize desert solitudes where man might follow. Small wonder, then, that this frontier-born Lanty, whose first infant cry had been answered by the yelp of wolf and scream of panther; whose father's rifle had been leveled across her cradle to cover the stealthy Indian who prowled outside—small wonder that she should feel herself equal to these "man's doin's," and prompt to take a part. For even in the first shock of the news of the capture she recalled the fact that the barn was old and rotten, that only that day the filly had kicked a board loose from behind her stall, which she, Lanty, had lightly returned to avoid "making a fuss." If his captors had not noticed it, or trusted only to their guards, she might make the opening wide enough to free him!

Two hours later the guard nearest the now sleeping house, a farm hand of the Fosters', saw his employer's daughter slip out and cautiously approach him. A devoted slave of Lanty's, and familiar with her impulses, he guessed her curiosity, and was not averse to satisfy it and the sense of his own importance. To her whispers of affected, half-terrified interest, he responded in whispers that the captive was really in the filly's stall, securely bound by his wrists behind his back, and his feet "hobbled" to a post. That Lanty couldn't see him, for it was dark inside, and he was sitting with his back to the wall, as he couldn't sleep comf'ble lyin' down. Lanty's eyes glowed, but her face was turned aside.

"And ye ain't reckonin' his friends will come and rescue him?" said Lanty, gazing with affected fearfulness in the darkness.

"Not much! There's two other guards down in the corral, and I'd fire my gun and bring 'em up."

But Lanty was gazing open-mouthed towards the ridge. "What's that wavin' on the ridge?" she said in awe-stricken tones.

She was pointing to the petticoat,—a vague, distant, moving object against the horizon.

"Why, that's some o' the wash on the line, ain't it?"

"Wash—*two days in the week!*" said Lanty sharply. "Wot's gone of you?"

"Thet's so," muttered the man, "and it wa'n't there at sundown, I'll swear! P'r'aps I'd better call the guard," and he raised his rifle.

"Don't," said Lanty, catching his arm. "Suppose it's nothin', they'll laugh at ye. Creep up softly and see; ye ain't afraid are ye? If ye are, give me yer gun, and *I'll* go."

This settled the question, as Lanty expected. The man cocked his piece, and bending low began cautiously to mount the acclivity. Lanty waited until his figure began to fade, and then ran like fire to the barn.

She had arranged every detail of her plan beforehand. Crouching beside the wall of the stall she hissed through a crack in thrilling whispers, "Don't move! Don't speak for your life's sake! Wait till I hand you back your knife, then do the best you can." Then slipping aside the loosened board she saw dimly the black outline of curling hair, back, shoulders, and tied wrists of the captive. Drawing the knife from her pocket, with two strokes of its keen cutting edge she severed the cords, threw the knife into the opening, and darted away. Yet in that moment she knew that the man was instinctively turning towards her. But it was one thing to free a horse-thief, and another to stop and "philander" with him.

She ran halfway up the ridge, and met the farm hand returning. It was only a bit of washing after all, and he was glad he hadn't fired his gun. On the other hand, Lanty confessed she had got "so skeert" being alone, that she came to seek him. She had the shivers; wasn't her hand cold? It was, but thrilling even in its coldness to the bashfully admiring man. And she was that weak and dizzy, he must let her lean on his arm going down; and they must go *slow*. She was sure he was cold too, and if he would wait at the back door she would give him a drink of whiskey. Thus Lanty, with her brain afire, her eyes and ears straining into the darkness, and the vague outline of the barn beyond. Another moment was protracted over the drink of whiskey, and then Lanty, with a faint archness, made him promise not to tell her mother of her escapade, and she promised on her part not to say anything about his "stalking a petticoat on the clothesline," and then shyly closed the door and regained her room. *He* must have got away by this time, or have been discovered; she believed they would not open the barn door until the return of the posse.

She was right. It was near daybreak when they returned, and, again crouching low beside her window, she heard, with a fierce joy, the sudden outcry, the oaths, the wrangling voices, the summoning of her father to the front door, and then the tumultuous sweeping away again of the whole posse, and a blessed silence falling over the rancho. And then Lanty went quietly to bed, and slept like a three-year child!

Perhaps that was the reason why she was able at breakfast to listen with lazy and even rosy indifference to the startling events of the night; to the sneers of the farm hands at the posse who had overlooked the knife when they searched their prisoner, as well as the stupidity of the corral guard who had never heard him make a hole "the size of a house" in the barn side! Once she glanced demurely at Silas Briggs—the farm hand—and the poor fellow felt consoled in his shame at the remembrance of their confidences.

But Lanty's tranquillity was not destined to last long. There was again the irruption of exciting news from the highroad; the Mexican leader had been recaptured, and was now safely lodged in Brownsville jail! Those who were previously loud in their praises of the successful horse-thief who had baffled the vigilance of his pursuers were now equally keen in their admiration of the new San Francisco deputy who, in turn, had outwitted the whole gang. It was *he* who was fertile in expedients; *he* who had studied the whole country, and even risked his life among the gang, and *he* who had again closed the meshes of the net around the escaped outlaw. He was already returning by way of the rancho, and might stop there a moment,—so that they could all see the hero. Such was the power of success on the country-side! Outwardly indifferent, inwardly bitter, Lanty turned away. She should not grace his triumph, if she kept in her room all day! And when there was a clatter of hoofs on the road again Lanty slipped upstairs.

But in a few moments she was summoned. Captain Lance Wetherby, Assistant Chief of Police of San Francisco, Deputy Sheriff and ex-United States scout, had requested to see Miss Foster a few moments alone. Lanty knew what it meant,—her secret had been discovered; but she was not the girl to shirk the responsibility! She lifted her little brown head proudly, and with the same resolute step with which she had left the house the night before, descended the stairs and entered the sitting-room. At first she saw nothing. Then a remembered voice struck her ear; she started, looked up, and gasping, fell back against the door. It was the stranger who had given her the dagger, the stranger she had met in the run!—the horse-thief himself! No! no! she saw it all now—she had cut loose the wrong man!

He looked at her with a smile of sadness—as he drew from his breast-pocket that dreadful dagger, the very sight of which Lanty now loathed! "This is the *second* time, Miss Foster," he said gently, "that I have taken this knife from Murietta, the Mexican bandit: once when I disarmed him three weeks ago, and he escaped, and last night, when he had again escaped and I recaptured him. After I lost it that night I understood from you that you had found it and were keeping it for me." He paused a moment and went on: "I don't ask you what happened last night. I don't condemn you for it; I can believe what a girl of your courage and sympathy might rightly do if her pity were excited; I only ask—why did you give *him* back that knife *I* trusted you with?"

"Why? Why did I?" burst out Lanty in a daring gush of truth, scorn, and temper. *"Because I thought you were that horse-thief. There!"*

He drew back astonished, and then suddenly came that laugh that Lanty remembered and now hailed with joy. "I believe you, by Jove!" he gasped. "That first night I wore the disguise in which I have tracked him and mingled with his gang. Yes! I see it all now—and more. I see that to *you* I owe his recapture!"

"To me!" echoed the bewildered girl. "How?"

"Why, instead of making for his cave he lingered here in the

{177}

confines of the ranch! He thought you were in love with him, because you freed him and gave him his knife, and stayed to see you!"

But Lanty had her apron to her eyes, whose first tears were filling their velvet depths. And her voice was broken as she said,—

"Then he—cared—a—good deal more for me—than some people!"

But there is every reason to believe that Lanty was wrong! At least later events that are part of the history of Foster's Rancho and the Foster family pointed distinctly to the contrary.

HEYDAY BOOKS publishes high quality and accessible books on California history, literature, natural history, and culture. For a free catalog, please contact us at P.O. Box 9145, Berkeley, CA 94709. Tel: (510) 549-3564; e-mail: heyday@heydaybooks.com

Related Titles from Heyday Books

No Rooms of Their Own:
Women Writers of Early California
by Ida Rae Egli
112 pages, paperback, with black & white photos
ISBN: 0-930588-54-1, $8.95

> "The journal entries, stories and poems by fifteen mid-19th century California women offer fresh and immediate perspectives on their lives and times."
>
> —*Publishers Weekly*

Life Amongst the Modocs:
Unwritten History
by Joaquin Miller
446 pages, paperback
ISBN: 0-930588-79-7, $14.95

> "A powerfully felt narrative of survival and warfare in the gold-digger slums and Indian encampments of northern California."
> —William Kittredge, *Northwest Review*

Highway 99:
A Literary Journey through California's Great Central Valley
Edited by Stan Yogi
448 pages, paperback, with black & white photos
ISBN: 0-930588-82-7, $16.00

> "A rich mix of poetry, fiction and journalism."
>
> —*Los Angeles Times*